Cap'n Eri

Joseph Crosby Lincoln

Kessinger Publishing reprints thousands of hard–to–find books!

Visit us at http://www.kessinger.net

CHAPTER I. A LAMB FOR THE SACRIFICE

"Perez," observed Captain Eri cheerfully, "I'm tryin' to average up with the mistakes of Providence."

The Captain was seated by the open door of the dining room, in the rocker with the patched cane seat. He was apparently very busy doing something with a piece of fishline and a pair of long−legged rubber boots. Captain Perez, swinging back and forth in the parlor rocker with the patch−work cushion, was puffing deliberately at a wooden pipe, the bowl of which was carved into the likeness of a very rakish damsel with a sailor's cap set upon the side of her once flaxen head. In response to his companion's remark he lazily turned his sunburned face toward the cane−seated rocker and inquired:

"What on airth are you doin' with them boots?"

Captain Eri tied a knot with his fingers and teeth and then held the boots out at arm's length.

"Why, Perez," he said, "I'm averagin' up, same as I told you. Providence made me a two−legged critter, and a two−legged critter needs two boots. I've always been able to find one of these boots right off whenever I wanted it, but it's took me so plaguey long to find the other one that whatever wet there was dried up afore I got out of the house. Yesterday when I wanted to go clammin' I found the left one on the mantelpiece, no trouble at all, but it was pretty nigh high water before I dug the other one out of the washb'iler. That's why I'm splicin' 'em together this way. I don't want to promise nothin' rash, but I'm in hopes that even Jerry can't lose 'em now."

"Humph!" grunted Captain Perez. "I don't think much of that plan. 'Stead of losin' one you'll lose both of 'em."

"Yes, but then I shan't care. If there ain't NO boots in sight; I'll go barefoot or stay at home. It's the kind of responsibleness that goes with havin' one boot that's wearin' me out. Where IS Jerry?"

"He went out to feed Lorenzo. I heard him callin' a minute ago. That cat ain't been home

Cap'n Eri

Joseph Crosby Lincoln

Table of Contents

sence noon, and Jerry's worried."

A stentorian shout of "Puss! puss! Come, kitty, kitty, kitty!" came from somewhere outside. Captain Eri smiled.

"I'm 'fraid Lorenzo's gittin' dissipated in his old age," he observed. Then, as a fat gray cat shot past the door, "There he is! Reg'lar prodigal son. Comes home when the fatted ca'f's ready."

A moment later Captain Jerry appeared, milk pitcher in hand. He entered the dining room and, putting the pitcher down on the table, pulled forward the armchair with the painted sunset on the back, produced his own pipe, and proceeded to hunt through one pocket after the other with a troubled expression of countenance.

"Where in tunket is my terbacker?" he asked, after finishing the round of pockets and preparing to begin all over again.

"I see it on the top of the clock a spell ago," said Captain Perez.

"Was that yours, Jerry?" exclaimed Captain Eri. "Well, that's too bad! I see it there and thought 'twas mine. Here 'tis, or what's left of it."

Captain Jerry took the remnant of a plug from his friend and said in an aggrieved tone:

"That's jest like you, Eri! Never have a place for nothin' and help yourself to anything you happen to want, don't make no odds whose 'tis. Why don't you take care of your terbacker, same's I do of mine?"

"Now see here, Jerry! I ain't so sure that is yours. Let me see it. Humph! I thought so! This is 'Navy Plug' and you always smoke 'Sailor's Sweetheart.' Talk about havin' a place for things!"

"That's MY terbacker, if you want to know," observed Captain Perez. "I've got yours, Eri. Here 'tis."

"Well, then, where IS mine?" said Captain Jerry somewhat snappishly.

3

Cap'n Eri

"Bet a dollar you've got it in your pocket," said Captain Eri.

"Bet ten dollars I ain't! I ain't quite a fool yit, Eri Hedge. I guess I know—well, I snum! I forgot that upper vest pocket!" and from the pocket mentioned Captain Jerry produced the missing tobacco.

There was a general laugh, in which Captain Jerry was obliged to join, and the trio smoked in silence for a time, while the expanse of water to the eastward darkened, and the outer beach became but a dusky streak separating the ocean from the inner bay. At length Captain Perez rose and, knocking the ashes from his pipe, announced that he was going to "show a glim."

"Yes, go ahead, Jerry!" said Captain Eri, "it's gittin' dark."

"It's darker in the grave," observed Captain Perez with lugubrious philosophy.

"Then for the land's sake let's have it light while we can! Here, Jerry! them matches is burnt ones. Try this, 'twon't be so damagin' to the morals."

Captain Jerry took the proffered match and lit the two bracket lamps, fastened to the walls of the dining room. The room, seen by the lamplight, was shiplike, but as decidedly not shipshape. The chronometer on the mantel was obscured by a thick layer of dust. The three gorgeous oil paintings—from the brush of the local sign painter—respectively representing the coasting packet Hannah M., Eri Hedge, Master, and the fishing schooners, Georgie Baker, Jeremiah Burgess, Master, and the Flying Duck, Perez Ryder, Master, were shrouded in a very realistic fog of the same dust. Even the imposing gilt-lettered set of "Lives of Great Naval Commanders," purchased by Captain Perez some months before, and being slowly paid for on an apparently never-ending installment plan, was cloaked with it. The heap of newspapers, shoved under the couch to get them out of the way, peeped forth in a tell-tale manner. The windows were not too clean and the floor needed sweeping. Incidentally the supper table had not been cleared. Each one of the three noted these things and each sighed. Then Captain Eri said, as if to change the subject, though no one had spoken:

"What started you talkin' about the grave, Perez? Was it them clam fritters of Jerry's?"

"No," answered the ex–skipper of the Flying Duck, pulling at his grizzled scrap of throat whisker and looking rather shamefaced. "You see, M'lissy Busteed dropped in a few minutes this mornin' while you fellers was out and—"

Both Captain Eri and Captain Jerry set up a hilarious shout.

"Haw! haw!" roared the former, slapping his knee. "I wouldn't be so fascinatin' as you be for no money, Perez. She'll have you yit; you can't git away! But say, I don't wonder you got to thinkin' 'bout the grave. Ten minutes of M'lissy gits me thinkin' of things way t'other side of that!"

"Aw, belay there, Eri" protested Captain Perez testily. "'Twan't my fault. I didn't see her comin' or I'd have got out of sight. She was cruisin' 'round the way she always does with a cargo of gabble, and, she put in here to unload. Talk! I never heard a woman talk the way she can! She'd be a good one to have on board in a calm. Git her talkin' abaft the mains'l and we'd have a twenty–knot breeze in a shake."

"What was it this time?" asked Captain Jerry.

"Oh, a little of everything. She begun about the 'beautiful' sermon that Mr. Perley preached at the last 'Come–Outers" meetin'. That was what started me thinkin' about the grave, I guess. Then she pitched into Seth Wingate's wife for havin' a new bunnit this season when the old one wan't ha'f wore out. She talked for ten minutes or so on that, and then she begun about Parker's bein' let go over at the cable station and about the new feller that's been signed to take his place. She's all for Parker. Says he was a 'perfectly lovely' man and that 'twas outrageous the way he was treated, and all that sort of thing."

"She ain't the only one that thinks so," observed Captain Jerry. "There's a heap of folks in this town that think Parker was a mighty fine feller."

"Yes," said Captain Eri, "and it's worth while noticin' who they be. Perez' friend, M'lissy, thinks so, and 'Squealer' Wixon and his gang think so, and 'Web' Saunders thinks so, and a lot more like them. Parker was TOO good a feller, that's what was the matter with him. His talk always reminded me of washday at the poorhouse, lots of soft soap with plenty of lye in it."

"Well, M'lissy says that the men over to the station—all except Langley, of course—are mad as all git−out because Parker was let go, and she says somebody told somebody else, and somebody else told somebody else, and somebody else told HER—she says it come reel straight—that the men are goin' to make it hot for the new feller when he comes. She says his name's Hazeltine, or somethin' like that, and that he's goin' to get here to−morrer or next day."

"Well," said Captain Eri, "it's a mercy M'lissy found it out. If that man should git here and she not know it aforehand 'twould kill her sure as fate, and think what a blow that would be to you, Perez."

He took his old−fashioned watch from his pocket and glanced at the dial.

"I mustn't be settin' round here much longer," he added. "John Baxter's goin' to have that little patch of cranberry swamp of his picked to−morrer, and he's expectin' some barrels down on to− night's train. John asked me to git Zoeth Cahoon to cart 'em down for him, but I ain't got nothin' special to do to−night, so I thought I'd hitch up and go and git 'em myself. You and Jerry can match cents to see who does the dishes. I did 'em last night, so it's my watch below."

"Well, _I_ shan't do 'em," declared Captain Perez. "Blessed if I'd do the durn things to−night if the President of the United States asked me to."

"Humph!" sputtered Captain Jerry. "I s'pose you fellers think I'll do 'em all the time. If you do you're mistook, that's all. 'Twan't last night you done 'em, Eri; 'twas the night afore. I done 'em last night, and I'm ready to take my chances agin if we match, but I'm jiggered if I let you shove the whole thing off onto me. I didn't ship for cook no more 'n the rest of you."

Neither of the others saw fit to answer this declaration of independence and there was a pause in the conversation. Then Captain Jerry said moodily:

"It ain't no use. It don't work."

"What don't work?" asked Captain Eri.

"Why, this plan of ours. I thought when we fellers give up goin' to sea reg'lar and settled down here to keep house ourselves and live economical and all that, that 'twas goin' to be fine. I thought I wouldn't mind doin' my share of the work a bit, thought 'twould be kind of fun to swab decks and all that. Well, 'twas for a spell, but 'tain't now. I'm so sick of it that I don't know what to do. And I'm sick of livin' in a pigpen, too. Look at them dead-lights! They're so dirty that when I turn out in the mornin' and go to look through 'em, I can't tell whether it's foul weather or fair."

Captain Eri looked at the windows toward which his friend pointed and signed assent.

"There's no use talkin'," he observed, "we've got to have a steward aboard this craft."

"Yes," said Captain Perez emphatically, "a steward or a woman."

"A WOMAN!" exclaimed Captain Eri. Then he shook his head solemnly and added, "There, Jerry! What did I tell you? M'lissy!"

But Captain Perez did not smile.

"I ain't foolin'," he said; "I mean it."

Captain Jerry thought of the spick-and-span days of his wife, dead these twenty years, and sighed again. "I s'pose we might have a housekeeper," he said.

"Housekeeper!" sneered Captain Eri. "Who'd you hire? Perez don't, seemin'ly, take to M'lissy, and there ain't nobody else in Orham that you could git, 'less 'twas old A'nt Zuby Higgins, and that would be actin' like the feller that jumped overboard when his boat sprung a leak. No, sir! If A'nt Zuby ships aboard here I heave up MY commission."

"Who said anything about A'nt Zuby or housekeepers either?" inquired Captain Perez. "I said we'd got to have a woman, and we have. One of us 'll have to git married, that's all."

"MARRIED!" roared the two in chorus.

"That's what I said, married, and take the others to board in this house. Look here now! When a shipwrecked crew's starvin' one of 'em has to be sacrificed for the good of the

7

rest, and that's what we've got to do. One of us has got to git married for the benefit of the other two."

Captain Eri shouted hilariously. "Good boy, Perez!" he cried. "Goin' to be the first offerin'?"

"Not unless it's my luck, Eri. We'll all three match for it, same as we do 'bout washin' the dishes."

"Where are you goin' to find a wife?" asked Captain Jerry.

"Now that's jest what I'm goin' to show you. I see how things was goin', and I've been thinkin' this over for a consid'rable spell. Hold on a minute till I overhaul my kit."

He went into the front bedroom, and through the open door they could see him turning over the contents of the chest with P. R. in brass nails on the lid. He scattered about him fish–lines, hooks, lead for sinkers, oilcloth jackets, whales' teeth, and various other articles, and at length came back bearing a much–crumpled sheet of printed paper. This he spread out upon the dining table, first pushing aside the dishes to make room, and, after adjusting his spectacles, said triumphantly:

"There! There she is! The Nup–ti–al Chime. A Journal of Matrimony. I see a piece about it in the Herald the other day, and sent a dime for a sample copy. It's chock–full of advertisements from women that wants husbands."

Captain Eri put on his spectacles and hitched his chair up to the table. After giving the pages of the Nuptial Chime a hurried inspection, he remarked:

"There seems to be a strong runnin' to 'vi–va–ci–ous brunettes' and 'blondes with tender and romantic dispositions.' Which of them kinds are you sufferin' for, Perez? Oh, say! here's a lady that's willin' to heave herself away on a young and handsome bachelor with a income of ten thousand a year. Seems to me you ought to answer that."

"Oh, hush up, Eri! 'Tain't likely I'd want to write to any of them in there. The thing for us to do would be to write out a advertisement of our own; tell what sort of woman we want, and then set back and wait for answers. Now, what do you say?"

Cap'n Eri

Captain Eri looked at the advocate of matrimony for a moment without speaking. Then he said: "Do you really mean it, Perez?"

"Sartin I do."

"What do you think of it, Jerry?"

"Think it's a good idee," said that ancient mariner decisively. "We've got to do somethin', and this looks like the only sensible thing."

"Then Eri's GOT to do it!" asserted Captain Perez dogmatically. "We agreed to stick together, and two to one's a vote. Come on now, Eri, we'll match."

Captain Eri hesitated.

"Come on, Eri!" ordered Captain Jerry. "Ain't goin' to mutiny, are you?"

"All right!" said Captain Eri, "I'll stick to the ship. Only," he added, with a quizzical glance at his companions, "it's got to be settled that the feller that's stuck can pick his wife, and don't have to marry unless he finds one that suits him."

The others agreed to this stipulation, and Captain Perez, drawing a long breath, took a coin from his pocket, flipped it in the air and covered it, as it fell on the table, with a big hairy hand. Captain Eri did likewise; so did Captain Jerry. Then Captain Eri lifted his hand and showed the coin beneath; it was a head. Captain Jerry's was a tail. Under Captain Perez' hand lurked the hidden fate. The Captain's lips closed in a grim line. With a desperate glance at the others he jerked his hand away.

The penny lay head uppermost. Captain Jerry was "stuck."

Captain Eri rose, glanced at his watch, and, taking his hat from the shelf where the dishes should have been, opened the door. Before he went out, however, he turned and said:

"Perez, you and Jerry can be fixin' up the advertisement while I'm gone. You can let me see it when I come back. I say, Jerry," he added to the "sacrifice," who sat gazing at the pennies on the table in a sort of trance, "don't feel bad about it. Why, when you come to think of it, it's a providence it turned out that way. Me and Perez are bachelors, and we'd be jest green hands. But you're a able seaman, you know what it is to manage a wife."

"Yes, I do," groaned Captain Jerry lugubriously. "Durn it, that's jest it!"

Captain Eri was chuckling as, lantern in hand, he passed around the corner of the little white house on the way to the barn. He chuckled all through the harnessing of Daniel, the venerable white horse. He was still chuckling as, perched on the seat of the "truck wagon," he rattled and shook out of the yard and turned into the sandy road that led up to the village. And an outsider, hearing these chuckles, and knowing what had gone before, might have inferred that perhaps Captain Eri did not view the "matching" and the matrimonial project with quite the deadly seriousness of the other two occupants of the house by the shore.

CHAPTER II. THE TRAIN COMES IN

There is in Orham a self-appointed committee whose duty it is to see the train come in. The committeemen receive no salary for their services; the sole compensation is the pleasure derived from the sense of duty done. Rain, snow, or shine, the committee is on hand at the station—the natives, of course, call it the "deepo"— to consume borrowed tobacco and to favor Providence with its advice concerning the running of the universe. Also it discusses local affairs with fluency and more or less point.

Mr. "Squealer" Wixon, a lifelong member of this committee, was the first to sight Captain Eri as the latter strolled across the tracks into the circle of light from the station lamps. The Captain had moored Daniel to a picket in the fence over by the freight-house. He had heard the clock in the belfry of the Methodist church strike eight as he drove by that edifice, but he heard no whistle from the direction of the West Orham woods, so he knew that the down train would arrive at its usual time, that is, from fifteen to twenty minutes behind the schedule.

"Hey!" shouted Mr. Wixon with enthusiasm. "Here's Cap'n Eri! Well, Cap, how's she headin'?"

"'Bout no'theast by no'th," was the calm reply. "Runnin' fair, but with lookout for wind ahead."

"Hain't got a spare chaw nowheres about you, have you, Cap'n?" anxiously inquired "Bluey" Batcheldor. Mr. Batcheldor is called "Bluey" for the same reason that Mr. Wixon is called "Squealer," and that reason has been forgotten for years.

Captain Eri obligingly produced a black plug of smoking tobacco, and Mr. Batcheldor bit off two-thirds and returned the balance. After adjusting the morsel so that it might interfere in the least degree with his vocal machinery, he drawled:

"I cal'late you ain't heard the news, Eri. Web Saunders has got his original-package license. It come on the noon mail."

The Captain turned sharply toward the speaker. "Is that a fact?" he asked. "Who told you?"

"See it myself. So did Squealer and a whole lot more. Web was showin' it round."

"We was wonderin'," said Jabez Smalley, a member of the committee whose standing was somewhat impaired, inasmuch as he went fishing occasionally and was, therefore, obliged to miss some of the meetings, "what kind of a fit John Baxter would have now. He's been pretty nigh distracted ever sence Web started his billiard room, callin' it a 'ha'nt of sin' and a whole lot more names. There ain't been a 'Come-Outers' meetin' 'sence I don't know when that he ain't pitched into that saloon. Now, when he hears that Web's goin' to sell rum, he'll bust a biler sure."

The committee received this prophecy with an hilarious shout of approval and each member began to talk. Captain Eri took advantage of this simultaneous expression of opinion to walk away. He looked in at the window of the ticket-office, exchanged greetings with Sam Hardy, the stationmaster, and then leaned against the corner of the building furthest removed from Mr. Wixon and his friends, lit his pipe and puffed thoughtfully with a troubled expression on his face.

From the clump of blackness that indicated the beginning of the West Orham woods came a long-drawn dismal "toot"; then two shorter ones. The committee sprang to its feet and looked interested. Sam Hardy came out of the ticket office. The stage-driver, a

11

sharp– looking boy of about fourteen, with a disagreeable air of cheap smartness sticking out all over him, left his seat in the shadow of Mr. Batcheldor's manly form, tossed a cigarette stump away and loafed over to the vicinity of the "depot wagon," which was backed up against the platform. Captain Eri knocked the ashes from his pipe and put that service–stained veteran in his pocket. The train was really "coming in" at last.

If this had been an August evening instead of a September one, both train and platform would have been crowded. But the butterfly summer maiden had flitted and, as is his wont, the summer man had flitted after her, so the passengers who alighted from the two coaches that, with the freight car, made up the Orham Branch train, were few in number and homely in flavor. There was a very stout lady with a canvas extension case and an umbrella in one hand and a bulging shawl–strap and a pasteboard box in the other, who panted and wheezed like the locomotive itself and who asked the brakeman, "What on airth DO they have such high steps for?" There was a slim, not to say gawky, individual with a chin beard and rubber boots, whom the committee hailed as "Andy" and welcomed to its bosom. There were two young men, drummers, evidently, who nodded to Hardy, and seemed very much at home. Also, there was another young man, smooth–shaven and square–shouldered, who deposited a suit–case on the platform and looked about him with the air of being very far from home, indeed.

The drummers and the stout lady got into the stage. The young man with the suit–case picked up the latter and walked toward the same vehicle. He accosted the sharp boy, who had lighted another cigarette.

"Can you direct me to the cable station?" he asked.

"Sure thing!" said the youth, and there was no Cape Cod twist to his accent. "Git aboard."

"I didn't intend to ride," said the stranger.

"What was you goin' to do? Walk?"

"Yes, if it's not far."

The boy grinned, and the members of the committee, who had been staring with all their might, grinned also. The young man's mention of the cable station seemed to have caused considerable excitement.

"Oh, it ain't too FAR!" said the stage-driver. Then he added: "Say, you're the new electrician, ain't you?"

The young man hesitated for a moment. Then he said, "Yes," and suggested, "I asked the way."

"Two blocks to the right; that's the main road, keep on that for four blocks, then turn to the left, and if you keep on straight ahead you'll get to the station."

"Blocks?" The stranger smiled. "I think you must be from New York."

"Do you?" inquired the youthful prodigy, climbing to the wagon seat. "Don't forget to keep straight ahead after you turn off the main road. Git dap! So long, fellers!" He leaned over the wheel, as the stage turned, and bestowed a wink upon the delighted "Squealer," who was holding one freckled paw over his mouth; then the "depot wagon" creaked away.

The square-shouldered young man looked after the equipage with an odd expression of countenance. Then he shrugged his shoulders, picked up the suitcase, and walked off the platform into the darkness.

Mr. Wixon removed the hand from his mouth and displayed a mammoth grin, that grew into a shriek of laughter in which every member of the committee joined.

"Haw! haw!" bellowed "Bluey," "so that's the feller that done Parker out of his job! Well, he may be mighty smart, but if that Joe Bartlett ain't smarter then I'm a skate, that's all! Smartest boy ever I see! 'If you keep on straight ahead you'll git to the station!' Gosh! he'll have to wear rubbers!"

"Maybe he's web-footed," suggested Smalley, and they laughed again.

A little later Captain Eri, with a dozen new, clean-smelling cranberry barrels in the wagon behind him, drove slowly down the "depot road." It was a clear night, but there was no moon, and Orham was almost at its darkest, which is very dark, indeed. The

13

"depot road"—please bear in mind that there are no streets in Orham—was full of ruts, and although Daniel knew his way and did his best to follow it, the cranberry barrels rattled and shook in lively fashion. There are few homes near the station, and the dwellers in them conscientiously refrain from showing lights except in the ends of the buildings furthest from the front. Strangers are inclined to wonder at this, but when they become better acquainted with the town and its people, they come to know that front gates and parlors are, by the majority of the inhabitants, restricted in their use to occasions such as a funeral, or, possibly, a wedding. For the average Orham family to sit in the parlor on a week evening would be an act bordering pretty closely on sacrilege.

It is from the hill by the Methodist church that the visitor to Orham gets his best view of the village. It is all about him, and for the most part below him. At night the lights in the houses show only here and there through the trees, but those on the beaches and at sea shine out plainly. The brilliant yellow gleam a mile away is from the Orham lighthouse on the bluff. The smaller white dot marks the light on Baker's Beach. The tiny red speck in the distance, that goes and comes again, is the flash–light at Setuckit Point, and the twinkle on the horizon to the south is the beacon of the lightship on Sand Hill Shoal.

It is on his arrival at this point, too, that the stranger first notices the sound of the surf. Being a newcomer, he notices this at once; after he has been in the village a few weeks, he ceases to notice it at all. It is like the ticking of a clock, so incessant and regular, that one has to listen intently for a moment or two before his accustomed ear will single it out and make it definite. One low, steady, continuous roar, a little deeper in tone when the wind is easterly, the voice of the old dog Ocean gnawing with foaming mouth at the bone of the Cape and growling as he gnaws.

It may be that the young man with the square shoulders and the suit–case had paused at the turn of the road by the church to listen to this song of the sea; at any rate he was there, and when Captain Eri steered Daniel and the cranberry barrels around the corner and into the "main road," he stepped out and hailed.

"I beg your pardon," he said; "I'm afraid I'm mixed in my directions. The stage–driver told me the way to the cable station, but I've forgotten whether he said to turn to the right when I reached here, or to the left."

Cap'n Eri

Captain Eri took his lantern from the floor of the wagon and held it up. He had seen the stranger when the latter left the train, but he had not heard the dialogue with Josiah Bartlett.

"How was you cal'latin' to go to the station?" he asked.

"Why, I intended to walk."

"Did you tell them fellers at the depot that you wanted to walk?"

"Certainly."

"Well, I swan! And they give you the direction?"

"Yes," a little impatiently; "why shouldn't they? So many blocks till I got to the main street, or road, and so many more, till I got somewhere else, and then straight on."

"Blocks, hey? That's Joe Bartlett. That boy ought to be mastheaded, and I've told Perez so more'n once. Well, Mister, I guess maybe you'd better not try to walk to the cable station to– night. You see, there's one thing they forgot to tell you. The station's on the outer beach, and there's a ha'f mile of pretty wet water between here and there."

The young man whistled. "You don't mean it!" he exclaimed.

"I sartin do, unless there's been an almighty drought since I left the house. I tell you what! If you'll jump in here with me, and don't mind waitin' till I leave these barrels at the house of the man that owns 'em, I'll drive you down to the shore and maybe find somebody to row you over. That is," with a chuckle, "if you ain't dead set on walkin'."

The stranger laughed heartily. "I'm not so stubborn as all that," he said. "It's mighty good of you, all the same."

"Don't say a word," said the Captain. "Give us your satchel. Now your flipper! There you are! Git dap, Dan'l!"

Daniel accepted the Captain's command in a tolerant spirit. He paddled along at a jog–trot for perhaps a hundred yards, and then, evidently feeling that he had done all that could be expected, settled back into a walk. The Captain turned towards his companion on the seat:

"I don't know as I mentioned it," he observed, "but my name is Hedge."

"Glad to meet you, Mr. Hedge," said the stranger. "My name is Hazeltine."

"I kind of jedged it might be when you said you wanted to git to the cable station. We heard you was expected."

"Did you? From Mr. Langley, I presume."

"No–o, not d'rectly. Of course, we knew Parker had been let go, and that somebody would have to take his place. I guess likely it was one of the operators that told it fust that you was the man, but anyhow it got as fur as M'lissy Busteed, and after that 'twas plain sailin'. You come from New York, don't you?"

"Yes."

"Well, you know how 'tis when a thing gits into the papers. Orham ain't big enough to have a paper of its own, so the Almighty give us M'lissy, I jedge, as a sort of substitute. She can spread a little news over more country than anybody I know. If she spreads butter the same way, she could make money keepin' boarders. Is this your fust visit to the Cape?"

"Yes. I hardly know why I'm here now. I have been with the Cable Company at their New York experimental station for some years, and the other day the General Manager called me into his office and told me I was expected to take the position of electrician here. I thought it might add to my experience, so I accepted."

"Humph! Did he say anything about the general liveliness of things around the station?"

Mr. Hazeltine laughed. "Why," he answered, "now that you speak of it, I remember that he began by asking me if I had any marked objection to premature burial."

Cap'n Eri

The Captain chuckled. "The outer beach in winter ain't exactly a camp—meeting for sociableness," he said. "And the idea of that Bartlett boy tellin' you how to walk there!"

"Is he a specimen of your Cape Cod youngsters?"

"Not exactly. He's a new shipment from New York. Grand—nephew of a messmate of mine, Cap'n Perez Ryder. Perez, he's a bachelor, but his sister's daughter married a feller named Bartlett. Maybe you knew him; he used to run a tugboat in the Sound."

Mr. Hazeltine, much amused, denied the acquaintance.

"Well, I s'pose you wouldn't, nat'rally," continued the Captain. "Anyhow, Perez's niece's husband died, and the boy sort of run loose, as yer might say. Went to school when he had to, and raised Ned when he didn't, near's I can find out. 'Lizabeth, that's his ma, died last spring, and she made Perez promise—he being the only relation the youngster had—to fetch the boy down here and sort of bring him up. Perez knows as much about bringing up a boy as a hen does about the Ten Commandments, and 'Lizabeth made him promise not to lick the youngster and a whole lot more foolishness. School don't commence here till October, so we got him a job with Lem Mullett at the liv'ry stable. He's boardin' with Lem till school opens. He ain't a reel bad boy, but he knows too much 'bout some things and not ha'f enough 'bout others. You've seen fellers like that, maybe?"

Hazeltine nodded. "There are a good many of that kind in New York, I'm afraid," he said.

Captain Eri smiled. "I shouldn't wonder," he observed. "The boys down here think Josiah's the whole crew, and the girls ain't fur behind. There's been more deviltry in this village sence he landed than there ever was afore. He needs somethin', and needs it bad, but I ain't decided jest what it is yit. Are you a married man?"

"No."

"Same here. Never had the disease. Perez, he's had symptoms every once in a while, but nothin' lastin'. Jerry's the only one of us three that's been through the mill. His wife died twenty year ago. I don't know as I told you, but Jerry and Perez and me are keepin' house down by the shore. That is, we call it keepin' house, but—"

Cap'n Eri

Here the Captain broke off and seemed to meditate.

Ralph Hazeltine forbore to interrupt, and occupied himself by scrutinizing the buildings that they were passing. They were nearing the center of the town now, and the houses were closer together than they had been on the "depot road," but never so close as to be in the least crowded. Each house had its ample front yard, and the new arrival could smell the box hedges and see, now and then, the whiteness of the kalsomined stones that bordered a driveway. It was too dark for the big seashells at the front steps to be visible, but they were there, all the same; every third house of respectability in Orham has them. There was an occasional shop, too, with signs like "Cape Cod Variety Store," or "The Boston Dry Goods Emporium," over their doors. On the platform of one a small crowd was gathered, and from the interior came shouts of laughter and the sound of a tin-panny piano.

"That's the billiard saloon," volunteered Captain Eri, suddenly waking from his trance. "Play pool, Mr. Hazeltine?"

"Sometimes."

"What d'ye play it with?"

"Why, with a cue, generally speaking."

"That so! Most of the fellers in there play it with their mouths. Miss a shot and then spend the rest of the evenin' tellin' how it happened."

"I don't think I should care to play it that way," said Ralph, laughing.

"Well, it has its good p'ints. Kind of all-round exercise; develops the lungs and strengthens the muscles, as the patent- medicine almanac says. Parker played it considerable."

"I judge that your opinion of my predecessor isn't a high one."

"Who? Oh, Parker! He was all right in his way. Good many folks in this town swore by him. I understand the fellers over at the station thought he was about the ticket."

"Mr. Langley included?"

"Oh, Mr. Langley, bein' manager, had his own ideas, I s'pose! Langley don't play pool much; not at Web Saunders' place, anyhow. We turn in here."

They rolled up a long driveway, very dark and overgrown with trees, and drew up at the back door of a good–sized two–story house. There was a light in the kitchen window.

"Whoa, Dan'l!" commanded the Captain. Then he began to shout, "Ship ahoy!" at the top of his lungs.

The kitchen door opened and a man came out, carrying a lamp, its light shining full upon his face. It was an old face, a stern face, with white eyebrows and a thin–lipped mouth. Just such a face as looked on with approval when the executioner held up the head of Charles I., at Whitehall. There was, however, a tremble about the chin that told of infirm health.

"Hello, John!" said Captain Eri heartily. "John, let me make you acquainted with Mr. Hazeltine, the new man at the cable station. Mr. Hazeltine, this is my friend, Cap'n John Baxter."

The two shook hands, and then Captain Eri said:

"John, I brought down them barrels for you. Hawkins got 'em here, same as he always does, by the skin of his teeth. Stand by now, 'cause I've got to deliver Mr. Hazeltine at the station, and it's gittin' late."

John Baxter said nothing, beyond thanking his friend for the good turn, but he "stood by," as directed, and the barrels were quickly unloaded. As they were about to drive out of the yard, Captain Eri turned in his seat and said:

"John, guess I'll be up some time to–morrow. I want to talk with you about that billiard–room business."

The lamp in Baxter's hand shook.

"God A'mighty's got his eye on that place, Eri Hedge," he shouted, "and on them that's runnin' it!"

"That's all right," said the Captain. "Then the job's in good hands, and we ain't got to worry. Good–night."

But, in spite of this assurance, Hazeltine noticed that his driver was silent and preoccupied until they reached the end of the road by the shore, when he brought the willing Daniel to a stand still and announced that it was time to "change cars."

It is a fifteen–minute row from the mainland to the outer beach, and Captain Eri made it on schedule time. Hazeltine protested that he was used to a boat, and could go alone and return the dory in the morning, but the Captain wouldn't hear of it. The dory slid up on the sand and the passenger climbed out. The sound of the surf on the ocean side of the beach was no longer a steady roar, it was broken into splashing plunges and hisses with, running through it, a series of blows like those of a muffled hammer. The wind was wet and smelt salty.

"There's the station," said the Captain, pointing to a row of lighted windows a quarter of a mile away. "It IS straight ahead this time, and the walkin's better'n it has been for the last few minutes. Good–night!"

The electrician put his hand in his pocket, hesitated, and then withdrew it, empty.

"I'm very much obliged to you for all this," he said. "I'm glad to have made your acquaintance, and I hope we shall see each other often."

"Same here!" said the Captain heartily. "We're likely to git together once in a while, seein' as we're next–door neighbors, right across the road, as you might say. That's my berth over yonder, where you see them lights. It's jest 'round the corner from the road we drove down last. Good–night! Good luck to you!"

And he settled himself for the row home.

CHAPTER III. THE "COME–OUTERS'" MEETING

The house where the three Captains lived was as near salt water as it could be and remain out of reach of the highest tides. When Captain Eri, after beaching and anchoring his dory and stabling Daniel for the night, entered the dining room he found his two messmates deep in consultation, and with evidences of strenuous mental struggle written upon their faces. Captain Perez's right hand was smeared with ink and there were several spatters of the same fluid on Captain Jerry's perspiring nose. Crumpled sheets of note paper were on the table and floor, and Lorenzo, who was purring restfully upon the discarded jackets of the two mariners, alone seemed to be enjoying himself.

"Well, you fellers look as if you'd had a rough v'yage," commented Captain Eri, slipping out of his own jacket and pulling his chair up beside those of his friends. "What's the trouble?"

"Gosh, Eri, I'm glad to see you!" exclaimed Captain Perez, drawing the hand, just referred to, across his forehead and thereby putting that portion of his countenance into mourning. "How do you spell conscientious?"

"I don't, unless it's owner's orders," was the answer. "What do you want to spell it for?"

"We've writ much as four hundred advertisements, I do believe!" said Captain Jerry, "and there ain't one of them fit to feed to a pig. Perez here, he's got such hifalutin' notions, that nothin' less than a circus bill 'll do him. _I_ don't see why somethin' plain and sensible like 'Woman wanted to do dishes and clean house for three men,' wouldn't be all right; but no, it's got to have more fancy trimmin's than a Sunday bunnit. Foolishness, I call it."

"You'd have a whole lot of women answerin' that advertisement, now wouldn't you?" snorted Captain Perez hotly. "'To do dishes for three men!' That's a healthy bait to catch a wife with, ain't it? I can see 'em comin'. I cal'late you'd stay single till Jedgment, and then you wouldn't git one. No, sir! The thing to do is to be sort of soft–soapy and high–toned. Let 'em think they're goin' to git a bargain when they git you. Make believe it's goin' to be a privilege to git sech a husband."

"Well, 'tis," declared the sacrifice indignantly. "They might git a dum–sight worse one."

Cap'n Eri

"I cal'late that's so, Jerry," said Captain Eri. "Still, Perez ain't altogether wrong. Guess you'd better keep the dishwashin' out of it. I know dishwashin' would never git ME; I've got so I hate the sight of soap and hot water as bad as if I was a Portugee. Pass me that pen."

Captain Perez gladly relinquished the writing materials, and Captain Eri, after two or three trials, by which he added to the paper decorations of the floor, produced the following:

"Wife Wanted—By an ex–seafaring man of steady habbits. Must be willing to Work and Keep House shipshape and aboveboard. No sea– lawyers need apply. Address—Skipper, care the Nuptial Chime, Boston, Mass."

The line relating to sea–lawyers was insisted upon by Captain Jerry. "That'll shut out the tonguey kind," he explained. The advertisement, with this addition, being duly approved, the required fifty cents was inclosed, as was a letter to the editor of the matrimonial journal requesting all answers to be forwarded to Captain Jeremiah Burgess, Orham, Mass. Then the envelope was directed and the stamp affixed.

"There," said Captain Eri, "that's done. All you've got to do now, Jerry, is to pick out your wife and let us know what you want for a weddin' present. You're a lucky man."

"Aw, let's talk about somethin' else," said the lucky one rather gloomily. "What's the news up at the depot, Eri?"

They received the tidings of the coming of Hazeltine with the interest due to such an event. Captain Eri gave them a detailed account of his meeting with the new electrician, omitting, however, in consideration for the feelings of Captain Perez, to mention the fact that it was the Bartlett boy who started that gentleman upon his walk to the cable station.

"Well, what did you think of him?" asked Captain Perez, when the recital was finished.

"Seemed to me like a pretty good feller," answered Captain Eri deliberately. "He didn't git mad at the joke the gang played on him, for one thing. He ain't so smooth–tongued as Parker used to be and he didn't treat Baxter and me as if Cape Codders was a kind of animals, the way some of the summer folks do. He had the sense not to offer to pay me for takin' him over to the station, and I liked that. Take it altogether, he seemed like a pretty decent chap—for a New Yorker," he added, as an after thought.

"But say," he said a moment later, "I've got some more news and it ain't good news, either. Web Saunders has got his liquor license."

"I want to know!" exclaimed Captain Perez.

"You don't tell me!" said Captain Jerry.

Then they both said, "What will John Baxter do now?" And Captain Eri shook his head dubiously.

The cod bit well next morning and Captain Eri did not get in from the Windward Ledge until afternoon. By the way, it may be well to explain that Captain Jerry's remarks concerning "settlin' down" and "restin'," which we chronicled in the first chapter must not be accepted too literally. While it is true that each of the trio had given up long voyages, it is equally true that none had given up work entirely. Some people might not consider it restful to rise at four every weekday morning and sail in a catboat twelve miles out to sea and haul a wet cod line for hours, not to mention the sail home and the cleaning and barreling of the catch. Captain Eri did that. Captain Perez was what he called "stevedore"—that is, general caretaker during the owner's absence, at Mr. Delancy Barry's summer estate on the "cliff road." As for Captain Jerry, he was janitor at the schoolhouse.

The catch was heavy the next morning, as has been said, and by the time the last fish was split and iced and the last barrel sent to the railway station it was almost supper time. Captain Eri had intended calling on Baxter early in the day, but now he determined to wait until after supper.

The Captain had bad luck in the "matching" that followed the meal, and it was nearly eight o'clock before he finished washing dishes. This distasteful task being completed, he set out for the Baxter homestead.

The Captain's views on the liquor question were broader than those of many Orham citizens. He was an abstainer, generally speaking, but his scruples were not as pronounced as those of Miss Abigail Mullett, whose proudest boast was that she had refused brandy when the doctor prescribed it as the stimulant needed to save her life. Over and over again has Miss Abigail told it in prayer–meeting; how she "riz up" in her bed, "expectin' every breath to be the last" and said, "Dr. Palmer, if it's got to be liquor or death, then death referred to!"—meaning, it is fair to presume, that death was preferred rather than the brandy. With much more concerning her miraculous recovery through the aid of a "terbacker and onion poultice."

On general principles the Captain objected to the granting of a license to a fellow like "Web" Saunders, but it was the effect that this action of the State authorities might have upon his friend John Baxter that troubled him most.

For forty–five years John Baxter was called by Cape Cod people "as smart a skipper as ever trod a plank." He saved money, built an attractive home for his wife and daughter, and would, in the ordinary course of events, have retired to enjoy a comfortable old age. But his wife died shortly after the daughter's marriage to a Boston man, and on a voyage to Manila, Baxter himself suffered from a sunstroke and a subsequent fever, that left him a physical wreck and for a time threatened to unsettle his reason. He recovered a portion of his health and the threatened insanity disappeared, except for a religious fanaticism that caused him to accept the Bible literally and to interpret it accordingly. When his daughter and her husband were drowned in the terrible City of Belfast disaster, it is an Orham tradition that John Baxter, dressed in gunny–bags and sitting on an ash–heap, was found by his friends mourning in what he believed to be the Biblical "sackcloth and ashes." His little baby granddaughter had been looked out for by some kind friends in Boston. Only Captain Eri knew that John Baxter's yearly trip to Boston was made for the purpose of visiting the girl who was his sole reminder of the things that might have been, but even the Captain did not know that the money that paid her board and, as she grew older, for her gowns and schooling, came from the bigoted, stern old hermit, living alone in the old house at Orham.

In Orham, and in other sections of the Cape as well, there is a sect called by the ungodly, "The Come–Outers." They were originally seceders from the Methodist churches who disapproved of modern innovations. They "come out" once a week to meet at the houses of the members, and theirs are lively meetings. John Baxter was a "Come–Outer," and ever since the enterprising Mr. Saunders opened his billiard room, the old man's tirades of righteous wrath had been directed against this den of iniquity. Since it became known that "Web" had made application for the license, it was a regular amusement for the unregenerate to attend the gatherings of the "Come–Outers" and hear John Baxter call down fire from Heaven upon the billiard room, its proprietor, and its patrons. Orham people had begun to say that John Baxter was "billiard–saloon crazy."

And John Baxter was Captain Eri's friend, a friendship that had begun in school when the declaimer of Patrick Henry's "Liberty or Death" speech on Examination Day took a fancy to and refused to laugh at the little chap who tremblingly ventured to assert that he loved "little Pussy, her coat is so warm." The two had changed places until now it was Captain Eri who protected and advised.

When the Captain rapped at John Baxter's kitchen door no one answered, and, after yelling "Ship ahoy!" through the keyhole a number of times, he was forced to the conclusion that his friend was not at home.

"You lookin' fer Cap'n Baxter?" queried Mrs. Sarah Taylor, who lived just across the road. "He's gone to Come–Outers' meetin', I guess. There's one up to Barzilla Small's to–night."

Mr. Barzilla Small lived in that part of the village called "down to the neck," and when the Captain arrived there, he found the parlor filled with the devout, who were somewhat surprised to see him.

"Why, how do you do?" said Mrs. Small, resplendent in black "alpaca" and wearing her jet earrings. "I snum if you ain't a stranger! We'll have a reel movin' meetin' to–night because Mr. Perley's here, and he says he feels the sperrit a–workin'. Set right down there by the what–not. Luther," to her oldest but three, "give Cap'n Hedge your chair. You can set on the cricket. Yes, you can! Don't answer back!"

"Aw, ma!" burst out the indignant Luther, "how d'yer think I'm goin' to set on that cricket? My laigs 'll be way up under my chin. Make Hart set on it; he's shorter'n me."

"Shan't nuther, Lute Small!" declared Hartwell, a freckle–faced youngster, who was the next step downward in the family stair of children. "Set on it yourself. Make him, ma, now! You said he'd have to."

Cap'n Eri

"Now, ma, I—"

"Be still, both of you! I sh'd think you'd be ashamed, with everybody here so! Oh, my soul and body!" turning to the company, "if it ain't enough to try a saint! Sometimes seems's if I SHOULD give up. You be thankful, Abigail," to Miss Mullett, who sat by the door, "that you ain't got nine in a family and nobody to help teach 'em manners. If Barzilla was like most men, he'd have some dis–CIP–line in the house; but no, I have to do it all, and—"

Mr. Small, thus publicly rebuked, rose from his seat in the corner by the melodeon and proclaimed in a voice that he tried hard not to make apologetic:

"Now, Luther, if I was you I'd be a good boy and mind ma."

Even this awe–inspiring command had little effect upon the reluctant Luther, but Captain Eri, who, smiling and bowing right and left, had been working his passage to the other side of the room, announced that he was all right and would "squeeze in on the sofy 'side of Cap'n Baxter." So there was peace once more, that is, as much peace as half a dozen feminine tongues, all busy with different subjects, would allow.

"Why, Eri" whispered John Baxter, "I didn't expect to see you here. I'm glad, though; Lord knows every God–fearin' man in this town has need to be on his knees this night. Have you heard about it?"

"Cap'n John means about the rum–sellin' license that Web Saunders has got," volunteered Miss Melissa Busteed, leaning over from her seat in the patent rocker that had been the premium earned by Mrs. Small for selling one hundred and fifty pounds of tea for a much– advertised house. "Ain't it awful? I says to Prissy Baker this mornin', soon 's I heard of it, 'Prissy,' s' I, 'there 'll be a jedgment on this town sure's you're a livin' woman,' s' I. Says she, 'That's so, M'lissy,' s' she, and I says—"

Well, when Miss Busteed talks, interruptions are futile, so Captain Eri sat silent, as the comments of at least one-tenth of the population of Orham were poured into his ears. The recitation was cut short by Mrs. Small's vigorous pounding on the center table.

Cap'n Eri

"We're blessed this evenin'," said the hostess with emotion, "in havin' Mr. Perley with us. He's goin' to lead the meetin'."

The Reverend Mr. Perley—Reverend by courtesy; he had never been ordained—stood up, cleared his throat with vigor, rose an inch or two on the toes of a very squeaky pair of boots, sank to heel level again and announced that everyone would join in singing, "Hymn number one hundred and ten, omitting the second and fourth stanzas: hymn number one hundred and ten, second and fourth stanzas omitted." The melodeon, tormented by Mrs. Lurania Bassett, shrieked and groaned, and the hymn was sung. So was another, and yet another. Then Mr. Perley squeaked to his tiptoes again, subsided, and began a lengthy and fervent discourse.

Mr. Perley had been a blacksmith in Ostable before he "got religion," and now spent the major portion of his time in "boardin' 'round" with "Come–Outers" up and down the Cape and taking part in their meetings. His services at such gatherings paid for his food and lodging. He had been a vigorous horseshoer in the old days; now he preached just as vigorously.

He spoke of the faithful few here gathered together. He spoke of the scoffing of those outside the pale and hinted at the uncomfortable future that awaited them. He ran over the various denominations one by one, and one by one showed them to be worshipers of idols and followers after strange gods. He sank hoarsely into the bass and quavered up into falsetto and a chorus of "Amens!" and "Hallelujahs!" followed him.

"Oh, brothers and sisters!" he shouted, "here we are a–kneelin' at the altar's foot and what's goin' on outside? Why, the Devil's got his clutches in our midst. The horn of the wicked is exalted. They're sellin' rum—RUM—in this town! They're a–sellin' rum and drinkin' of it and gloryin' in their shame. But the Lord ain't asleep! He's got his eye on 'em! He's watchin' 'em! And some of these fine days he'll send down fire out of Heaven and wipe 'em off the face of the earth!" ("Amen! Glory! Glory! Glory!")

John Baxter was on his feet, his lean face working, the perspiration shining on his forehead, his eyes gleaming like lamps under his rough white eyebrows, and his clenched fists pounding the back of the chair in front of him. His hallelujahs were the last to cease. Captain Eri had to use some little force to pull him down on the sofa again.

27

Then Mrs. Small struck up, "Oh, brother, have you heard?" and they sang it with enthusiasm. Next, Miss Mullett told her story of the brandy and the defiance of the doctor. Nobody seemed much interested except a nervous young man with sandy hair and a celluloid collar, who had come with Mr. Tobias Wixon and was evidently a stranger. He had not heard it before and seemed somewhat puzzled when Miss Abigail repeated the "Death referred to" passage.

There was more singing. Mrs. Small "testified." So did Barzilla, with many hesitations and false starts and an air of relief when it was over. Then another hymn and more testimony, each speaker denouncing the billiard saloon. Then John Baxter arose and spoke.

He began by saying that the people of Orham had been slothful in the Lord's vineyard. They had allowed weeds to spring up and wax strong. They had been tried and found wanting.

"I tell you, brothers and sisters," he declaimed, leaning over the chair back and shaking a thin forefinger in Mr. Perley's face, "God has given us a task to do and how have we done it? We've set still and let the Devil have his way. We've talked and talked, but what have we done? Nothin'! Nothin' at all; and now the grip of Satan is tighter on the town than it ever has been afore. The Lord set us a watch to keep and we've slept on watch. And now there's a trap set for every young man in this c'munity. Do you think that that hell–hole down yonder is goin' to shut up because we talk about it in meetin'? Do you think Web Saunders is goin' to quit sellin' rum because we say he ought to? Do you think God's goin' to walk up to that door and nail it up himself? No, sir! He don't work that way! We've talked and talked, and now it's time to DO. Ain't there anybody here that feels a call? Ain't there axes to chop with and fire to burn? I tell you, brothers, we've waited long enough! I—old as I am—am ready. Lord, here I am! Here I am—"

He swayed, broke into a fit of coughing, and sank back upon the sofa, trembling all over and still muttering that he was ready. There was a hushed silence for a moment or two, and then a storm of hallelujahs and shouts. Mr. Perley started another hymn, and it was sung with tremendous enthusiasm.

Just behind the nervous young man with the celluloid collar sat a stout individual with a bald head. This was Abijah Thompson, known by the irreverent as "Barking" Thompson, a nickname bestowed because of his peculiar habit of gradually puffing up, like a frog, under religious excitement, and then bursting forth in an inarticulate shout, disconcerting to the uninitiated. During Baxter's speech and the singing of the hymn his expansive red cheeks had been distended like balloons, and his breath came shorter and shorter. Mr. Perley had arisen and was holding up his hand for silence, when with one terrific "Boo!" "Barking" Thompson's spiritual exaltation exploded directly in the ear of the nervous stranger.

The young man shot out of his chair as if Mr. Thompson had fired a dynamite charge beneath him. "Oh, the Devil!" he shrieked, and then subsided, blushing to the back of his neck.

Somehow this interruption took the spirit out of the meeting. Giggles from Luther and the younger element interfered with the solemnity of Mr. Perley's closing remarks, and no one else was brave enough to "testify" under the circumstances. They sang again, and the meeting broke up. The nervous young man was the first one to leave.

Captain Eri got his friend out of the clutches of the "Come−Outers" as quickly as possible, and piloted him down the road toward his home. John Baxter was silent and absent−minded, and most of the Captain's cheerful remarks concerning Orham affairs in general went unanswered. As they turned in at the gate the elder man said:

"Eri, do you believe that man's law ought to be allowed to interfere with God's law?"

"Well, John, in most cases it's my jedgment that it pays to steer pretty close to both of 'em."

"S'pose God called you to break man's law and keep His; what would you do?"

"Guess the fust thing would be to make sure 'twas the Almighty that was callin'. I don't want to say nothin' to hurt your feelin's, but I should advise the feller that thought that he had that kind of a call to 'beware of imitations,' as the soap folks advertise."

"Eri, I've got a call."

"Now, John Baxter, you listen. You and me have been sailin' together, as you might say, for forty odd years. I ain't a religious man 'cordin' to your way of thinkin', but I've generally found that the Lord runs things most as well as us folks could run 'em. When there's a leak at one end of the schooner it don't pay to bore a hole at the other end to let the water out. Don't you worry no more about Web Saunders and that billiard saloon. The s'lectmen 'll attend to them afore very long. Why don't you go up to Boston for a couple of weeks? 'Twill do you good."

"Do you think so, Eri? Well, maybe 'twould—maybe 'twould. Sometimes I feel as if my head was kind of wearin' out. I'll think about it."

"Better not think any more; better go right ahead."

"Well, I'll see. Good−night."

"Good−night, John."

"Perez," said Captain Eri, next day, "seems to me some kinds of religion is like whisky, mighty bad for a weak head. I wish somebody 'd invent a gold cure for Come−Outers."

CHAPTER IV. A PICTURE SENT AND A CABLE TESTED

Something over a fortnight went by and the three captains had received no answers from the advertisement in the Nuptial Chime. The suspense affected each of them in a different manner. Captain Jerry was nervous and apprehensive. He said nothing, and asked no questions, but it was noticeable that he was the first to greet the carrier of the "mail box" when that individual came down the road, and, as the days passed and nothing more important than the Cape Cod Item and a patent−medicine circular came to hand, a look that a suspicious person might have deemed expressive of hope began to appear in his face.

Captain Perez, on the contrary, grew more and more disgusted with the delay. He spent a good deal of time wondering why there were no replies, and he even went so far as to suggest writing to the editor of the Chime. He was disposed to lay the blame upon Captain Eri's advertisement, and hinted that the latter was not "catchy" enough.

Cap'n Eri

Captain Eri, alone of the trio, got any amusement out of the situation. He pretended to see in Captain Jerry an impatient bridegroom and administered comfort in large doses by suggesting that, in all probability, there had been so many replies that it had been found necessary to charter a freight–car to bring them down.

"Cheer up, Jerry!" he said. "It's tough on you, I know, but think of all them poor sufferin' females that's settin' up nights and worryin' for fear they won't be picked out. Why, say, when you make your ch'ice you'll have to let the rest know right off; 'twould be cruelty to animals not to. You ought to put 'em out of their misery quick's possible."

Captain Jerry's laugh was almost dismal.

The first batch of answers from the Chime came by an evening mail. Captain Eri happened to beat the post–office that night and brought them home himself. They filled three of his pockets to overflowing, and he dumped them by handfuls on the dining table, under the nose of the pallid Jerry.

"What did I tell you, Jerry?" he crowed. "I knew they was on the way. What have you got to say about my advertisement now, Perez?"

There were twenty–six letters altogether. It was surprising how many women were willing, even anxious, to ally themselves with "an ex–seafaring man of steady habbits." But most of the applicants were of unsatisfactory types. As Captain Perez expressed it, "There's too many of them everlastin' 'blondes' and things."

There was one note, however, that even Captain Eri was disposed to consider seriously. It was postmarked Nantucket, was written on half a sheet of blue–lined paper, and read as follows:

"MR. SKIPPER:

"Sir: I saw your advertisements in the paper and think perhaps you might suit me. Please answer these questions by return mail. What is your religious belief? Do you drink liquor? Are you a profane man? If you want to, you might send me your real name and a photograph. If I think you will suit maybe we might sign articles.

Yours truly,

"MARTHA B. SNOW.

"NANTUCKET, MASS."

"What I like about that is the shipshape way she puts it," commented Captain Perez. "She don't say that she 'jest adores the ocean.'"

"She's mighty handy about takin' hold and bossin' things; there ain't no doubt of that," said Captain Eri. "Notice it's us that's got to suit her, not her us. I kind of like that 'signin' articles,' too. You bet she's been brought up in a seagoin' family."

"I used to know a Jubal Snow that hailed from Nantucket," suggested Perez; "maybe she's some of his folks."

'Tain't likely," sniffed Captain Jerry. "There's more Snows in Nantucket than you can shake a stick at. You can't heave a rock without hittin' one."

"I b'lieve she's jest the kind we want," said Captain Perez with conviction.

"What do you say, Jerry?" asked Captain Eri. "You're goin' to be the lucky man, you know."

"Oh, I don't know. What's the use of hurryin'? More 'n likely the next lot of letters 'll have somethin' better yit."

"Now, that's jest like you, Jerry Burgess!" exclaimed Perez disgustedly. "Want to put off and put off and put off. And the house gittin' more like the fo'castle on a cattleboat every day."

"I don't b'lieve myself you'd do much better, Jerry," said Captain Eri seriously. "I like that letter somehow. Seems to me it's worth a try."

"Oh, all right! Have it your own way. Of course, _I_ ain't got nothin' to say. I'm only the divilish fool that's got to git married and keep boarders; that's all _I_ am!"

Cap'n Eri

"Be careful! She asked if you was a profane man."

"Aw, shut up! You fellers are enough to make a minister swear. _I_ don't care what you do. Go ahead and write to her if you want to, only I give you fair warnin', I ain't goin' to have her if she don't suit. I ain't goin' to marry no scarecrow."

Between them, and with much diplomacy, they soothed the indignant candidate for matrimony until he agreed to sign his name to a letter to the Nantucket lady. Then Captain Perez said:

"But, I say, Jerry; she wants your picture. Have you got one to send her?"

"I've got that daguerreotype I had took when I was married afore."

He rummaged it out of his chest and displayed it rather proudly. It showed him as a short, sandy–haired youth, whose sunburned face beamed from the depths of an enormous choker, and whose head was crowned with a tall, flat–brimmed silk hat of a forgotten style.

"I s'pose that might do," said Cap'n Perez hesitatingly.

"Do! 'Twill HAVE to do, seein' it's all he's got," said Captain Eri. "Good land!" he chuckled; "look at that hat! Say, Jerry, she'll think you done your seafarin' in Noah's ark."

But Captain Jerry was oblivious to sarcasm just then. He was gazing at the daguerreotype in a sentimental sort of way, blowing the dust from the glass, and tilting it up and down so as to bring it to the most effective light.

"I swan!" he mused, "I don't know when I've looked at that afore. I remember when I bought that hat, jest as well. Took care of it and brushed it—my! my! I don't know but it's somewheres around now. I thought I was jest about the ticket then, and—and I wa'n't BAD lookin', that's a fact!"

This last with a burst of enthusiasm.

Cap'n Eri

"Ho, ho! Perez," roared Captain Eri; "Jerry's fallin' in love with his own picture. Awful thing for one so young, ain't it?"

"I ain't such a turrible sight older 'n you be, Eri Hedge," sputtered the prospective bridegroom with righteous indignation. Then he added in a rather crestfallen tone, "But I am a heap older 'n I was when I had that daguerreotype took. See here; if I send that Nantucket woman this picture won't she notice the difference when she sees me?"

"What if she does?" broke in Captain Perez. "You can tell her how 'twas. Talk her over. A feller that's been married, like you, ought to be able to talk ANY woman over."

Captain Jerry didn't appear sanguine concerning his ability to "talk her over," but his fellow-conspirators made light of his feeble objections, and the daguerreotype, carefully wrapped, was mailed the next morning, accompanied by a brief biographical sketch of the original and his avowed adherence to the Baptist creed and the Good Templar's abstinence.

"I hope she'll hurry up and answer," said the impatient Captain Perez. "I want to get this thing settled one way or another. Don't you, Jerry?"

"Yes," was the hesitating reply. "One way or another."

Captain Eri had seen John Baxter several times since the evening of the "Come-Outers'" meeting. The old man was calmer apparently, and was disposed to take the billiard-saloon matter less seriously, particularly as it was reported that the town selectmen were to hold a special meeting to consider the question of allowing Mr. Saunders to continue in business. The last-named gentleman had given what he was pleased to call a "blow-out" to his regular patrons in celebration of the granting of the license, and "Squealer" Wixon and one or two more spent a dreary day and night in the town lock-up in consequence. Baxter told the Captain that he had not yet made up his mind concerning the proposed Boston trip, but he thought "more 'n likely" he should go.

Captain Eri was obliged to be content with this assurance, but he determined to keep a close watch on his friend just the same.

34

Cap'n Eri

He had met Ralph Hazeltine once or twice since the latter's arrival in Orham, and, in response to questions as to how he was getting on at the station, the new electrician invariably responded, "First– rate." Gossip, however, in the person of Miss Busteed, reported that the operators were doing their best to keep Mr. Hazeltine's lot from being altogether a bed of roses, and there were dark hints of something more to come.

On the morning following the receipt of the letter from the Nantucket lady, Captain Eri was busy at his fish shanty, putting his lines in order and sewing a patch on the mainsail of his catboat. These necessary repairs had prevented his taking the usual trip to the fishing grounds. Looking up from his work, he saw, through the open door, Ralph Hazeltine just stepping out of the cable–station skiff. He tucked his sail needle into the canvas and hailed the young man with a shouted "Good–morning!"

"How do you do, Cap'n Hedge?" said Hazeltine, walking toward the shanty. "Good weather, isn't it?"

"Tip–top. Long 's the wind stays westerly and there ain't no Sunday–school picnics on, we don't squabble with the weather folks. The only thing that 'll fetch a squall with a westerly wind is a Sunday–school picnic. That 'll do it, sure as death. Busy over across?"

"Pretty busy just now. The cable parted day before yesterday, and I've been getting things ready for the repair ship. She was due this morning, and we're likely to hear from her at any time."

"You don't say! Cable broke, hey? Now it's a queer thing, but I've never been inside that station since 'twas built. Too handy, I guess. I've got a second cousin up in Charlestown, lived there all his life, and he's never been up in Bunker Hill monument yit. Fust time I landed in Boston I dug for that monument, and I can tell you how many steps there is in it to this day. If that cable station was fifty mile off I'd have been through it two weeks after it started up, but bein' jest over there, I ain't ever done it. Queer, ain't it?"

"Perhaps you'd like to go over with me. I'm going up to the post– office, and when I come back I should be glad of your company."

"Well, now, that's kind of you. I cal'late I will. You might sing out as you go past. I've got a ha'f–hour job on this sail and then it's my watch below."

Cap'n Eri

The cable station at Orham is a low whitewashed building with many windows. The vegetation about it is limited exclusively to "beach grass" and an occasional wild–plum bush. The nearest building which may be reached without a boat is the life–saving station, two miles below. The outer beach changes its shape every winter. The gales tear great holes in its sides, and then, as if in recompense, throw up new shoals and build new promontories. From the cable– station doorway in fair weather may be counted the sails of over one hundred vessels going and coming between Boston and New York. They come and go, and, alas! sometimes stop by the way. Then the life–saving crews are busy and the Boston newspapers report another wreck. All up and down the outer beach are the sun–whitened bones of schooners and ships; and all about them, and partially covering them, is sand, sand, sand, as white and much coarser than granulated sugar.

Hazeltine's post–office trip and other errands had taken much more time than he anticipated, and more than two hours had gone by before he called for Captain Eri. During the row to the beach the electrician explained to the Captain the processes by which a break in the cable is located and repaired.

"You see," he said, "as soon as the line breaks we set about finding where it is broken. To do this we use an instrument called the Wheatstone bridge. In this case the break is about six hundred miles from the American shore. The next thing is to get at the company's repair ship. She lies, usually, at Halifax when she isn't busy, and that is where she was this time. We wired her and she left for the spot immediately. It was up to me to get ready the testing apparatus—we generally set up special instruments for testing. Judging by the distance, the ship should have been over the break early this morning. She will grapple for the broken cable ends, and as soon as she catches our end she'll send us a message. It's simple enough."

"Like takin' wormwood tea—easy enough if you've been brought up that way. I think I'd make more money catchin' codfish, myself," commented the Captain dryly.

Ralph laughed. "Well, it really is a very simple matter," he said. "The only thing we have to be sure of is that our end of the line is ready by the time the ship reaches the break. If the weather is bad the ship can't work, and so, when she does work, she works quick. I had my instruments in condition yesterday, so we're all right this time."

They landed at the little wharf and plodded through the heavy sand.

"Dismal–looking place, isn't it?" said Hazeltine, as he opened the back door of the station.

"Well, I don't know; it has its good p'ints," replied his companion. "Your neighbors' hens don't scratch up your garden, for one thing. What do you do in here?"

"This is the room where we receive and send. This is the receiver."

The captain noticed with interest the recorder, with its two brass supports and the little glass tube, half filled with ink, that, when the cable was working, wrote the messages upon the paper tape traveling beneath it.

"Pretty nigh as finicky as a watch, ain't it?" he observed.

"Fully as delicate in its way. Do you see this little screw on the centerpiece? Turn that a little, one way or the other, and the operator on the other side might send until doomsday, we wouldn't know it. I'll show you the living rooms and the laboratory now."

Just then the door at the other end of the room opened, and a man, whom Captain Eri recognized as one of the operators, came in. He started when he saw Hazeltine and turned to go out again. Ralph spoke to him:

"Peters," he said, "where is Mr. Langley?"

"Don't know," answered the fellow gruffly.

"Wait a minute. Tell me where Mr. Langley is."

"I don't know where he is. He went over to the village a while ago."

"Where are the rest of the men?"

"Don't know."

The impudence and thinly veiled hostility in the man's tone were unmistakable. Hazeltine hesitated, seemed about to speak, and then silently led the way to the hall.

Cap'n Eri

"I'll show you the laboratory later on," he said. "We'll go up to the testing room now." Then he added, apparently as much to himself as to his visitor, "I told those fellows that I wouldn't be back until noon."

There was a door at the top of the stairs. Ralph opened this quietly. As they passed through, Captain Eri noticed that Peters had followed them into the hall and stood there, looking up.

The upper hall had a straw matting on the floor. There was another door at the end of the passage, and this was ajar. Toward it the electrician walked rapidly. From the room behind the door came a shout of laughter; then someone said:

"Better give it another turn, hadn't I, to make sure? If two turns fixes it so we don't hear for a couple of hours, another one ought to shut it up for a week. That's arithmetic, ain't it?"

The laugh that followed this was cut short by Hazeltine's throwing the door wide open.

Captain Eri, close at the electrician's heels, saw a long room, empty save for a few chairs and a table in the center. Upon this table stood the testing instruments, exactly like those in the receiving room downstairs. Three men lounged in the chairs, and standing beside the table, with his fingers upon the regulating screw at the centerpiece of the recorder, was another, a big fellow, with a round, smooth–shaven face.

The men in the chairs sprang to their feet as Hazeltine came in. The face of the individual by the table turned white and his fingers fell from the regulating screw, as though the latter were red hot. The Captain recognized the men; they were day operators whom he had met in the village many times. Incidentally, they were avowed friends of the former electrician, Parker. The name of the taller one was McLoughlin.

No one spoke. Ralph strode quickly to the table, pushed McLoughlin to one side and stooped over the instruments. When he straightened up, Captain Eri noticed that his face also was white, but evidently not from fear. He turned sharply and looked at the four operators, who were doing their best to appear at ease and not succeeding. The electrician looked them over, one by one. Then he gave a short laugh.

Cap'n Eri

"You damned sneaks!" he said, and turned again to the testing apparatus.

He began slowly to turn the regulating screw on the recorder. He had given it but a few revolutions when the point of the little glass siphon, that had been tracing a straight black line on the sliding tape, moved up and down in curving zigzags. Hazeltine turned to the operator.

"Palmer," he said curtly, "answer that call."

The man addressed seated himself at the table, turned a switch, and clicked off a message. After a moment the line on the moving tape zigzagged again. Ralph glanced at the zigzags and bit his lip.

"Apologize to them," he said to Palmer. "Tell them we regret exceedingly that the ship should have been kept waiting. Tell them our recorder was out of adjustment."

The operator cabled the message. The three men at the end of the room glanced at each other; this evidently was not what they expected.

Steps sounded on the stairs and Peters hurriedly entered.

"The old man's comin'," he said.

Mr. Langley, the superintendent of the station, had been in the company's employ for years. He had been in charge of the Cape Cod station since it was built, and he liked the job. He knew cable work, too, from A to Z, and, though he was a strict disciplinarian, would forgive a man's getting drunk occasionally, sooner than condone carelessness. He was eccentric, but even those who did not like him acknowledged that he was "square."

He came into the room, tossed a cigar stump out of the window, and nodded to Captain Eri.

"How are you, Captain Hedge?" he said. Then, stepping to the table, he picked up the tape.

39

"Everything all right, Mr. Hazeltine?" he asked. "Hello! What does this mean? They say they have been calling for two hours without getting an answer. How do you explain that?"

It was very quiet in the room when the electrician answered.

"The recorder here was out of adjustment, sir," he said simply.

"Out of adjustment! I thought you told me everything was in perfect order before you left this morning."

"I thought so, sir, but I find the screw was too loose. That would account for the call not reaching us."

"Too loose! Humph!" The superintendent looked steadfastly at Hazeltine, then at the operators, and then at the electrician once more.

"Mr. Hazeltine," he said at length, "I will hear what explanations you may have to make in my office later on. I will attend to the testing myself. That will do."

Captain Eri silently followed his young friend to the back door of the station. Hazeltine had seen fit to make no comment on the scene just described, and the captain did not feel like offering any. They were standing on the steps when the big operator, McLoughlin, came out of the building behind them.

"Well," he said gruffly to the electrician. "Shall I quit now or wait until Saturday?"

"What?"

"Shall I git out now or wait till Saturday night? I suppose you'll have me fired."

Then Hazeltine's pent-up rage boiled over.

"If you mean that I'll tell Mr. Langley of your cowardly trick and have you discharged—No! I don't pay my debts that way. But I'll tell you this,—you and your sneaking friends. If you try another game like that,—yes, or if you so much as speak to

40

me, other than on business while I'm here, I WILL fire you—out of the window. Clear out!"

"Mr. Hazeltine," said Captain Eri a few moments later, "I hope you don't mind my sayin' that I like you fust–rate. Me and Perez and Jerry ain't the biggest bugs in town, but we like to have our friends come and see us. I wish you'd drop in once 'n a while."

"I certainly will," said the young man, and the two shook hands. That vigorous handshake was enough of itself to convince Ralph Hazeltine that he had made, at any rate, one friend in Orham.

And we may as well add here that he had made two. For that evening Jack McLoughlin said to his fellow conspirators:

"He said he'd fire me out of the window,—ME, mind you! And, by thunder! I believe he'd have DONE it too. Boys, there ain't any more 'con' games played on that kid while I'm around—Parker or no Parker. He's white, that's what HE is!"

CHAPTER V. THE WOMAN FROM NANTUCKET

Conversation among the captains was, for the next two days, confined to two topics, speculation as to how soon they might expect a reply from the Nantucket female and whether or not Mr. Langley would discharge Hazeltine. On the latter point Captain Eri was decided.

"He won't be bounced," said the Captain; "now you just put that down in your log. Langley ain't a fool, and he can put two and two together as well as the next feller. If I thought there was any need of it, I'd just drop him a hint myself, but there ain't, so I shan't put my oar in. But I wish you two could have heard that youngster talk to that McLoughlin critter; 'twould have done you good. That boy's all right."

Captain Jerry was alone when the expected letter came. He glanced at the postmark, saw that it was Nantucket, and stuck the note behind the clock. He did his best to forget it, but he looked so guilty when Captain Perez returned at supper time that that individual suspected something, made his friend confess, and, a little later when Captain Eri came in, the envelope, bearing many thumb—prints, was propped up against the sugar bowl in the middle of the table.

"We didn't open it, Eri," said Perez proudly. "We did want to, but we thought all hands ought to be on deck when anything as important as this was goin' to be done."

"He's been holdin' it up to the light for the last ha'f hour," sneered Captain Jerry. "Anybody 'd think it had a million dollars in it. For the land's sake, open it, Eri, 'fore he has a fit!"

Captain Eri picked up the letter, looked it over very deliberately, and then tore off the end of the envelope. The inclosure was another sheet of note paper like the first epistle. The Captain took out his spectacles, wiped them, and read the following aloud:

"CAPTAIN JEREMIAH BURGESS.

"Sir: I like your looks well enough, though it don't pay to put too much dependence in looks, as nobody knows better than me. Besides, I judge that picture was took quite a spell ago. Anyway, you look honest, and I am willing to risk money enough to carry me to Orham and back, though the dear land knows I ain't got none to throw away. If we don't agree to sign articles, I suppose likely you will be willing to stand half the fare. That ain't any more than right, the way I look at it. I shall come to Orham on the afternoon train, Thursday. Meet me at the depot.

"Yours truly,

"MARTHA B. SNOW.

"P. S.—I should have liked it better if you was a Methodist, but we can't have everything just as we want it in this world."

Nobody spoke for a moment after the reading of this intensely practical note. Captain Eri whistled softly, scratched his head, and then read the letter over again to himself. At length Captain Perez broke the spell.

"Jerusalem!" he exclaimed. "She don't lose no time, does she?"

Cap'n Eri

"She's pretty prompt, that's a fact," assented Captain Eri.

Captain Jerry burst forth in indignation:

"Is THAT all you've got to say?" he inquired with sarcasm, "after gittin' me into a scrape like this? Well now, I tell you one thing, I—"

"Don't go on your beam ends, Jerry," interrupted Captain Eri. "There ain't no harm done yit."

"Ain't no harm done? Why how you talk, Eri Hedge! Here's a woman that I ain't never seen, and might be a hundred years old, for all I know, comin' down here to—morrow night to marry me by main force, as you might say, and you set here and talk about—"

"Now, hold on, hold on, Jerry! She ain't goin' to marry you unless you want her to, 'tain't likely. More I think of it, the more I like the woman's way of doin' things. She's got sense, there's no doubt of that. You can't sell HER a cat in a bag. She's comin' down here to see you and talk the thing over, and I glory in her spunk."

"Wants me to pay her fare! I see myself doin' it! I've got ways enough to spend my money without paying fares for Nantucket folks."

"If you and she sign articles, as she calls it, you'll have to pay more than fares," said Captain Perez, in a matter—of—fact tone. "I think same as Eri does; she's a smart woman. We'll have to meet her at the depot, of course."

"Well _I_ won't! Cheeky thing! Let her find out where I am! I cal'late she'll have to do some huntin'."

"Now, see here, Jerry," said Captain Eri, "you was jest as anxious to have one of us get married as anybody else. You haven't got to marry the woman unless you want to, but you have got to help us see the thing through. I wish myself that we hadn't been quite so pesky anxious to give her the latitude and longitude, and had took some sort of an observation ourselves; but we didn't, and now we've got to treat her decent. You'll be at that depot along with Perez and me."

43

Cap'n Eri

When Captain Eri spoke in that tone his two cronies usually obeyed orders. Even the rebellious Jerry, who had a profound respect for his younger friend, gave in after some grumbling.

They sat up until late, speculating concerning the probable age and appearance of the expected visitor. Captain Perez announced that he didn't know why it was, but he had a notion that she was about forty and slim. Captain Jerry, who was in a frame of mind where agreement with anyone was out of the question, gave it as his opinion that she was thirty odd and rather plump. Captain Eri didn't hazard a guess, but suggested that they wait and see.

But even Captain Eri's calmness was more or less assumed, for he did not go fishing the next morning, but stayed about the house, whittling at the model of a clipper ship and tormenting Captain Jerry. The model was one that he had been at work upon at odd times ever since he gave up sea–going. It had never been completed for the very good reason that when one part was finished the Captain tore another part to pieces, and began over again. It was a sort of barometer of his feelings, and when his companions saw him take down the clipper and go to work, they knew he was either thinking deeply upon a perplexing problem or was troubled in his mind.

Captain Perez sang a good deal, principally confining his musical efforts to a ballad with a chorus of,

"Storm along, John; John, storm along; Ain't I glad my day's work's done!"

Also, he glanced at his watch every few minutes and then went to consult the chronometer to make sure of the time.

Captain Jerry went up to the schoolhouse and gave its vacant rooms a thorough sweeping for no particular reason except to be doing something. His appetite was poor, and he actually forgot to feed Lorenzo, a hitherto unheard–of slight, and one that brought down upon him a long lecture from Captain Eri, who vowed that loss of memory was a sure sign of lovesickness.

They started for the railway station immediately after supper. As they passed John Baxter's house they noticed a light in an upper chamber, and wondered if the old man was

44

ill. Captain Eri would have stopped to find out, but Captain Perez insisted that it could be done just as well when they came back, and expressed a fear that they might miss the train. Captain Jerry hadn't spoken since they left home, and walked gloomily ahead with his hands in his pockets.

Mr. "Web" Saunders, fat and in his pink–striped shirtsleeves, sat upon the steps of his saloon as they went by. He wished them an unctuous good–evening. The oily smoothness of Mr. Saunders' voice cannot be described with plain pen and ink; it gurgled with sweetness, like molasses poured from a jug. This was not a special tone put on for the occasion; no one except his wife ever heard him speak otherwise.

The response from the three captains was not enthusiastic, but Mr. Saunders continued to talk of the weather, the fishing, and the cranberry crop until a customer came and gave them a chance to get away.

"Slick! slick! slick!" commented Captain Eri, as they hurried along. "Blessed if he don't pretty nigh purr. I like a cat fust– rate, but I'm always suspicious of a cat–man. You know he's got claws, but you can't tell where he's goin' to use 'em. When a feller like that comes slidin' around and rubbin' his head against my shin, I always feel like keepin' t'other foot ready for a kick. You're pretty sartin to need it one time or another."

The train was nearly an hour late this evening, owing to a hot box, and the "ex–seafaring man" and his two friends peered anxiously out at it from around the corner of the station. The one coach stopped directly under the lights, and they could see the passengers as they came down the steps. Two or three got out, but these were men. Then came an apparition that caused Captain Jerry to gasp and clutch at Perez for support.

Down the steps of the car came a tall, coal–black negress, and in her hand was a canvas extension case, on the side of which was blazoned in two–inch letters the fateful name, "M. B. Snow, Nantucket."

Captain Eri gazed at this astounding spectacle for a full thirty seconds. Then he woke up.

"Godfrey domino!" he ejaculated. "BLACK! BLACK! Run! Run for your lives, 'fore she sees us!"

This order was superfluous. Captain Jerry was already half—way to the fence, and going at a rate which bid fair to establish a record for his age. The others fell into his wake, and the procession moved across country like a steeplechase.

They climbed over stone walls and splashed into meadows. They took every short cut between the station and their home. As they came in sight of the latter, Captain Perez' breath gave out almost entirely.

"Heave to!" he gasped. "Heave to, or I'll founder. I wouldn't run another step for all the darkies in the West Indies."

Captain Eri paused, but it was only after a struggle that Captain Jerry was persuaded to halt.

"I shan't do it, Eri!" he vowed wildly. "I shan't do it! There ain't no use askin' me; I won't marry that black woman! I won't, by thunder!"

"There! there! Jerry!" said Captain Eri soothingly. "Nobody wants you to. There ain't no danger now. She didn't see us."

"Ain't no danger! There you go again, Eri Hedge! She'll ask where I live and come right down in the depot wagon. Oh! Lordy! Lordy!"

The frantic sacrifice was about to bound away again, when Captain Eri caught him by the arm.

"I'll tell you what," he said, "we'll scoot for Eldredge's shanty and hide there till she gits tired and goes away. P'raps she won't come, anyhow."

The deserted fish shanty, property of the heirs of the late Nathaniel Eldredge, was situated in a hollow close to the house. In a few moments the three were inside, with a sawhorse against the door. Then Captain Eri pantingly sat down on an overturned bucket and laughed until the tears came into his eyes.

"That's it, laff!" almost sobbed Captain Jerry. "Set there and tee—hee like a Bedlamite. It's what you might expect. Wait till the rest of the town finds out about this; they'll do the laffin' then, and you won't feel so funny. We'll never hear the last of it in this world. If that darky comes down here, I'll—I'll drown her; I will—"

"I don't blame Jerry," said Perez indignantly. "I don't see much to laff at. Oh, my soul and body there she comes now."

They heard the rattle of a heavy carriage, and, crowding together at the cobwebbed window, saw the black shape of the "depot wagon" rock past. They waited, breathless, until they saw it go back again up the road.

"Did you lock the dining–room door, Perez?" asked Captain Eri.

"Course I didn't. Why should I?"

It was a rather senseless question. Nobody locks doors in Orham except at bedtime.

"Humph!" grunted Captain Eri. "She'll see the light in the dining room, and go inside and wait, more 'n likely. Well, there's nothin' for us to do but to stay here for a while, and then, if she ain't gone, one of us 'll have to go up and tell her she won't suit and pay her fare home, that's all. I think Jerry ought to be the one," he added mischievously. "He bein' the bridegroom, as you might say."

"Me!" almost shouted the frantic Captain Jerry. "You go to grass! You fellers got me into this scrape, and now let's see you git me out of it. I don't stir one step."

They sat there in darkness, the silence unbroken, save for an occasional chuckle from the provoking Eri. Perez, however, was meditating, and observed, after a while:

"Snow! That's a queer name for a darky, ain't it?"

"That colored man up at Barry's place was named White," said Captain Jerry, "and he was black as your hat. Names don't count."

"They say colored folks make good cooks, Jerry," slyly remarked Eri. "Maybe you'd better think it over."

47

Cap'n Eri

The unlucky victim of chance did not deign an answer, and the minutes crept slowly by. After a long while they heard someone whistling. Perez went to the window to take an observation.

"It's a man," he said disappointedly. "He's been to our house, too. My land! I hope he didn't go in. It's that feller Hazeltine; that's who 'tis."

"Is it?" exclaimed Eri eagerly. "That's so! so 'tis. Let's give him a hail."

Before he could be stopped he had pulled the saw–horse from the door, had opened the latter a little way, and, with his face at the opening, was whistling shrilly.

The electrician looked up and down the dark road in a puzzled sort of way, but evidently could not make up his mind from what quarter the whistles came.

"Mr. Hazeltine!" hailed the Captain, in what might be called a whispered yell or a shouted whisper. "Mr. Hazeltine! Here, on your lee bow. In the shanty."

The word "shanty" was the only part of the speech that brought light to Ralph's mind, but that was sufficient; he came down the hill, left the road, and plunged through the blackberry vines to the door.

"Who is it?" he asked. "Why, hello, Captain! What on earth—"

Captain Eri signaled him to silence, and then, catching his arm, pulled him into the shanty and shut the door. Captain Jerry hastened to set the saw–horse in place again.

"Mr. Hazeltine," said Captain Eri, "let me make you acquainted with Cap'n Perez and Cap'n Jerry, shipmates of mine. You've heard me speak of 'em."

Ralph, in the darkness, shook two big hands and heard whispered voices express themselves as glad to know him.

"You see," continued Eri in a somewhat embarrassed fashion, "we're sort of layin' to, as yer might say, waitin' to git our bearin's. We ain't out of our heads; I tell you that, 'cause I know that's what it looks like."

48

The bewildered Hazeltine laughed and said he was glad to hear it. To tell the truth, he had begun to think that something or other had suddenly driven his nearest neighbors crazy.

"I—I—I don't know how to explain it to you," the Captain stumbled on. "Fact is, I guess I won't jest yit, if you don't mind. It does sound so pesky ridic'lous, although it ain't, when you understand it. What we want to know is, have you been to our house and is there anybody there?"

"Why, yes, I've been there. I rowed over and dropped in for a minute, as you suggested the other day. The housekeeper—I suppose it was the housekeeper—that opened the door, said you were out, and I—"

He was interrupted by a hopeless groan.

"I knew it!" wailed Captain Jerry. "I knew it! And you said there wa'n't no danger, Eri!"

"Hush up, Jerry, a minute, for the love of goodness! What was she doin', Mr. Hazeltine, this woman you thought was the housekeeper? Did she look as if she was gettin' ready to go out? Did she have her bunnit on?"

"No. She seemed to be very much at home. That's why I thought—"

But again Captain Jerry broke in, "Well, by mighty!" he ejaculated. "That's nice, now, ain't it! SHE goin' away! You bet she ain't! She's goin' to stay there and wait, if it's forever. She's got too good a thing. Jest as like 's not, M'lissy Busteed, or some other gab machine like her, 'll be the next one to call, and if they see that great black critter! Oh! my soul!"

"Black!" said Ralph amazedly. "Why, the woman at your house isn't black. She's as white as I am, and not bad-looking for a woman of her age."

"WHAT?" This was the trio in chorus. Then Captain Eri said:

"Mr. Hazeltine, now, honest and true, is that a fact?"

"Of course it's a fact."

Cap'n Eri

The Captain wiped his forehead. "Mr. Hazeltine," he said, "if anybody had told me a fortn't ago that I was one of the three biggest fools in Orham, I'd have prob'ly rared up some. As 'tis now, I cal'late I'd thank him for lettin' me off so easy. You'll have to excuse us to–night, I'm afraid. We're in a ridic'lous scrape that we've got to git out of all alone. I'll tell you 'bout it some day. Jest now wish you'd keep this kind of quiet to oblige me."

Hazeltine saw that this was meant as a gentle hint for his immediate departure, and although he had a fair share of curiosity, felt there was nothing else to do. He promised secrecy, promised faithfully to call again later in the week, and then, the sawhorse having been removed by Captain Perez,—Captain Jerry was apparently suffering from a sort of dazed paralysis,—he went away. As soon as he had gone, Captain Eri began to lay down the law.

"Now then," he said, "there's been some sort of a mistake; that's plain enough. More 'n likely, the darky took the wrong satchel when she got up to come out of the car. That woman at the house is the real Marthy Snow all right, and we've got to go right up there and see her. Come on!"

But Captain Jerry mutinied outright. He declared that the sight of that darky had sickened him of marrying forever, and that he would not see the candidate from Nantucket, nor any other candidate. No persuasion could budge him. He simply would not stir from that shanty until the house had been cleared of female visitors.

"Go and see her yourself, if you're so set on it," he declared. "I shan't!"

"All right," said Captain Eri calmly. "I will. I'll tell her you're bashful, but jest dyin' to be married, and that she can have you if she only waits long enough."

With this he turned on his heel and walked out.

"Hold on, Eri!" shouted the frantic Jerry. "Don't you do it! Don't you tell her that! Land of love, Perez, do you s'pose he will?"

"I don't know," was the answer in a disgusted tone. "You hadn't ought to have been so pig–headed, Jerry."

Cap'n Eri

Captain Eri, with set teeth and determination written on his face, walked straight to the dining-room door. Drawing a long breath, he opened it and stepped inside. A woman, who had been sitting in Captain Perez' rocker, rose as he entered.

The woman looked at the Captain and the Captain looked at her. She was of middle age, inclined to stoutness, with a pair of keen eyes behind brass-rimmed spectacles, and was dressed in a black "alpaca" gown that was faded a little in places and had been neatly mended in others. She spoke first.

"You're not Cap'n Burgess?" she said.

"No, ma'am," said the Captain uneasily. "My name is Hedge. I'm a sort of messmate of his. You're Miss Snow?"

"Mrs. Snow. I'm a widow."

They shook hands. Mrs. Snow calmly expectant; the Captain very nervous and not knowing how to begin.

"I feel as if I knew you, Cap'n Hedge," said the widow, as the Captain slid into his own rocker. "The boy on the depot wagon told me a lot about you and Cap'n Ryder and Cap'n Burgess."

"Did, hey?" The Captain inwardly vowed vengeance on his chum's grandnephew. "Hope he gave us a clean bill."

"Well, he didn't say nothin' against you, if that's what you mean. If he had, I don't think it would have made much diff'rence. I've lived long enough to want to find out things for myself, and not take folks' say-so."

The lady seeming to expect some sort of answer to this statement, Captain Eri expressed his opinion that the plan of finding out things for one's self was a good "idee." Then, after another fidgety silence, he observed that it was a fine evening. There being no dispute on this point, he endeavored to think of something else to say. Mrs. Snow, however, saved him the trouble.

"Cap'n Hedge," she said, "as I'm here on what you might call a bus'ness errand, and as I've been waitin' pretty nigh two hours already, p'raps we'd better talk about somethin' besides fine evenin's. I've got to be lookin' up a hotel or boardin' house or somewheres to stay to-night, and I can't wait much longer. I jedge you got my letter and was expectin' me. Now, if it ain't askin' too much, I'd like to know where Cap'n Burgess is, and why he wa'n't at the depot to meet me."

This was a leading question, and the Captain was more embarrassed than ever. However, he felt that something had to be done and that it was wisest to get it over with as soon as possible.

"Well, ma'am," he said, "we—we got your letter all right, and, to tell you the truth, we was at the depot—Perez and me and Jerry."

"You WAS! Well, then, for the land of goodness, why didn't you let me know it? Such a time as I had tryin' to find out where you lived and all!"

The Captain saw but one plausible explanation, and that was the plain truth. Slowly he told the story of the colored woman and the extension case. The widow laughed until her spectacles fell off.

"Well, there!" she exclaimed. "If that don't beat all! I don't blame Cap'n Burgess a mite. Poor thing! I guess I'd have run, too, if I'd have seen that darky. She was settin' right in the next seat to me, and she had a shut-over bag consid'rable like mine, and when she got up to git out, she took mine by mistake. I was a good deal put out about it, and I expect I talked to her like a Dutch uncle when I caught up with her. Dear! dear! Where is Cap'n Burgess?"

"He's shut up in a fish shanty down the road, and he's so upsot that I dunno's he'll stir from there tonight. Jerry ain't prejudiced, but that darky was too much for him."

And then they both laughed, the widow because of the ludicrous nature of the affair and the Captain because of the relief that the lady's acceptance of it afforded his mind.

Mrs. Snow was the first to become grave. "Cap'n Hedge," she said, "there's one or two things I must say right here. In the first place, I ain't in the habit of answerin' advertisements from folks that wants to git married; I ain't so hard up for a man as all that comes to. Next thing, I didn't come down here with my mind made up to marry Cap'n Burgess, not by no means. I wanted to see him and talk with him, and tell him jest all about how things was with me and find out about him and then—why, if everything was shipshape, I might, p'raps, think about—"

"Jest so, ma'am, jest so," broke in her companion. "That's about the way we felt. You see, there's prob'ly a long story on both sides, and if you'll excuse me I'll go down to the shanty and see if I can't git Jerry up here. It'll be a job, I'm 'fraid, but—"

"No, you shan't either. I'll tell you what we'll do. It's awful late now and I must be gittin' up to the tavern. S'pose, if 'tain't too much trouble, you walk up there with me and I'll stay there to–night and to–morrer I'll come down here, and we'll all have a common–sense talk. P'raps by that time your friend 'll have the darky woman some off his mind, too."

Needless to say Captain Eri agreed to this plan with alacrity. The widow carefully tied on a black, old–fashioned bonnet, picked up a fat, wooden–handled umbrella and the extension case, and said that she was ready.

They walked up the road together, the Captain carrying the extension case. They talked, but not of matrimonial prospects. Mrs. Snow knew almost as much about the sea and the goings and comings thereon as did her escort, and the conversation was salty in the extreme. It developed that the Nantucket lady had a distant relative who was in the life–saving service at Cuttyhunk station, and as the Captain knew every station man for twenty miles up and down the coast, wrecks and maritime disasters of all kinds were discussed in detail.

At the Traveler's Rest Mrs. Snow was introduced by the unblushing Eri as a cousin from Provincetown, and, after some controversy concerning the price of board and lodging, she was shown up to her room. Captain Eri walked home, absorbed in meditation. Whatever his thoughts were they were not disagreeable, for he smiled and shook his head more than once, as if with satisfaction. As he passed John Baxter's house he noticed that the light in the upper window was still burning.

Captain Perez was half asleep when Eri opened the door of the shanty. Captain Jerry, however, was very much awake and demanded to be told things right away. His friend briefly explained the situation.

"I don't care if she stays here till doomsday," emphatically declared the disgruntled one, "I shan't marry her. What's she like, anyhow?"

He was surprised at the enthusiasm of Captain Eri's answer.

"She's a mighty good woman; that's what I think she is, and she'd make a fust–class wife for any man. I hope you'll say so, too, when you see her. There ain't nothin' hity–tity about her, but she's got more common–sense than any woman I ever saw. But there! I shan't talk another bit about her to–night. Come on home and turn in."

And go home and turn in they did, but not without protestation from the pair who had yet to meet the woman from Nantucket.

CHAPTER VI. THE SCHOOLHOUSE BELL RINGS

"All hands on deck! Turn out there! Turnout!"

Captain Eri grunted and rolled over in his bed; for a moment or two he fancied himself back in the fo'castle of the Sea Mist, the bark in which he had made his first voyage. Then, as he grew wider awake, he heard, somewhere in the distance, a bell ringing furiously.

"Turn out, all hands! Turn out!"

Captain Eri sat up. That voice was no part of a dream. It belonged to Captain Jerry, and the tone of it meant business. The bell continued to ring.

"Aye, aye, Jerry! What's the matter?" he shouted.

"Fire! There's a big fire up in the village. Look out of the window, and you can see. They're ringing the schoolhouse bell; don't you hear it?"

The Captain, wide awake enough by this time, jumped out of bed, carrying the blankets with him, and ran to the window. Opening it, he thrust out his head. The wind had changed to the eastward, and a thick fog had come in with it. The house was surrounded by a wet, black wall, but off to the west a red glow shone through it, now brighter and now fainter. The schoolhouse bell was turning somersaults in its excitement.

Only once, since Captain Jerry had been janitor, had the schoolhouse bell been rung except in the performance of its regular duties. That once was on a night before the Fourth of July, when some mischievous youngsters climbed in at a window and proclaimed to sleeping Orham that Young America was celebrating the anniversary of its birth. Since then, on nights before the Fourth, Captain Jerry had slept in the schoolhouse, armed with a horsewhip and an ancient navy revolver. The revolver was strictly for show, and the horsewhip for use, but neither was called into service, for even if some dare–devil spirits did venture near the building, the Captain's snores, as he slumbered by the front door, were danger signals that could not be disregarded.

But there was no flavor of the Fourth in the bell's note this night. Whoever the ringer might be, he was ringing as though it was his only hope for life, and the bell swung back and forth without a pause. The red glow in the fog brightened again as the Captain gazed at it.

Captain Jerry came tumbling up the stairs, breathless and half dressed.

"Where do you make it out to be?" he panted.

"Somewhere's nigh the post–office. Looks 's if it might be Weeks's store. Where's Perez?"

Captain Eri had lighted a lamp and was pulling on his boots, as he spoke.

"Here I be!" shouted the missing member of the trio from the dining room below. "I'm all ready. Hurry up, Eri!"

Captain Eri jumped into his trousers, slipped into a faded pea– jacket and clattered downstairs, followed by the wildly excited Jerry.

"Good land, Perez!" he cried, as he came into the dining room, "I thought you said you was all ready!"

Captain Perez paused in the vain attempt to make Captain Jerry's hat cover his own cranium and replied indignantly, "Well, I am, ain't I?"

"Seems to me I'd put somethin' on my feet besides them socks, if I was you. You might catch cold."

Perez glanced down at his blue—yarn extremities in blank astonishment. "Well, now," he exclaimed, "if I hain't forgot my boots!"

"Well, git 'em on, and be quick. There's your hat. Give Jerry his."

The excited Perez vanished through the door of his chamber, and Captain Eri glanced at the chronometer; the time was a quarter after two.

They hurried out of the door and through the yard. The wind, as has been said, was from the east, but there was little of it and, except for the clanging of the bell, the night was very still. The fog was heavy and wet, and the trees and bushes dripped as if from a shower. There was the salt smell of the marshes in the air, and the hissing and splashing of the surf on the outer beach were plainly to be heard. Also there was the clicking sound of oars in row—locks.

"Somebody is comin' over from the station," gasped Captain Jerry. "Don't run so, Eri. It's too dark. I've pretty nigh broke my neck already."

They passed the lily pond, where the frogs had long since adjourned their concert and gone to bed, dodged through the yard of the tightly shuttered summer hotel, and came out at the corner of the road, having saved some distance by the "short—cut."

"That ain't Weeks's store," declared Captain Perez, who was in the lead. "It's Web Saunders's place; that's what it is."

Captain Eri paused and looked over to the left in the direction of the Baxter homestead. The light in the window was still burning.

They turned into the "main road" at a dog trot and became part of a crowd of oddly dressed people, all running in the same direction.

"Web's place, ain't it?" asked Eri of Seth Wingate, who was lumbering along with a wooden bucket in one hand and the pitcher of his wife's best washstand set in the other.

"Yes," breathlessly answered Mr. Wingate, "and it's a goner, they tell me. Every man's got to do his part if they're going to save it. I allers said we ought to have a fire department in this town."

Considering that Seth had, for the past eight years, persistently opposed in town–meeting any attempt to purchase a hand engine, this was a rather surprising speech, but no one paid any attention to it then.

The fire was in the billiard saloon sure enough, and the back portion of the building was in a blaze when they reached it. Ladders were placed against the eaves, and a line of men with buckets were pouring water on the roof. The line extended to the town pump, where two energetic youths in their shirtsleeves were working the handle with might and main. The houses near at hand were brilliantly illuminated, and men and women were bringing water from them in buckets, tin pails, washboilers, and even coalscuttles.

Inside the saloon another hustling crowd was busily working to "save" Mr. Saunders' property. A dozen of the members had turned the biggest pool table over on its back and were unscrewing the legs, heedless of the fact that to attempt to get the table through the front door was an impossibility and that, as the back door was in the thickest of the fire, it, too, was out of the question. A man appeared at the open front window of the second story with his arms filled with bottles of various liquids, "original packages" and others. These, with feverish energy, he threw one by one into the street, endangering the lives of everyone in range and, of course, breaking every bottle thrown. Some one of the cooler heads calling his attention to these facts, he retired and carefully packed all the empty bottles, the only ones remaining, into a peach basket and tugged the latter downstairs and to a safe place on a neighboring piazza. Then he rested from his labors as one who had done all that might reasonably be expected.

Mr. Saunders himself, lightly attired in a nightshirt tucked into a pair of trousers, was rushing here and there, now loudly demanding more water, and then stopping to swear at the bottle–thrower or some other enthusiast. "Web's" smoothness was all gone, and the language he used was, as Abigail Mullett said afterward, "enough to bring down a jedgment on anybody."

Captain Eri caught him by the sleeve as he was running past and inquired, "How'd it start, Web?"

"How'd it START? I know mighty well HOW it started, and 'fore I git through I'll know WHO started it. Somebody 'll pay for this, now you hear me! Hurry up with the water, you—"

He tore frantically away to the pump and the three captains joined the crowd of volunteer firemen. Captain Eri, running round to the back of the building, took in the situation at once. Back of the main portion of the saloon was an ell, and it was in this ell that the fire had started. The ell, itself, was in a bright blaze, but the larger building in front was only just beginning to burn. The Captain climbed one of the ladders to the roof and called to the men at work there.

"That shed's gone, Ben," he said. "Chuck your water on the main part here. Maybe, if we had some ropes we might be able to pull the shed clear, and then we could save the rest."

"How'd you fasten the ropes?" was the panted reply. "She's all ablaze, and a rope would burn through in a minute if you tied it anywheres."

"Git some grapples and anchors out of Rogers' shop. He's got a whole lot of 'em. Keep on with the water bus'ness. I'll git the other stuff."

He descended the ladder and explained his idea to the crowd below. There was a great shout and twenty men and boys started on a run after ropes, while as many more stormed at the door of Nathaniel Rogers' blacksmith shop. Rogers was the local dealer in anchors and other marine ironwork. The door of the shop was locked and there was a yell for axes to burst it open.

Then arose an agonized shriek of "Don't chop! don't chop!" and Mr. Rogers himself came struggling to the defense of his property. In concert the instant need was explained to him, but he remained unconvinced.

"We can't stay here arguin' all night!" roared one of the leaders. "He's got to let us in. Go ahead and chop! I'll hold him."

"I give you fair warnin', Squealer Wixon! If you chop that door, I'll have the law onto you. I just had that door painted, and— STOP! I've got the key in my pocket!"

It was plain that the majority were still in favor of chopping, as affording a better outlet for surplus energy, but they waited while Mr. Rogers, still protesting, produced the key and unlocked the door. In another minute the greater portion of the ironwork in the establishment was on its way to the fire.

The rope–seekers were just returning, laden with everything from clothes–lines to cables. Half a dozen boat anchors and a grapnel were fastened to as many ropes, and the crowd pranced gayly about the burning ell, looking for a chance to make them fast. Captain Eri found a party with axes endeavoring to cut a hole through the side of the saloon in order to get out the pool table. After some endeavor he persuaded them to desist and they came around to the rear and, taking turns, ran in close to the shed and chopped at it until the fire drove them away. At last they made a hole close to where it joined the main building, large enough to attach the grapnel. Then, with a "Yo heave ho!" everyone took hold of the rope and pulled. Of course the grapnel pulled out with only a board or two, but they tried again, and, this time getting it around a beam, pulled a large portion of the shed to the ground.

Meanwhile, another ax party had attached an anchor to the opposite side, and were making good progress. In due time the shed yawned away from the saloon, tottered, and collapsed in a shower of sparks. A deluge of water soon extinguished these. Then everyone turned to the main building, and, as the fire had not yet taken a firm hold of this, they soon had it under control.

Captain Eri worked with the rest until he saw that the worst was over. Then he began the search that had been in his mind since he first saw the blaze. He found Captain Jerry and Captain Perez perspiringly passing buckets of water from hand to hand in the line, and, calling them to one side, asked anxiously:

"Have either of you fellers seen John Baxter tonight?"

Cap'n Eri

Captain Perez looked surprised, and then some of the trouble discernible in Eri's face was apparent in his own.

"Why, no," he replied slowly, "I ain't seen him, now you speak of it. Everybody in town's here, too. Queer, ain't it?

"Haven't you seen him, either, Jerry?"

Captain Jerry answered with a shake of the head. "But then," he said, "Perez and me have been right here by the pump ever sence we come. He might be 'most anywheres else, and we wouldn't see him. Want me to ask some of the other fellers?"

"No!" exclaimed his friend, almost fiercely. "Don't you mention his name to a soul, nor let 'em know you've thought of him. If anybody should ask, tell 'em you guess he's right around somewheres. You two git to work ag'in. I'll let you know if I want you."

The pair took up their buckets, and the Captain walked on from group to group, looking carefully at each person. The Reverend Perley and some of his flock were standing by themselves on a neighboring stoop, and to them the searcher turned eagerly.

"Why, Cap'n Eri!" exclaimed Miss Busteed, the first to identify him, "how you've worked! You must be tired pretty nigh to death. Ain't it awful! But it's the Lord's doin's; I'm jest as sure of that as I can be, and I says so to Mr. Perley. Didn't I, Mr. Perley? I says—"

"Lookin' for anybody, Cap'n?" interrupted the reverend gentleman.

"No," lied the Captain calmly, "jest walkin' around to git cooled off a little. Good—night."

There was the most likely place, and John Baxter was not there. Certainly every citizen in Orham, who was able to crawl, would be out this night, and if the old puritan hermit of the big house was not present to exult over the downfall of the wicked, it would be because he was ill or because— The Captain didn't like to think of the other reason.

Mrs. "Web" Saunders, quietly weeping, was seated on a knoll near the pump. Three of the Saunders' hopefuls, also weeping, but not quietly, were seated beside her. Another,

60

the youngest of the family, was being rocked soothingly in the arms of a stout female, who was singing to it as placidly as though fires were an every day, or night, occurrence. The Captain peered down, and the stout woman looked up.

"Why, Mrs. Snow!" exclaimed Captain Eri.

The lady from Nantucket made no immediate reply. She rose, however, shook down the black "alpaca" skirt, which had been folded up to keep it out of the dew, and, still humming softly to the child, walked off a little way, motioning with her head for the Captain to follow. When she had reached a spot sufficiently remote from Mrs. Saunders, she whispered:

"How d'ye do, Cap'n Hedge? I guess the wust is over now, isn't it? I saw you workin' with them ropes; you must be awful tired."

"How long have you been here?" asked the Captain somewhat astonished at her calmness.

"Oh, I come right down as soon as I heard the bell. I'm kind of used to fires. My husband's schooner got afire twice while I was with him. He used to run a coal vessel, you know. I got right up and packed my bag, 'cause I didn't know how the fire might spread. You never can tell in a town like this. Ssh'h, dearie," to the baby, "there, there, it's all right. Lay still."

"How'd you git acquainted with her?" nodding toward the wife of the proprietor of the scorched saloon.

"Oh, I see the poor thing settin' there with all them children and nobody paying much attention to her, so I went over and asked if I couldn't help out. I haven't got any children of my own, but I was number three in a fam'ly of fourteen, so I know how it's done. Oh! that husband of hers! He's a nice one, he is! Would you b'lieve it, he come along and she spoke to him, and he swore at her somethin' dreadful. That's why she's cryin'. Poor critter, I guess by the looks she's used to it. Well, I give HIM a piece of my mind. He went away with a flea in his ear. I do despise a profane man above all things. Yes, the baby's all right, Mrs. Saunders. I'm a-comin'. Good-night, Cap'n Hedge. I s'pose I shall see you all in the mornin'. You ought to be careful and not stand still much this damp night. It's bad

Cap'n Eri

when you're het up so."

She went back, still singing to the baby, to where Mrs. Saunders sat, and the Captain looked after her in a kind of amazed fashion.

"By mighty!" he muttered, and then repeated it. Then he resumed his search.

He remembered that there had been a number of people on the side of the burning shed opposite that on which he had been employed, and he determined to have one look there before going to the Baxter homestead. Almost the first man he saw as he approached the dying fire was Ralph Hazeltine. The electrician's hands and face were blackened by soot, and the perspiration sparkled on his forehead.

"Hello, Captain!" he said, holding out his hand. "Lively for a while, wasn't it? They tell me you were the man who suggested pulling down the shed. It saved the day, all right enough."

"You look as if you'd been workin' some yourself. Was you one of the fellers that got that anchor in on this side?"

"He was THE one," broke in Mr. Wingate, who was standing at Hazeltine's elbow. "He waded in with an ax and stayed there till I thought he'd burn the hair off his head. Web ought to pay you and him salvage, Eri. The whole craft would have gone up if it hadn't been for you two."

"I wonder if they got that pool table out," laughed Ralph. "They did everything but saw it into chunks."

"I never saw Bluey Bacheldor work so afore," commented the Captain. "I wish somebody'd took a photograph of him. I'll bet you could sell 'em round town for curiosities. Well, I can't be standin' here."

"If you're going home I'll go along with you. I may as well be getting down toward the station. The excitement is about over."

"I ain't goin' right home, Mr. Hazeltine. I've got an errand to do. Prob'ly I'll be goin' pretty soon, though."

"Oh, all right! I'll wait here a while longer then. See you later perhaps."

The fog had lifted somewhat and as the Captain, running silently, turned into the "shore road," he saw that the light in the Baxter homestead had not been extinguished. The schoolhouse bell had ceased to ring, and the shouts of the crowd at the fire sounded faintly. There were no other sounds.

Up the driveway Captain Eri hurried. There were no lights in the lower part of the house and the dining–room door was locked. The kitchen door, however, was not fastened and the Captain opened it and entered. Shutting it carefully behind him, he groped along to the entrance of the next room.

"John!" he called softly. There was no answer, and the house was perfectly still save for the ticking of the big clock. Captain Eri scratched a match and by its light climbed the stairs. His friend's room was empty. The lamp was burning on the bureau and a Bible was open beside it. The bed had not been slept in.

Thoroughly alarmed now, the Captain, lamp in hand, went through one room after the other. John Baxter was not at home, and he was not with the crowd at the fire. Where was he? There was, of course, a chance that his friend had passed him on the way or that he had been at the fire, after all, but this did not seem possible. However, there was nothing to do but go back, and this time the Captain took the path across the fields.

The Baxter house was on the "shore road," and the billiard room and post–office were on the "main road." People in a hurry sometimes avoided the corner by climbing the fence opposite the Baxter gate, going through the Dawes' pasture and over the little hill back of the livery stable, and coming out in the rear of the post–office and close to the saloon.

Captain Eri, worried, afraid to think of the fire and its cause, and only anxious to ascertain where his friend was and what he had been doing that night, trotted through the pasture and over the hill. Just as he came to the bayberry bushes on the other side he stumbled and fell flat.

63

He knew what it was that he had stumbled over the moment that he fell across it, and his fingers trembled, so that he could scarcely scratch the match that he took from his pocket. But it was lighted at last and, as its tiny blaze grew brighter, the Captain saw John Baxter lying face downward in the path, his head pointed toward his home and his feet toward the billiard saloon.

CHAPTER VII. CAPTAIN ERI FINDS A NURSE

For a second, only, Captain Eri stood there motionless, stooping over the body of his friend. Then he sprang into vigorous action. He dropped upon his knees and, seizing the shoulder of the prostrate figure, shook it gently, whispering, "John! John!" There was no answer and no responsive movement, and the Captain bent his head and listened. Breath was there and life; but, oh, so little of either! The next thought was, of course, to run for help and for a doctor, but he took but a few steps when a new idea struck him and he came back.

Lighting another match he examined the fallen man hurriedly. The old "Come–Outer" lay in the path with his arms outstretched, as if he had fallen while running. He was bare–headed, and there was no sign of a wound upon him. One coat–sleeve was badly scorched, and from a pocket in the coat protruded the neck of a bottle. The bottle was empty, but its odor was strong; it had contained kerosene. The evidence was clear, and the Captain knew that what he had feared was the truth.

For a moment he stood erect and pondered as to what was best to do. Whatever it was, it must be done quickly, but if the doctor and those that might come with him should find the burned coat and the tell–tale bottle, it were better for John Baxter that consciousness and life never were his again. There might, and probably would, be suspicion; but here was proof absolute that meant prison and disgrace for a man whom all the community had honored and respected.

Captain Eri weighed the chances, speculated on the result, and then did what seemed to him right. He threw the bottle as far away from the path as he could and then stripped off the coat, and, folding it into a small bundle, hid it in the bushes near by. Then he lifted the limp body, and turned it so that the gray head was toward the billiard saloon instead of from it.

Cap'n Eri

Perez and Jerry were still busy with the water buckets when their friend came panting up the knoll to the pump.

"Hello, Eri!" said the former, wiping his forehead with his arm. "It's 'bout out, ain't it? Why, what's the matter?"

"Nothin'; nothin' to speak of. Put down them buckets, and you and Jerry come with me. I've got somethin' that I want you to do."

Nodding and exchanging congratulations with acquaintances in the crowd on the success of the fire–fighting, Captain Eri led his messmates to a dark corner under a clump of trees. Then he took each of them by the arm and whispered sharply:

"Dr. Palmer's somewheres in this crowd. I want each of you fellers to go diff'rent ways and look for him. Whichever one finds him fust can bring him up to the corner by the post–office. Whistle when you git there and the rest of us 'll come. Don't stop to ask questions. I ain't hurt, but John Baxter's had a stroke or somethin'. I can't tell you no more now. Hurry! And say, don't you mention to a soul what the matter is."

A sea–faring life has its advantages. It teaches prompt obedience, for one thing. The two mariners did not hesitate an instant, but bolted in opposite directions. Captain Eri watched them go, and then set off in another. He was stopped every few moments and all sorts of questions and comments concerning the fire and its cause were fired at him, but he put off some inquiries with a curt "Don't know" and others with nods or negatives, and threaded his way from one clump of townspeople to another. As he came close to the blackened and smoking billiard saloon, Ralph Hazeltine caught him by the arm.

"Hello!" said the electrician. "Haven't you gone home yet?"

"No, not yit. Say, I'll ask you, 'cause I cal'late you can keep your mouth shut if it's necessary: Have you seen the Doctor anywheres 'round lately? He was here, 'cause I saw him when I fust come."

"Who, Dr. Palmer? No; I haven't seen him. Is anyone hurt? Can I help?"

"I guess not. John Baxter's sick, but—oh, Lord! Here comes Wingate. He'll talk for a week."

Seth, panting and excited, was pushing his way toward them, shouting the Captain's name at the top of his voice.

"Hey, Eri!" he hailed. "I want to know if you'll sign a petition to git the town a fire ingyne? I've been talkin' to a couple of the s'lectmen and they—"

"Oh, Mr. Wingate," interrupted Ralph, "Mr. Mullett's been looking for you. He's over there by the pump, I think."

"Who, Lem Mullett? Is that so! He's jest the feller I want to see. See you later, Eri."

The Captain grinned appreciatively as the convert to the hand–engine proposal disappeared.

"That wasn't so bad," he said. "I'm much obliged. Hey! There's the whistle. Come on, Mr. Hazeltine, if you ain't in a special hurry. Maybe we WILL need you."

They reached the corner by the post–office to find Dr. Palmer, who had practiced medicine in Orham since he received his diploma, waiting for them. Captain Perez, who had discovered the physician on the Nickerson piazza, was standing close by with his fingers in his mouth, whistling with the regularity of a foghorn.

"Cut it short, Perez!" commanded Eri. "We're here now."

"Yes, but Jerry ain't." And the whistling began again.

"Dry up, for the land's sake! D'you want to fetch the whole tribe here? There's Jerry, now. Come on, Doctor."

John Baxter was lying just as the Captain had left him, and the others watched anxiously as the doctor listened at the parted lips, and thrust his hand inside the faded blue waistcoat.

"He's alive," he said after a moment, "but unconscious. We must get him home at once."

"He heard the bell and was runnin' to the fire when he was took," said Captain Jerry. "Run out in his shirt sleeves, and was took when he got as fur as here."

"That's the way I figger it," said Eri unblushingly. "Lift him carefully, you fellers. Now then!"

"I warned him against over–exertion or excitement months ago," said the Doctor, as they bore the senseless burden toward the big house, now as black as the grave that was so near its owner. "We must find someone to take care of him at once. I don't believe the old man has a relation within a hundred miles."

"Why don't we take him to our house?" suggested Captain Jerry. "'Twouldn't seem so plaguey lonesome, anyhow."

"By mighty!" ejaculated Captain Eri in astonishment. "Well, Jerry, I'll be switched if you ain't right down brilliant once in a while. Of course we will. He can have the spare room. Why didn't I think of that, I wonder?"

And so John Baxter, who had not paid a visit in his native village since his wife died, came at last to his friend's home to pay what seemed likely to be a final one. They carried him up the stairs to the spare room, as dismal and cheerless as spare rooms in the country generally are, undressed him as tenderly as their rough hands would allow, robed him in one of Captain Jerry's nightshirts— the buttons that fastened it had been sewed on by the Captain himself, and were all sizes and colors—and laid him in the big corded bedstead. The Doctor hastened away to procure his medicine case. Ralph Hazeltine, having been profusely thanked for his services and promising to call the next day, went back to the station, and the three captains sat down by the bedside to watch and wait.

Captain Eri was too much perturbed to talk, but the other two, although sympathetically sorry for the sufferer, were bursting with excitement and curiosity.

"Well, if THIS ain't been a night!" exclaimed Captain Jerry. "Seem's if everything happened at once. Fust that darky and then the fire and then this. Don't it beat all?

Cap'n Eri

"Eri," said Captain Perez anxiously, "was John layin' jest the same way when you found him as he was when we come?"

"Right in the same place," was the answer.

"I didn't say in the same place. I asked if he was layin' the same way."

"He hadn't moved a muscle. Laid jest as if he was dead."

It will be noticed that Captain Eri was adhering strictly to the truth. Luckily, Perez seemed to be satisfied, for he asked no further questions, but observed, "It's a good thing we've got a crowd to swear how we found him. There's a heap of folks in this town would be sayin' he set that fire if 'twa'n't for that."

"Some of 'em will be sayin' it anyhow," remarked Jerry.

"Some folks 'll say anything but their prayers," snapped Eri savagely. "They won't say it while I'm around. And look here! if you hear anybody sayin' it, you tell 'em it's a lie. If that don't keep 'em quiet, let me know."

"Oh, all right. WE know he didn't set it. I was jest sayin'—"

"Well, don't say it."

"My, you're techy! Guess fires and colored folks don't agree with you. What are we goin' to do now? If John don't die, and the Lord knows I hope he won't, he's likely to be sick here a long spell. Who are we goin' to git to take care of him? That's what I want to know. Somebody's got to do it and we ain't fit. If Jerry 'd only give in and git married now—"

But Captain Jerry's protest against matrimony was as obstinate as ever. Even Perez gave up urging after a while and conversation lagged again. In a few minutes the Doctor came back, and his examination of the patient and demands for glasses of water, teaspoons, and the like, kept Perez and Jerry busy. It was some time before they noticed that Captain Eri had disappeared. Even then they did not pay much attention to the circumstance, but watched the physician at work and questioned him concerning the nature of their guest's illness.

"D'you think he'll die, Doctor?" inquired Jerry in a hushed voice, as they came out of the sick room into the connecting chamber.

"Can't say. He has had a stroke of paralysis, and there seem to be other complications. If he regains consciousness I shall think he has a chance, but not a very good one. His pulse is a little stronger. I don't think he'll die to-night, but if he lives he will need a good nurse, and I don't know of one in town."

"Nor me neither," said Captain Perez.

"Well, A'nt Zuby might come," suggested Jerry, "but I should hate to have her nuss me, and as for bein' WELL in a house where she was—whew!"

"A'nt Zuby!" sneered his messmate. "If Lorenzo had a fit and they called A'nt Zuby he'd have another one and die. A'nt Zuby! I'd 'bout as soon have M'lissy and be done with it."

"Yes, I don't doubt YOU WOULD," was the anything but gentle retort.

What Perez would have said to this thrust must be surmised, for just then the dining-room door opened and closed again.

"There's Eri," said Captain Jerry. Then he added in an alarmed whisper, "Who on airth has he got with him?"

They heard their friend's voice warning someone to be careful of the top step, and then the chamber door opened and Captain Eri appeared. There were beads of perspiration on his forehead, and he was carrying a shabby canvas extension-case. Captain Jerry gazed at the extension-case with bulging eyes.

Captain Eri put down the extension-case and opened the door wide. A woman came in; a stout woman dressed in black "alpaca" and wearing brass-rimmed spectacles. Captain Jerry gasped audibly.

Cap'n Eri

"Dr. Palmer," said Captain Eri, "let me make you acquainted with Mrs. Snow of Nantucket. Mrs. Snow, this is Dr. Palmer."

The Doctor and the lady from Nantucket shook hands, the former with a puzzled expression on his face.

"Perez," continued the Captain, "let me make you known to Mrs. Snow—Mrs. Marthy B. Snow,"—this with especial emphasis,—"of Nantucket. Mrs. Snow, this is Cap'n Perez Ryder."

They shook hands; Captain Perez managed to say that he was glad to meet Mrs. Snow. Captain Jerry said nothing, but he looked like a criminal awaiting the fall of the drop.

"Doctor," continued the Captain, paying no attention to the signals of distress displayed by his friend, "I heard you say a spell ago that John here needed somebody to take care of him. Well, Mrs. Snow—she's a—a—sort of relation of Jerry's"—just a suspicion of a smile accompanied this assertion—"and she's done consid'rable nussin' in her time. I've been talkin' the thing over with her and she's willin' to look out for John till he gits better."

The physician adjusted his eyeglasses and looked the volunteer nurse over keenly. The lady paid no attention to the scrutiny, but calmly removed her bonnet and placed it on the bureau. The room was Captain Eri's, and the general disarrangement of everything movable was only a little less marked than in those of his companions. Mrs. Snow glanced over the heap of odds and ends on the bureau and picked up a comb. There were some teeth in it, but they were distant neighbors.

"I don't use that comb very much," said Captain Eri rather apologetically. "I gin'rally use the one downstairs."

The new-found relative of Captain Jerry said nothing, but, laying down the ruin, marched over to the extension-case, opened it, and took out another comb—a whole one. With this she arranged the hair on her forehead. It, the hair, was parted in the middle and drawn back smoothly at the sides, and Captain Eri noticed that it was brown with a little gray in it. When the last stray wisp was in place, she turned calmly to the Doctor and said:

Cap'n Eri

"Cap'n Baxter's in here, I s'pose. Shall I walk right in?"

The man of medicine seemed a little surprised at the lady's command of the situation, but he said:

"Why, yes, ma'am; I guess you may. You have nursed before, I think the Captain said."

"Five years with my husband. He had slow consumption. Before that with my mother, and most of my brothers and sisters at one time or another. I've seen consid'rable sickness all my life. More of that than anything else, I guess. Now, if you'll come in with me, so's to tell me about the medicine and so on."

With a short "Humph!" the physician followed her into the sick room, while the three mariners gazed wide–eyed in at the door. They watched, as Doctor Palmer explained medicines and gave directions. It did not need an expert to see that the new nurse understood her business.

When the Doctor came out his face shone with gratification.

"She'll do," he said emphatically. "If all your relatives are like that, Cap'n Burgess, I'd like to know 'em; 'twould help me in my business." Then he added in response to a question, "He seems to be a little better just now. I think there will be no change for a while; if there should be, send for me. I'll call in the morning. Gracious! it's almost daylight now."

They saw him to the door and then came back upstairs. Mrs. Snow was busy, arranging the pillows, setting the room in something like order, and caring for her patient's garments, that had been tossed helter–skelter on the floor in the hurry of undressing. She came to the door as they entered Captain Eri's chamber.

"Mrs. Snow," said the Captain, "you'd better sleep in my room here long's you stay. I'll bunk in with Perez downstairs. I'll git my dunnage out of here right off. I think likely you'll want to clean up some."

The lady from Nantucket glanced at the bureau top and seemed about to say something, but checked herself. What she did say was:

71

Cap'n Eri

"P'raps you'd better introduce me to Cap'n Burgess. I don't think we've ever met, if we ARE relations."

Captain Eri actually blushed a little. "Why, of course," he said. "Excuse me, ma'am. Jerry, this is Mrs. Snow. I don't know what's got into me, bein' so careless."

The sacrifice shook the nurse's hand and said something, nobody knew exactly what. Mrs. Snow went on to say, "Now, I want you men to go right on to bed, for I know you're all tuckered out. We can talk to—morrow—I mean to—day, of course: I forgot 'twas next—door to daylight now. I shall set up with Cap'n Baxter, and if I need you I'll call you. I'll call you anyway when I think it's time. Good—night."

They protested, of course, but the lady would not listen. She calmly seated herself in the rocker by the bed and waved to them to go, which two of them reluctantly did after a while. The other one had gone already. It would be superfluous to mention his name.

Downstairs again and in Perez' room Captain Eri came in for a questioning that bade fair to keep up forever. He shut off all inquiries, however, with the announcement that he wouldn't tell them a word about it till he'd had some sleep. Then he would explain the whole thing, and they could decide whether he had done right or not. There were all sorts of things to be considered, he said, and they had better take a nap now while they could.

"Well, I'd jest like to ask you this, Eri Hedge," demanded Captain Jerry. "What in time did you tell the Doctor that she was a relation of mine for? That was a nice thing to do, wa'n't it? I'll have to answer more fool questions 'bout that than a little. What sort of a relation shall I tell folks she is? Jest tell me that, will you?"

"Oh, tell 'em she's a relation by marriage," was the answer, muffled by the bed clothes. "Maybe that 'll be true by the time they ask you."

"I'll BET it won't!" snorted the rebel.

Captain Perez fell asleep almost immediately. Captain Jerry, tired out, did the same, but Captain Eri's eyes did not close. The surf pounded and grumbled. A rooster, early astir, crowed somewhere in the distance. Daniel thumped the side of his stall and then subsided for another nap. The gray morning light brightened the window of the little house.

72

Then Captain Eri slid silently out of bed, dressed with elaborate precautions against noise, put on his cap, and tiptoed out of the house. He walked through the dripping grass, climbed the back fence and hurried to the hill where John Baxter had fallen. Once there, he looked carefully around to be sure that no one was watching. Orham, as a rule, is an early riser, but this morning most of the inhabitants, having been up for the greater part of the night, were making up lost sleep and the Captain was absolutely alone.

Assured of this, he turned to the bush underneath which he had hidden the burned coat, pushed aside the drenched boughs with their fading leaves and reached down for the tell–tale garment.

And then he made an unpleasant discovery. The coat was gone.

He spent an agitated quarter of an hour hunting through every clump of bushes in the immediate vicinity, but there was no doubt of it. Someone had been there before him and had taken the coat away.

CHAPTER VIII. HOUSEKEEPER AND BOOK AGENT

There was a knock on the door of Captain Perez's sleeping apartment.

"Cap'n Hedge," said Mrs. Snow, "Cap'n Hedge! I'm sorry to wake you up, but it's 'most ten o'clock and—"

"What? Ten o'clock! Godfrey scissors! Of all the lazy—I'll be out in a jiffy. Perez, turn out there! Turn out, I tell you!"

Captain Eri had fallen asleep in the rocker where he had seated himself upon his return from the fruitless search for the coat. He had had no intention of sleeping, but he was tired after his strenuous work at the fire, and had dropped off in the midst of his worry. He sprang to his feet, and tried to separate dreams from realities.

"Land of love, Perez!" he ejaculated. "Here you and me have been sleepin' ha'f the forenoon. We'd ought to be ashamed of ourselves. Let's git dressed quicker 'n chain lightnin'."

"Dressed?" queried Perez, sitting up in bed. "I should think you was dressed now, boots and all. What are you talkin' 'bout?"

The Captain glanced down at his clothes and seemed as much surprised as his friend. He managed to pull himself together, however, and stammered:

"Dressed? Oh, I'm dressed, of course. It's you I'm tryin' to git some life into."

"Well, why didn't you call a feller, 'stead of gittin' up and dressin' all by yourself. I never see such a critter. Where's my socks?"

To avoid further perplexing questions Captain Eri went into the dining room. The table was set, really set, with a clean cloth and dishes that shone. The knives and forks were arranged by the plates, not piled in a heap for each man to help himself. The Captain gasped.

"Well, I swan to man!" he said. "Has Jerry had a fit or what's struck him? I ain't seen him do anything like this for I don't know when."

"Oh, Cap'n Burgess didn't fix the table, if that's what you mean," said the new nurse. "Cap'n Baxter seemed to be sleepin' or in a stupor like, and the Doctor, when he come, said I might leave him long enough to run downstairs for a few minutes, so—"

"The Doctor? Has the Doctor been here this mornin'?"

"Yes, he come 'bout an hour ago. Now, if you wouldn't mind goin' up and stayin' with Cap'n Baxter for a few minutes while I finish gettin' breakfast. I've been up and down so many times in the last ha'f hour, I don't know's I'm sartin whether I'm on my head or my heels."

The Captain went upstairs in a dazed state. As he passed through what had been his room he vaguely noticed that the bureau top was clean, and that most of the rubbish that had ornamented it had disappeared.

The sick man lay just as he had left him, his white face as colorless as the clean pillow case against which it rested. Captain Eri remembered that the pillow cases in the spare

74

room had looked a little yellow the night before, possibly owing to the fact that, as the room had not been occupied for months, they had not been changed. He reasoned that the improvement was another one of the reforms instituted by the lady from Nantucket.

He sat down in the rocker by the bed and thought, with a shiver, of the missing coat. There were nine chances out of ten that whoever found it would recognize it as belonging to the old "Come–Outer." The contents of the pocket would be almost certain to reveal the secret if the coat itself did not. It remained to be seen who the finder was and what he would do. Meanwhile there was no use worrying. Having come to this conclusion the Captain, with customary philosophy, resolved to think of something else.

Mrs. Snow entered and announced that breakfast was ready and that he must go down at once and eat it while it was hot. She, having breakfasted some time before, would stay with the patient until the meal was over. Captain Eri at first flatly declined to listen to any such arrangement, but the calm insistence of the Nantucket visitor prevailed as usual. The Captain realized that the capacity for "bossin' things," that he had discerned in the letter, was even more apparent in the lady herself. One thing he did insist upon, however, and this was that Mrs. Snow should "turn in" as soon as breakfast was over. One of the three would take the watch in the sick room while the other two washed the dishes. The nurse was inclined to balk on the dishwashing proposition, saying that she could do it herself after she had had a wink or two, but this the Captain wouldn't hear of. He went away, however, with an unsettled conviction that, although he and his partners might wash the dishes, Mrs. Snow would wash them again as soon as she had an opportunity. "She didn't say so, but she sort of looked it," he explained afterward.

He found his friends seated at the table and feasting on hot biscuits, eggs, and clear, appetizing coffee. They greeted him joyously.

"Hey, Eri!" hailed Captain Perez. "Ain't this gay? Look at them eggs; b'iled jest to a T. Ain't much like Jerry's h'af raw kind."

"Humph! You needn't say nothin', Perez," observed Captain Jerry, his mouth full of biscuit. "When you was cook, you allers b'iled 'em so hard they'd dent the barn if you'd fired 'em at it. How's John, Eri?"

Cap'n Eri

Captain Eri gave his and the Doctor's opinion of his friend's condition and then said, "Now, we've got to have some kind of a settlement on this marryin' question. Last night, when I was up in the room there, it come acrost me all of a sudden that, from what I'd seen of this Nantucket woman, she'd be jest the sort of nurse that John needed. So I skipped out while you fellers was busy with the Doctor, found her at the hotel, explained things to her, and got her to come down. That's all there is to that. I ain't made no arrangement with her, and somethin's got to be done. What do you think of her, jedgin' by what you've seen?"

Captain Perez gave it as his opinion that she was "all right," and added, "If Jerry here wa'n't so pigheaded all at once, he'd marry her without waitin' another minute."

Eri nodded. "That's my idee," he said emphatically.

But Captain Jerry was as obstinate as ever. He simply would not consider immediate marriage. In vain his comrades reminded him of the original compact, and the fact that the vote was two to one against him; he announced that he had changed his mind, and that that was all there was about it.

At length Captain Eri lost patience.

"Jerry," he exclaimed, "you remind me of that old white hen we used to have. When we didn't want her to set she'd set on anything from a doorknob to a rock, couldn't keep her off; but when we give in finally and got a settin' of eggs for her, she wouldn't come nigher to 'em than the other end of the hen–yard. Now you might as well make up your mind that somethin's got to be done. This Mrs. Snow ain't nobody's fool. We put out a bait that anybody with sense would say couldn't catch nothin' but sculpin, and, by mighty, we hooked a halibut! If the woman was anything like what you'd think she'd be, answerin' an advertisement like that, I'd be the fust to say let her go, but she ain't; she's all right, and we need her to nuss John besides."

"Tell you what we might do," said Perez slowly; "we might explain to her that Jerry don't feel that 'twould be right to think of marryin' with Cap'n Baxter so sick in the house and that, if she's willin', we'll put it off till he dies or gets better. Meantime, we'll pay her so much to stay here and nuss. Seems to me that's about the only way out of it."

Cap'n Eri

So they agreed to lay this proposal before the Nantucket lady, Captain Jerry reluctantly consenting. Then Captain Eri took up another subject.

John Baxter, as has been said, had one relative, a granddaughter, living somewhere near Boston. Captain Eri felt that this granddaughter should be notified of the old man's illness at once. The difficulty was that none of them knew the young lady's address.

"Her fust name's Elizabeth, same as her mothers was," said Eri, "and her dad's name was Preston. They called her Elsie. John used to write to her every once in a while. P'raps Sam would know where she lived."

"Jest' cause Sam's postmaster," observed Perez, "it don't foller that he reads the name on every letter that goes out and remembers 'em besides."

"Well, if he don't," said Captain Jerry decidedly, "Mary Emma does. She reads everything, postals and all."

Miss Mary Emma Cahoon was the assistant at the post−office, and was possessed of a well−developed curiosity concerning other people's correspondence.

"Humph!" exclaimed Captain Eri, "that's so. We'll write the letter, and I'll ask Mary Emma for the address when I go up to mail it."

So Captain Perez went upstairs to take Mrs Snow's place as nurse, while that lady "turned in." Captain Jerry went into the kitchen to wash the dishes, and Captain Eri sat down to write the note that should inform Elizabeth Preston of her grandfather's illness. It was a very short note, and merely stated the fact without further information. Having had some experience in that line, the Captain placed very little reliance upon the help to be expected from relatives.

Dr. Palmer had spread the news as he went upon his round of visits that morning, and callers began to drop in to inquire after the sick man. Miss Busteed was one of the first arrivals, and, as Captain Eri had seen her through the window, he went upstairs and took Perez' place as temporary nurse. To Perez, therefore, fell the delightful task of entertaining the voluble female for something like an hour, while she talked fire, paralysis, and general gossip at express speed.

77

Cap'n Eri

Ralph Hazeltine came in a little later, and was introduced to Mrs. Snow, that lady's nap having been but a short one. Ralph was favorably impressed with the capable appearance of the new nurse, and so expressed himself to Captain Eri as they walked together toward the post–office.

"I like her," he said emphatically. "She's quiet and sensible and cheerful besides. She looks as if trouble didn't trouble her very much."

"I jedge she's seen enough of it in her time, too," observed the Captain reflectively. "Queer thing how trouble acts different on folks. Kind of like hot weather, sours milk, but sweetens apples. She's one of the sweetened kind. And yet, I cal'late she can be pretty sharp, too, if you try to tread on her toes. Sort of a sweet pickle, hey?" and he laughed.

Miss Cahoon remembered the Preston girl's address. It was Cambridge, Kirkland Street, but the number, she did declare, had skipped her mind. The Captain said he would chance it without the number, so the letter was posted. Then, with the electrician, he strolled over to inspect the remains of the billiard saloon.

There was a small crowd gathered about the building, prominent among its members being the "train committee," who were evidently holding a special session on this momentous occasion. The busy "Squealer," a trifle enlivened by some of Mr. Saunders' wet goods that had escaped the efforts of the volunteer salvage corps, hailed the new arrivals as brother heroes.

"Well now, Cap'n Eri!" he exclaimed, shaking hands vigorously. "And Mr. Hazeltine, too! How're you feelin' after last night? I says to Web, I says, 'There's folks in this town besides me that kept you from losin' the whole thing and you ought to thank 'em,' I says. 'One of 'em 's Cap'n Eri and t'other one's Mr. Hazeltine. If we three didn't work, then _I_ don't know,' I says."

"Web found out how the fire started yit?" inquired the Captain with apparent unconcern.

"No, he hain't for sure. There was a lot of us thought old Baxter might have set it, but they tell me it couldn't have been him, cause he was took down runnin' to the fire. Web, he's sort of changed his tune, and don't seem to think anybody set it; thinks it catched itself."

Mr. Saunders, his smooth self again, with all traces of mental disturbance gone from his face and all roughness from his tongue, came briskly up, smiling as if the burning of his place of business was but a trifling incident, a little annoying, of course, but not worth fretting about. He thanked the Captain and Hazeltine effusively for their service of the previous night, and piled the weight of his obligations upon them until, as Captain Eri said afterwards, "the syrup fairly dripped off his chin." The Captain broke in upon the sugary flow as soon as he could.

"How d'you think it started, Web?" he asked.

"Well," replied Mr. Saunders slowly, "I kind of cal'late she started herself. There was some of the boys in here most of the evenin', and, jest like's not, a cigar butt, or a match, or somethin' dropped somewheres and got to smolderin', and smoldered along till bime–by—puff!" An expressive wave of a fat hand finished the sentence.

"Humph!" grunted the Captain. "Changed your mind sence last night. Seems to me I heard you then swearin' you knew 'twas set and who set it."

"Well, ye–es. I was considerable shook up last night and maybe I said things I hadn't ought to. You see there's been a good deal of hard feelin's towards me in town and for a spell I thought some feller'd tried to burn me out. But I guess not; I guess not. More I think of it, more I think it catched itself. Seems to me I remember smellin' sort of a scorchin' smell when I was lockin' up. Oh, say! I was mighty sorry to hear 'bout Cap'n Baxter bein' took sick. The old man was dreadful down on liquor, but I laid that to his religion and never had no hard feelin's against him. How's he gittin' along?"

Captain Eri brusquely replied that his friend was "'bout the same," and asked if Mr. Saunders intended to rebuild. "Web" didn't know just yet. He was a poor man, didn't carry much insurance, and so on. Thought likely he should fix up again if it didn't cost too much. Did the Doctor say whether Captain Baxter would pull through or not?

Captain Eri gave an evasive answer and turned away. He was silent for some little time, and when Ralph commented on "Web's" overnight change of manner, his rejoinder was to the effect that "ile was bound to rise, but that didn't mean there wa'n't dirty water underneath." On the way home he asked Hazeltine concerning the trouble at the cable station, and how Mr. Langley had treated the matter.

Ralph replied that Mr. Langley had said nothing to him about it. It was his opinion that the old gentleman understood the affair pretty well, and was not disposed to blame him. As for the men, they had been as docile as lambs, and he thought the feeling toward himself was not as bitter as it had been. All of which his companion said he was glad to hear.

They separated at the gate, and the Captain entered the house to find Mrs. Snow wielding a broom and surrounded by a cloud of dust. Perez was upstairs with the patient, and Captain Jerry, whose habits had been considerably upset by the sweeping, was out in the barn.

That evening the situation was explained to Mrs. Snow by Captain Eri, in accordance with the talk at the breakfast table. The lady from Nantucket understood and respected Captain Jerry's unwillingness to discuss the marriage question while John Baxter's condition continued critical, and she agreed to act as nurse and housekeeper for a while, at least, for the sum of six dollars a week. This price was fixed only after considerable discussion by the three mariners, for Captain Eri was inclined to offer eight, and Captain Jerry but four.

When Ralph Hazeltine called late in the afternoon of the following day, the dining room was so transformed that he scarcely knew it. The dust had disappeared; the chronometer was polished till it shone; the table was covered with a cloth that was snow—white, and everything movable had the appearance of being in its place. Altogether, there was an evidence of order that was almost startling.

Captain Eri came to the door in response to his knock, and grinned appreciatively at his caller's look of wonder.

"I don't wonder you're s'prised," he said, with a chuckle. "I ain't begun to git over it yit, myself, and Lorenzo's so shook up he ain't been in the house sence breakfast time. He's out in the barn, keepin' Dan'l comp'ny and waitin' for the end of the world to strike, I cal'late."

Ralph laughed. "Mrs. Snow?" he inquired.

"Mrs. Snow," answered the Captain. "It beats all what a woman can do when she's that kind of a woman. She's done more swabbin' decks and overhaulin' runnin' riggin' than a new mate on a clipper. The place is so all–fired clean that I feel like brushin' myself every time I go to set down."

"How's Captain Baxter?" asked Hazeltine.

"Seems to be some better. He come to a little this mornin', and seemed to know some of us, but he ain't sensed where he is yit, nor I don't b'lieve he will fur a spell. Set down and keep me comp'ny. It's my watch jest now. Perez, he's over to Barry's; Jerry's up to the schoolhouse, and Mrs. Snow's run up to the post–office to mail a letter. John's asleep, so I can stay downstairs a little while, long's the door's open. What's the news uptown? Web changed his mind ag'in 'bout the fire?"

It appeared that Mr. Saunders had not changed his mind, at least so current gossip reported. And it may be remarked here that, curiously enough, the opinion that the fire "caught itself" came at last to be generally accepted in the village. For some weeks Captain Eri was troubled with thoughts concerning the missing coat, but, as time passed, and the accusing garment did not turn up, he came to believe that some boy must have found it and that it had, in all probability, been destroyed. There were, of course, some persons who still suspected John Baxter as the incendiary, but the old man's serious illness and respect for his former standing in the community kept these few silent. The Baxter house had been locked up and the Captain had the key.

Hazeltine and his host chatted for a few minutes on various topics. The gilt titles on the imposing "Lives of Great Naval Commanders," having received their share of the general dusting, now shone forth resplendent, and the Captain noticed Ralph's eye as it involuntarily turned toward them.

"Noticin' our library?" he chuckled. "Perez' property, that is. 'Gusty Black talked him into buyin' 'em. Never met 'Gusty, did you? No, I guess likely not. She lives over to the Neck, and don't git down to the village much. 'Gusty's what you call a business woman. She' always up to somethin' to make a dollar, and she's as slick a talker as ever was, I guess. She never give Perez no rest till he signed the deed for them books. Told him they'd give liter'ry tone to the shebang. Perez started to read 'em out loud when they fust come, but he had to stop so often to spell out the furrin names that me and Jerry used to go to sleep.

That made him mad, and he said, liter'ry tone be durned; he wa'n't goin' to waste his breath readin' us to sleep; so they've been on the shelf ever sence."

Ralph laughed. "So you have book agents, too?" he said.

"Well, we've got 'Gusty," was the reply, "and she's enough to keep us goin'. Gits round reg'lar as clockwork once a month to collect the two dollars from Perez. It's her day now, and I told Perez that that was why he sneaked off to Barry's. You see, 'Gusty's after him to buy the history of Methuselah, or some old critter, and he don't like to see her. She's after me, too, but I'm 'fraid she don't git much encouragement."

After they had talked a little longer, the Captain seemed to remember something, for he glanced at his watch and said, "Mr. Hazeltine, I wonder if I could git you to do me a favor. I really ought to go down and see to my shanty. Ain't been there since day afore yesterday, and there's so many boys 'round, I'm 'fraid to leave it unlocked much longer. I thought some of the folks would be back 'fore this, but if you could stay here long enough for me to run down there a minute or two, I'd be ever so much obliged. I'll step up and see how John is."

He went upstairs and returned to report that the patient was quiet and seemed to be asleep.

"If you hear him groan, or anything," he said, "jest come to the door and whistle. Whistle anyway, if you want me. Ain't nobody likely to come, 'less it's 'Gusty or the Reverend Perley come to ask 'bout John. If it's a middlin' good–lookin' young woman with a satchel, that's 'Gusty. Don't whistle; tell her I'm out. I'll be back in a jiffy, but you needn't tell either of them so unless your conscience hurts you TOO much."

After the Captain had gone Ralph took down a volume of the "Great Commanders" and sat down in a chair by the table to look it over. He was smiling over the gaudy illustrations and flamboyant descriptions of battles, when there was a step on the walk outside and knock at the door. "Which is it," he thought, "'Gusty or the Reverend?"

Obviously it was Miss Black. She stood on the mica slab that formed the step and looked up at him as he swung the door open. She had a small leather bag in her hand, just as the Captain had said she would have, but it flashed across Mr. Hazeltine's mind that the rest of the description was not a fair one; she was certainly much more than "middlin' good–lookin'!"

"Is Captain Hedge in?" she asked.

Now, from his friend's hints, Ralph had expected to hear a rather sharp and unpleasant voice,—certain disagreeable remembrances of former encounters with female book agents had helped to form the impression perhaps,—but Miss Black's voice was mellow, quiet, and rather pleasing than otherwise.

"No," said Mr. Hazeltine, obeying orders with exactitude. "Captain Hedge is out just now."

"'Gusty"—somehow the name didn't seem to fit—was manifestly disappointed.

"Oh, dear!" she said, and then added, "Will he be back soon?"

Now this was a question unprovided for. Ralph stammered, and then miserably equivocated. He really couldn't say just when the Captain would return.

"Oh, dear!" said the young lady again. Then she seemed to be waiting for some further observation on the part of the gentleman at the door. None being forthcoming, she seemed to make up her mind to act on her own initiative.

"I think I will come in and wait," she said with decision. And come in she did, Mr. Hazeltine not knowing exactly what to do, under the circumstances.

Now this was much more in keeping with the electrician's preconceived ideas of a book agent's behavior; nevertheless, when he turned and found the young lady standing in the middle of the floor, he felt obliged to be at least decently polite.

"Won't you take a chair?" he asked.

"Thank you," said the caller, and took one.

Cap'n Eri

The situation was extremely awkward, but Ralph felt that loyalty to Captain Eri forbade his doing anything that might urge the self– possessed Miss Black to prolong her visit, so for a time he said nothing. The young lady looked out of the window and Mr. Hazeltine looked at her. He was more than ever of the opinion that the "middlin'" term should be cut out of her description. He rather liked her appearance, so he decided. He liked the way she wore her hair; so simple an arrangement, but so effective. Also he liked her dress. It was the first tailor–made walking suit he had seen since his arrival in Orham. And worn by a country book agent, of all people.

Just then Miss Black turned and caught him intently gazing at her. She colored, apparently with displeasure, and looked out of the window again. Mr. Hazeltine colored also and fidgeted with the book on the table. The situation was confoundedly embarrassing. He felt that he must say something now, so he made the original observation that it had been a pleasant day.

To this the young lady agreed, but there was no enthusiasm in her tone. Then Ralph, nervously fishing for another topic, thought of the book in his hand.

"I was just reading this," he said. "I found it quite interesting."

The next moment he realized that he had said what, of all things, was the most impolitic. It was nothing less than a bid for a "canvass," and he fully expected to be confronted with the necessary order blanks without delay. But, strangely enough, the book lady made no such move. She looked at him, it is true, but with an expression of surprise and what seemed to be amusement on her face. He was certain that her lips twitched as she said calmly:

"Did you? I am glad to hear it."

This dispassionate remark was entirely unexpected, and the electrician, as Captain Eri would have said, "lost his bearings" completely.

"Yes—er, yes," he stammered. "Very interesting indeed. I—I suppose you must take a good many orders in the course of a week."

"A good many ORDERS?"

"Why, yes. Orders for the books, I mean. The books—the 'Great Naval Lives'—er—these books here."

"I beg your pardon, but who do you think I am?"

And it was then that the perception of some tremendous blunder began to seize upon Mr. Hazeltine. He had been red before; now, he felt the redness creeping over his scalp under his hair.

"Why, why, Miss Black, I suppose; that is, I—"

Just here the door opened and Captain Eri came in. He took off his cap and then, seeing the visitor, remained standing, apparently waiting for an introduction. But the young lady did not keep him waiting long.

"Are you Captain Eri Hedge?" she asked.

"Yes'm," answered the Captain.

"Oh, I'm SO glad. Your letter came this morning, and I hurried down on the first train. I'm Elizabeth Preston."

CHAPTER IX. ELSIE PRESTON

Perhaps, on the whole, it is not surprising that Captain Eri didn't grasp the situation. Neither his two partners nor himself had given much thought to the granddaughter of the sick man in the upper room. The Captain knew that there was a granddaughter, hence his letter; but he had heard John Baxter speak of her as being in school somewhere in Boston, and had all along conceived of her as a miss of sixteen or thereabouts. No wonder that at first he looked at the stylishly gowned young woman, who stood before him with one gloved hand extended, in a puzzled, uncomprehending way.

"Excuse me, ma'am," he said slowly, mechanically swallowing up the proffered hand in his own mammoth fist, "but I don't know's I jest caught the name. Would you mind sayin' it ag'in?"

Cap'n Eri

"Elizabeth Preston," repeated the visitor. "Captain Baxter's granddaughter. You wrote me that he was ill, you know, and I—"

"What!" roared the Captain, delighted amazement lighting up his face like a sunrise. "You don't mean to tell me you're 'Liz'beth Baxter's gal Elsie! Well! Well! I want to know! If this don't beat all! Set down! Take your things right off. I'm mighty glad to see you."

Captain Eri's hand, with Miss Preston's hidden in it, was moving up and down as if it worked by a clock–work arrangement. The young lady withdrew her fingers from the trap as soon as she conveniently could, but it might have been noticed that she glanced at them when she had done so, as if to make sure that the original shape remained.

"Thank you, Captain Hedge," she said. "And now, please tell me about grandfather. How is he? May I see him?"

The Captain's expression changed to one of concern.

"Why, now, Miss Preston," he said, "your grandpa is pretty sick. Oh, I don't mean he's goin' to die right off or anything like that," he added hastily. "I mean he's had a stroke of palsy, or somethin', and he ain't got so yit that he senses much of what goes on. Now I don't want to frighten you, you know, but really there's a chance—a leetle mite of a chance—that he won't know you. Don't feel bad if he don't, now will you?"

"I knew he must be very ill from your letter," said the girl simply. "I was afraid that he might not be living when I reached here. They told me at the station that he was at your house and so I came. He has been very good to me and I—"

Her voice broke a little and she hesitated. Captain Eri was a picture of nervous distress.

"Yes, yes, I know," he said hastily. "Don't you worry now. He's better; the Doctor said he was consid'rably better to–day; didn't he, Mr. Hazeltine? Why, what am I thinkin' of? Let me make you known to Mr. Hazeltine; next–door neighbor of ours; right acrost the road," and he waved toward the bay.

86

Ralph and Miss Preston shook hands. The electrician managed to utter some sort of formality, but he couldn't have told what it was. He was glad when the Captain announced that, if Mr. Hazeltine would excuse them, he guessed Miss Preston and he would step upstairs and see John. The young lady took off her hat and jacket, and Captain Eri lighted a lamp, for it was almost dark by this time. As its light shone upon the visitor's face and hair the crimson flush before mentioned circumnavigated the electrician's head once more, and his bump of self-esteem received a finishing blow. That any man supposed to possess two fairly good eyes and a workable brain could have mistaken her for an Orham Neck book agent by the name of "'Gusty—'Gusty Black!" Heavens!

"I'll be down in a few minutes, Mr. Hazeltine," said the Captain. "Set still, won't you?"

But Mr. Hazeltine wouldn't sit still. He announced that it was late and he must be going. And go he did, in spite of his host's protestations.

"Look out for the stairs," cautioned the Captain, leading the way with the lamp. "The feller that built 'em must have b'lieved that savin' distance lengthens out life. Come to think of it, I wouldn't wonder if them stairs was the reason why me and Jerry and Perez took this house. They reminded us so of the shrouds on a three-master."

Elsie Preston did her best to smile as her companion rattled on in this fashion, but both the smile and the Captain's cheerfulness were too plainly assumed to be convincing, and they passed down the hall in silence. At the open door of the sick room Captain Eri paused.

"He's asleep," he whispered, "and, remember, if he wakes up and doesn't know you, you needn't feel bad."

Elsie slipped by him and knelt by the bed, looking into the white, old face on the pillow. Somehow the harsh lines had faded out of it, and it looked only old and pitiful.

The Captain watched the tableau for a moment or two, and then tiptoed into the room and placed the lamp on the bureau.

"Now, I think likely," he said in a rather husky whisper, "that you'd like to stay with your grandpa for a little while, so I'll go downstairs and see about supper. No, no, no!" he added, holding up his hand as the girl spoke some words of protest, "you ain't goin' nowheres to supper. You're goin' to stay right here. If you want me, jest speak."

And he hurried downstairs and into the kitchen, clearing his throat with vigor and making a great to–do over the scratching of a match.

Mrs. Snow returned a few minutes later and to her the news of the arrival was told, as it was also to Perez and Jerry when they came. Mrs. Snow took charge of the supper arrangements. When the meal was ready, she said to Captain Eri:

"Now, I'll go upstairs and tell her to come down. I'll stay with Cap'n Baxter till you're through, and then p'raps, if one of you'll take my place, I'll eat my supper and wash the dishes. You needn't come up now. I'll introduce myself."

Some few minutes passed before Miss Preston came down. When she did so her eyes were wet, but her manner was cheerful, and the unaffected way in which she greeted Captain Perez and Captain Jerry, when these two rather bashful mariners were introduced by Eri, won them at once.

The supper was a great success. It was Saturday night, and a Saturday night supper to the average New Englander means baked beans. The captains had long ago given up this beloved dish, because, although each had tried his hand at preparing it, none had wholly succeeded, and the caustic criticisms of the other two had prevented further trials. But Mrs. Snow's baked beans were a triumph. So, also, was the brown bread.

"I snum," exclaimed Captain Perez, "if I don't b'lieve I'd sooner have these beans than turkey. What do you say, Jerry?"

"I don't know but I had," assented the sacrifice, upon whose countenance sat a placidity that had not been there since the night of the "matching." "'Specially if the turkey was like the one we tried to cook last Thanksgivin'. 'Member that, Eri?"

Captain Eri, his mouth full, grunted an emphatic assent.

"Tell me," said Miss Preston, who had eaten but little, but was apparently getting more satisfaction from watching her companions, "did you three men try to keep house here alone?"

"Yes," answered Eri dryly. "We tried. First we thought 'twas goin' to be fine; then we thought we'd like it better after we got used to it; finally we decided that by the time we got used to it we'd die, like the horse that was fed on sawdust."

"And so you hired Mrs. Snow to keep house for you? Well, I don't see how you could have made a better choice; she's a dear, good woman; I'm sure of it. And now I want to thank you all for what you've done for grandfather. Mrs. Snow told me all about it; you've been so kind that I—"

"That's all right! that's all right!" hastily interrupted Captain Eri. "Pity if we couldn't help out a shipmate we've sailed with for years and years. But you'd ought to have tried some of OUR cookin'. Tell her about the sugar cake you made, Perez. The one that killed the yaller chicken."

So Captain Perez told it, and then their visitor set them all laughing by relating some queer housekeeping experiences that she and a school friend had had while camping at Chautauqua. Somehow each one felt at home with her. As Captain Eri said afterwards, "She didn't giggle, and then ag'in she didn't talk down at you."

As they rose from the table the young lady asked a question concerning the location of the hotel. The Captain made no answer at the time, but after a short consultation with the remainder of the triumvirate, he came to her as she stood by the window and, laying his hand on her shoulder, said:

"Now, Elsie—I hope you don't mind my callin' you Elsie, but I've been chums with your grandpa so long seems's if you must be a sort of relation of mine—Elsie, you ain't goin' to no hotel, that is, unless you're real set on it. Your grandpa's here and we're here, and there's room enough. I don't want to say too much, but I'd like to have you b'lieve that me and Perez and Jerry want you to stay right in this house jest as long's you stop in Orham. Now you will, won't you?"

And so it was settled, and Captain Perez harnessed Daniel and went to the station for the trunk.

That evening, just before going to bed, the captains stood by the door of the sick room watching Elsie and the lady from Nantucket as they sat beside John Baxter's bed. Mrs. Snow was knitting, and Elsie was reading. Later, as Captain Eri peered out of the dining–room window to take a final look at the sky in order to get a line on the weather, he said slowly:

"Fellers, do you know what I was thinkin' when I see them two women in there with John? I was thinkin' that it must be a mighty pleasant thing to know that if you're took sick somebody like that 'll take care of you."

Perez nodded. "I think so, too," he said.

But if this was meant to influence the betrothed one, it didn't succeed, apparently, for all Captain Jerry said was:

"Humph! 'Twould take more than that to make me hanker after a stroke of palsy."

And with the coming of Elsie Preston and Mrs. Snow life in the little house by the shore took on a decided change. The Nantucket lady having satisfied herself that John Baxter's illness was likely to be a long one, wrote several letters to persons in her native town, which letters, although she did not say so, were supposed by the captains to deal with the care of her property while she was away. Having apparently relieved her mind by this method, and evidently considering the marriage question postponed for the present, she settled down to nurse the sick man and to keep house as, in her opinion, a house should be kept. The captains knew nothing of her past history beyond what they had gathered from stray bits of her conversation. She evidently did not consider it necessary to tell anything further, and, on the other hand, asked no questions.

In her care of Baxter she was more like a sister than a hired nurse. No wife could have been more tender in her ministrations or more devotedly anxious for the patient's welfare.

In her care of the house, she was neatness itself. She scoured and swept and washed until the rooms were literally spotless. Order was Heaven's first law, in her opinion, and she expected everyone else to keep up to the standard. Captain Perez and Captain Eri soon got used to the change and gloried in it, but to Captain Jerry it was not altogether welcome.

Cap'n Eri

"Oh, cat's foot!" he exclaimed one day, after hunting everywhere for his Sunday tie, and at length finding it in his bureau drawer. "I can't git used to this everlastin' spruced-up bus'ness. Way it used to be, this necktie was likely to be 'most anywheres 'round, and if I looked out in the kitchen or under the sofy, I was jest as likely to find it. But now everything's got a place and is in it."

"Well, that's the way it ought to be, ain't it?" said Eri. "Then all you've got to do is look in the place."

"Yes, and that's jest it, I'm always forgittin' the place. My shoes is sech a place; my hankerchers is sech a place; my pipe is sech a place; my terbacker is another place. When I want my pipe I look where my shoes is, and when I want my shoes I go and look where I found my pipe. How a feller's goin' to keep run of 'em is what _I_ can't see."

"You was the one that did most of the growlin' when things was the old way."

"Yes, but jest 'cause a man don't want to live in a pigpen it ain't no sign he wants to be put under a glass case."

Elsie's influence upon the house and its inmates had become almost as marked as Mrs. Snow's. The young lady was of an artistic bent, and the stiff ornaments in the shut-up parlor and the wonderful oil-paintings jarred upon her. Strange to say, even the wax-dipped wreath that hung in its circular black frame over the whatnot did not appeal to her. The captains considered that wreath—it had been the principal floral offering at the funeral of Captain Perez's sister, and there was a lock of her hair framed with it— the gem of the establishment. They could understand, to a certain degree, why Miss Preston objected to the prominence given the spatter-work "God bless our Home" motto, but her failure to enthuse over the wreath was inexplicable.

But by degrees they became used to seeing the blinds open at the parlor windows the week through, and innovations like muslin curtains and vases filled with late wild flowers came to be at first tolerated and then liked. "Elsie's notions," the captains called them.

There were some great discussions on art, over the teacups after supper. Miss Preston painted very prettily in water-colors, and her sketches were received with enthusiastic praise by the captains and Mrs. Snow. But one day she painted a little picture of a fishing

91

boat and, to her surprise, it came in for some rather sharp criticism.

"That's a pretty picture, Elsie," said Captain Eri, holding the sketch at arm's length and squinting at it with his head on one side, "but if that's Caleb Titcomb's boat, and I jedge 'tis, it seems to me she's carryin' too much sail. What do you think, Jerry?"

Captain Jerry took the painting from his friend and critically examined it, also at arm's length.

"Caleb's boat ain't got no sech sail as that," was his deliberate comment. "She couldn't carry it and stand up that way. Besides, the way I look at it, she's down by the head more 'n she'd ought to be."

"But I didn't try to get it EXACTLY right," said the bewildered artist. "The boat's sails were so white, and the water was so blue, and the sand so yellow that I thought it made a pretty picture. I didn't think of the size of the sail."

"Well, I s'pose you wouldn't, nat'rally," observed Captain Perez, who was looking over Jerry's shoulder. "But you have to be awful careful paintin' vessels. Now you jest look at that picture," pointing to the glaring likeness of the Flying Duck, that hung on the wall. "Jest look at them sails, every one of 'em drawin' fine; and them ropes, every one in JEST the right place. That's what I call paintin'."

"But don't you think, Captain Perez, that the waves in that picture would be better if they weren't so all in a row, like a picket fence?"

"Well, now, that ain't it. That's a picture of the A1 two-masted schooner Flyin' Duck, and the waves is only thrown in, as you might say. The reel thing is the schooner, rigged jest right, trimmed jest right, and colored jest the way the Flyin' Duck was colored. You understand them waves was put there jest 'cause there had to be some to set the schooner in, that's all."

"But you needn't feel bad, Elsie," said Captain Jerry soothingly. "'Tain't to be expected that you could paint vessels like Eben Lothrop can. Eben he used to work in a shipyard up to East Boston once, and when he was there he had to paint schooners and things, reely put the paint onto 'em I mean, so, of course, when it come to paintin' pictures of

92

Cap'n Eri

'em, why—"

And Captain Jerry waved his hand.

So, as there was no answer to an argument like this, Miss Preston gave up marine painting for the time and began a water–color of the house and its inmates. This was an elaborate affair, and as the captains insisted that each member of the family, Daniel and Lorenzo included, should pose, it seemed unlikely to be finished for some months, at least.

Ralph Hazeltine called on the afternoon following Elsie's arrival, and Captain Eri insisted on his staying to tea. It might have been noticed that the electrician seemed a trifle embarrassed when Miss Preston came into the room, but as the young lady was not embarrassed in the least, and had apparently forgotten the mistaken–identity incident, his nervousness soon wore off.

But it came back again when Captain Eri said:

"Oh, I say, Mr. Hazeltine, I forgot to ask you, did 'Gusty come yesterday?"

Ralph answered, rather hurriedly, that she did not. He endeavored to change the subject, but the Captain wouldn't let him.

"Well, there!" he exclaimed amazedly; "if 'Gusty ain't broke her record! Fust time since Perez was took with the 'Naval Commander' disease that she ain't been on hand when the month was up, to git her two dollars. Got so we sort of reckoned by her like an almanac. Kind of thought she was sure, like death and taxes. And now she has gone back on us. Blessed if I ain't disapp'inted in 'Gusty!"

"Who is she?" inquired Mrs. Snow. "One of those book–agent critters?"

"Well, if you called her that to her face, I expect there'd be squalls, but I cal'late she couldn't prove a alibi in court."

Now it may have been Mr. Hazeltine's fancy, but he could have sworn that there was just the suspicion of a twinkle in Miss Preston's eye as she asked, innocently enough:

Cap'n Eri

"Is she a young lady, Captain Eri?"

"Well, she hopes she is," was the deliberate answer. "Why?"

"Does she look like me?"

"Like YOU? Oh, my soul and body! Wait till you see her. What made you ask that?"

"Oh, nothing! I was a little curious, that's all. Have you seen her, Mr. Hazeltine?"

Ralph stammered, somewhat confusedly, that he hadn't had the pleasure. The Captain glanced from the electrician to Miss Preston and back again. Then he suddenly realized the situation.

"Ho! ho!" he roared, slapping his knee and rocking back and forth in his chair. "Don't for the land's sake tell me you took Elsie here for 'Gusty Black! Don't now! Don't!"

"He asked me if I had taken many orders," remarked the young lady demurely.

When the general hilarity had abated a little Ralph penitently explained that it was dark, that Captain Eri had said Miss Black was young, and that she carried a bag.

"So I did, so I did," chuckled the Captain. "I s'pose 'twas nat'ral enough, but, oh dear, it's awful funny! Now, Elsie, you'd ought to feel flattered. Wait till you see 'Gusty's hat, the one she got up to Boston."

"Am I forgiven, Miss Preston?" asked Hazeltine, as he said good– night.

"Well, I don't know," was the rather non–committal answer. "I think I shall have to wait until I see 'Gusty."

But Mr. Hazeltine apparently took his forgiveness for granted, for his calls became more and more frequent, until his dropping in after supper came to be a regular occurrence. Young people of the better class are scarce in Orham during the fall and winter months, and Ralph found few congenial companions. He liked the captains and Mrs. Snow, and Elsie's society was a relief after a day with the operators at the station. Mr. Langley was entirely absorbed in his business, and spent his evenings in his room, reading and smoking.

So September and October passed and November came. School opened in October and the captains had another boarder, for Josiah Bartlett, against his wishes, gave up his position as stage–driver, and was sent to school again. As the boy was no longer employed at the livery stable, Captain Perez felt the necessity of having him under his eye, and so Josiah lived at the house by the shore, a cot being set up in the parlor for his use. His coming made more work for Mrs. Snow, but that energetic lady did not seem to mind, and even succeeded in getting the youngster to do a few "chores" about the place, an achievement that won the everlasting admiration of Captain Perez, who had no governing power whatever over the boy, and condoned the most of his faults or scolded him feebly for the others.

John Baxter continued to waver between this world and the next. He had intervals of consciousness in which he recognized the captains and Elsie, but these rational moments were few and, although he talked a little, he never mentioned recent events nor alluded to the fire.

The fire itself became an old story and gossip took up other subjects. The "Come–Outers" held a jubilee service because of the destruction of the saloon, but, as "Web" soon began to rebuild and repair, their jollification was short–lived. As for Mr. Saunders, he was the same unctuous, smiling personage that he had formerly been. It was a curious fact, and one that Captain Eri noted, that he never ceased to inquire after John Baxter's health, and seemed honestly glad to hear of the old man's improvement. He asked a good many questions about Elsie, too, but received little satisfaction from the Captain on this subject.

CHAPTER X. MATCHMAKING AND LIFE–SAVING

Captain Jerry sat behind the woodshed, in the sunshine, smoking and thinking. He had done a good deal of the first ever since he was sixteen years old; the second was, in a measure, a more recent acquirement. The Captain had things on his mind.

It was one of those perfect, springlike mornings that sometimes come in early November.

Cap'n Eri

The sky was clear blue, and the air was so free from haze that the houses at Cranberry Point could be seen in every detail. The flag on the cable station across the bay stood out stiff in the steady breeze, and one might almost count the stripes. The pines on Signal Hill were a bright green patch against the yellow grass. The sea was a dark sapphire, with slashes of silver to mark the shoals, and the horizon was notched with sails. The boats at anchor in front of the shanties swung with the outgoing tide.

Then came Captain Eri, also smoking.

"Hello!" said Captain Jerry. "How is it you ain't off fishin' a mornin' like this?"

"Somethin' else on the docket," was the answer. "How's matchmakin' these days?"

Now this question touched vitally the subject of Captain Jerry's thoughts. From a placid, easygoing retired mariner, recent events had transformed the Captain into a plotter, a man with a "deep-laid scheme," as the gentlemanly, cigarette-smoking villain of the melodrama used to love to call it. To tell the truth, petticoat government was wearing on him. The marriage agreement, to which his partners considered him bound, and which he saw no way to evade, hung over him always, but he had put this threat of the future from his mind so far as possible. He had not found orderly housekeeping the joy that he once thought it would be, but even this he could bear. Elsie Preston was the drop too much.

He liked Mrs. Snow, except in a marrying sense. He liked Elsie better than any young lady he had ever seen. The trouble was, that between the two, he, as he would have expressed it, "didn't have the peace of a dog."

Before Elsie came, a game of checkers between Perez and himself had been the regular after-supper amusement. Now they played whist, Captain Eri and Elsie against him and his former opponent. As Elsie and her partner almost invariably won, and as Perez usually found fault with him because they lost, this was not an agreeable change. But it was but one. He didn't like muslin curtains in his bedroom, because they were a nuisance when he wanted to sit up in bed and look out of the window; but the curtains were put there, and everybody else seemed to think them beautiful, so he could not protest. Captain Perez and Captain Eri had taken to "dressing up" for supper, to the extent of putting on neckties and clean collars. Also they shaved every day. He stuck to the old "twice-a-week" plan for a while, but looked so scrubby by contrast that out of mere

96

self–respect he had to follow suit. Obviously two females in the house were one too many. Something had to be done.

Ralph Hazeltine's frequent calls gave him the inspiration he was looking for. This was to bring about a marriage between Ralph and Miss Preston. After deliberation he decided that if this could be done the pair would live somewhere else, even though John Baxter was still too ill to be moved. Elsie could come in every day, but she would be too busy with her own establishment to bother with the "improvement" of theirs. It wasn't a very brilliant plan and had some vital objections, but Captain Jerry considered it a wonder.

He broached it to his partners, keeping his real object strictly in the background and enlarging upon his great regard for Ralph and Elsie, and their obvious fitness for each other. Captain Perez liked the scheme well enough, provided it could be carried out. Captain Eri seemed to think it better to let events take their own course. However, they both agreed to help if the chance offered.

So, when Mr. Hazeltine called to spend the evening, Captain Jerry would rise from his chair and, with an elaborate cough and several surreptitious winks to his messmates, would announce that he guessed he would "take a little walk," or "go out to the barn," or something similar. Captain Perez would, more than likely, go also. As for Captain Eri, he usually "cal'lated" he would step upstairs, and see how John was getting along.

But in spite of this loyal support, the results obtained from Captain Jerry's wonderful plan had not been so startlingly successful as to warrant his feeling much elated. Ralph and Elsie were good friends and seemed to enjoy each other's society, but that was all that might be truthfully said, so far.

Captain Jerry, therefore, was a little discouraged as he sat in the sunshine and smoked and pondered. He hid his discouragement, however, and in response to Captain Eri's question concerning the progress of the matchmaking, said cheerfully:

"Oh, it's comin' along, comin' along. Kind of slow, of course, but you can't expect nothin' diff'rent. I s'pose you noticed he was here four times last week?"

"Why, no," said Captain Eri, "I don't know's I did."

97

"Well, he was, and week a fore that 'twas only three. So that's a gain, ain't it?"

"Sartin."

"I didn't count the time he stopped after a drink of water neither. That wasn't a real call, but—"

"Oh, it ought to count for somethin'! Call it a ha'f a time. That would make four times and a ha'f he was here."

Captain Jerry looked suspiciously at his friend's face, but its soberness was irreproachable, so he said:

"Well, it's kind of slow work, but, as I said afore, it's comin' along, and I have the satisfaction of knowin' it's all for their good."

"Yes, like the feller that ate all the apple–dumplin's so's his children wouldn't have the stomach–ache. But say, Jerry, I come out to ask if you'd mind bein' housekeeper to–day. Luther Davis has been after me sence I don't know when to come down to the life– savin' station and stay to dinner. His sister Pashy—the old maid one—is down there, and it's such a fine day I thought I'd take Perez and Elsie and Mrs. Snow and, maybe, Hazeltine along. Somebody's got to stay with John, and I thought p'raps you would. I'd stay myself only Luther asked me so particular, and you was down there two or three months ago. When Josiah comes back from school he'll help you some, if you need him."

Captain Jerry didn't mind staying at home, and so Eri went into the house to make arrangements for the proposed excursion. He had some difficulty in persuading Mrs. Snow and Elsie to leave the sick man, but both were tired and needed a rest, and there was a telephone at the station, so that news of a change in the patient's condition could be sent almost immediately. Under these conditions, and as Captain Jerry was certain to take good care of their charge, the two were persuaded to go. Perez took the dory and rowed over to the cable station to see if Mr. Hazeltine cared to make one of the party. When he returned, bringing the electrician with him, Daniel, harnessed to the carryall, was standing at the side door, and Captain Eri, Mrs. Snow, and Elsie were waiting.

Ralph glanced at the carryall, and then at those who were expected to occupy it.

"I think I'd better row down, Captain," he said. "I don't see how five of us are going to find room in there."

"What, in a carryall?" exclaimed the Captain. "Why, that's what a carryall's for. I've carried six in a carryall 'fore now. 'Twas a good while ago, though," he added with a chuckle, "when I was consid'rable younger 'n I am now. Squeezin' didn't count in them days, 'specially if the girls wanted to go to camp–meetin'. I cal'late we can fix it. You and me'll set on the front seat, and the rest in back. Elsie ain't a very big package, and Perez, he's sort of injy–rubber; he'll fit in 'most anywheres. Let's try it anyhow."

And try it they did. While it was true that Elsie was rather small, Mrs. Snow was distinctly large, and how Captain Perez, in spite of his alleged elasticity, managed to find room between them is a mystery. He, however, announced that he was all right, adding, as a caution:

"Don't jolt none, Eri, 'cause I'm kind of hangin' on the little aidge of nothin'."

"I'll look out for you," answered his friend, picking up the reins. "All ashore that's goin' ashore. So long, Jerry. Git dap, Thousand Dollars!"

Daniel complacently accepted this testimony to his monetary worth and jogged out of the yard. Fortunately appearances do not count for much in Orham, except in the summer, and the spectacle of five in a carryall is nothing out of the ordinary. They turned into the "cliff road," the finest thoroughfare in town, kept in good condition for the benefit of the cottagers and the boarders at the big hotel. The ocean was on the left, and from the hill by the Barry estate—Captain Perez' charge—they saw twenty miles of horizon line with craft of all descriptions scattered along it.

Schooners there were of all sizes, from little mackerel seiners to big four– and five–masters. A tug with a string of coal barges behind it was so close in that they could make out the connecting hawsers. A black freight steamer was pushing along, leaving a thick line of smoke like a charcoal mark on the sky. One square– rigger was in sight, but far out.

"What do you make of that bark, Perez?" inquired Captain Eri, pointing to the distant vessel. British, ain't she?"

Cap'n Eri

Captain Perez leaned forward and peered from under his hand. "French, looks to me," he said.

"Don't think so. Way she's rigged for'ard looks like Johnny Bull. Look at that fo'tops'l."

"Guess you're right, Eri, now I come to notice it. Can you make out her flag? Wish I'd brought my glass."

"Great Scott, man!" exclaimed Ralph. "What sort of eyes have you got? I couldn't tell whether she had a flag or not at this distance. How do you do it?"

"'Cordin' to how you're brought up, as the goat said 'bout eatin' shingle–nails," replied Captain Eri. "When you're at sea you've jest got to git used to seein' things a good ways off and knowin' 'em when you see 'em, too."

"I remember, one time," remarked Mrs. Snow, "that my brother Nathan—he's dead now—was bound home from Hong Kong fust mate on the bark Di'mond King. 'Twas the time of the war and the Alabama was cruisin' 'round, lookin' out for our ships. Nate and the skipper—a Bangor man he was—was on deck, and they sighted a steamer a good ways off. The skipper spied her and see she was flyin' the United States flag. But when Nate got the glass he took one look and says, 'That Yankee buntin' don't b'long over that English hull,' he says. You see he knew she was English build right away. So the skipper pulled down his own flag and h'isted British colors, but 'twa'n't no use; the steamer was the Alabama sure enough, and the Di'mond King was burned, and all hands took pris'ners. Nate didn't git home for ever so long, and everybody thought he was lost."

This set the captains going, and they told sea–stories until they came to the road that led down to the beach beneath the lighthouse bluff. The lifesaving station was in plain sight now, but on the outer beach, and that was separated from them by a two–hundred–yard stretch of water.

"Well," observed Captain Eri, "here's where we take Adam's bridge."

"Adam's bridge?" queried Elsie, puzzled.

100

"Yes; the only kind he had, I cal'late. Git dap, Daniel! What are you waitin' for? Left your bathin' suit to home?"

Then, as Daniel stepped rather gingerly into the clear water, he explained that, at a time ranging from three hours before low tide to three hours after, one may reach the outer beach at this point by driving over in an ordinary vehicle. The life–savers add to this time–limit by using a specially built wagon, with large wheels and a body considerably elevated.

"Well, there now!" exclaimed the lady from Nantucket, as Daniel splashingly emerged on the other side. "I thought I'd done about everything a body could do with salt water, but I never went ridin' in it afore."

The remainder of the way to the station was covered by Daniel at a walk, for the wheels of the heavy carryall sank two inches or more in the coarse sand as they turned. The road wound between sand dunes, riven and heaped in all sorts of queer shapes by the wind, and with clumps of the persevering beach grass clinging to their tops like the last treasured tufts of hair on partially bald heads. Here and there, half buried, sand–scoured planks and fragments of spars showed, relics of wrecks that had come ashore in past winters.

"Five years ago," remarked Captain Eri, "there was six foot of water where we are now. This beach changes every winter. One good no'theaster jest rips things loose over here; tears out a big chunk of beach and makes a cut–through one season, and fills in a deep hole and builds a new shoal the next. I've heard my father tell 'bout pickin' huckleberries when he was a boy off where them breakers are now. Good dry land it was then. Hey! there's Luther. Ship ahoy, Lute!"

The little brown life–saving station was huddled between two sand– hills. There was a small stable and a henhouse and yard just behind it. Captain Davis, rawboned and brown–faced, waved a welcome to them from the side door.

"Spied you comin', Eri," he said in a curiously mild voice, that sounded odd coming from such a deep chest. "I'm mighty glad to see you, too? Jump down and come right in. Pashy 'll be out in a minute. Here she is now."

Cap'n Eri

Miss Patience Davis was as plump as her brother was tall. She impressed one as a comfortable sort of person. Captain Eri did the honors and everyone shook hands. Then they went into the living room of the station.

What particularly struck Mrs. Snow was the neatness of everything. The brass on the pump in the sink shone like fire as the sunlight from the window struck it. The floor was white from scouring. There were shelves on the walls and on these, arranged in orderly piles, were canned goods of all descriptions. The table was covered with a figured oilcloth.

Two or three men, members of the crew, were seated in the wooden chairs along the wall, but rose as the party came in. Captain Davis introduced them, one after the other. Perhaps the most striking characteristic of these men was the quiet, almost bashful, way in which they spoke; they seemed like big boys, as much as anything, and yet the oldest was nearly fifty.

"Ever been in a life-saving station afore?" asked Captain Eri.

Elsie had not. Ralph had and so had Mrs. Snow, but not for years.

"This is where we keep the boat and the rest of the gear," said Captain Davis, opening a door and leading the way into a large, low-studded room. "Them's the spare oars on the wall. The reg'lar ones are in the boat."

The boat itself was on its carriage in the middle of the room. Along the walls on hooks hung the men's suits of oilskins and their sou'westers. The Captain pointed out one thing after another, the cork jackets and life-preservers, the gun for shooting the life line across a stranded vessel, the life car hanging from the roof, and the "breeches buoy."

"I don't b'lieve you'd ever git me into that thing," said the Nantucket lady decidedly, referring to the buoy. "I don't know but I'd 'bout as liefs be drownded as make sech a show of myself."

"Took off a bigger woman than you one time," said Captain Davis. "Wife of a Portland skipper, she was, and he was on his fust v'yage in a brand-new schooner jest off the stocks. Struck on the Hog's Back off here and then drifted close in and struck again. We got 'em all, the woman fust. That was the only time we've used the buoy sence I've been at the station. Most of the wrecks are too fur off shore and we have to git out the boat."

He took them upstairs to the men's sleeping rooms and then up to the little cupola on the roof.

"Why do you have ground–glass windows on this side of the house?" asked Elsie, as they passed the window on the landing.

Captain Davis laughed.

"Well, it is pretty nigh ground–glass now," he answered, "but it wa'n't when it was put in. The sand did that. It blows like all possessed when there's a gale on."

"Do you mean that those windows were ground that way by the beach sand blowing against them?" asked Ralph, astonished.

"Sartin. Git a good no'therly wind comin' up the beach and it fetches the sand with it. Mighty mean stuff to face, sand blowin' like that is; makes you think you're fightin' a nest of yaller– jackets."

With the telescope in the cupola they could see for miles up and down the beach and out to sea. An ocean tug bound toward Boston was passing, and Elsie, looking through the glass, saw the cook come out of the galley, empty a pan over the side, and go back again.

"Let me look through that a minute," said Captain Eri, when the rest had had their turn. He swung the glass around until it pointed toward their home away up the shore.

"Perez," he called anxiously, "look here quick!"

Captain Perez hastily put his eye to the glass, and his friend went on:

"You see our house?" he said. "Yes; well, you see the dinin'–room door. Notice that chair by the side of it?"

"Yes, what of it?"

"Well, that's the rocker that Elsie made the velvet cushion for. I want you to look at the upper southeast corner of that cushion, and see if there ain't a cat's hair there. Lorenzo's possessed to sleep in that chair, and—"

"Oh, you git out!" indignantly exclaimed Captain Perez, straightening up.

"Well, it was a pretty important thing, and I wanted to make sure. I left that chair out there, and I knew what I'd catch if any cat's hairs got on that cushion while I was gone. Ain't that so, Mrs. Snow?"

The housekeeper expressed her opinion that Captain Eri was a "case," whatever that may be.

They had clam chowder for dinner—a New England clam chowder, made with milk and crackers, and clams with shells as white as snow. They were what the New Yorker calls "soft–shell" clams, for a Fulton Market chowder is a "quahaug soup" to the native of the Cape.

Now that chowder was good; everybody said so, and if the proof of the chowder, like that of the pudding, is in the eating of it, this one had a clear case. Also, there were boiled striped bass, which is good enough for anybody, hot biscuits, pumpkin pie, and beach–plum preserves. There was a running fire of apologies from Miss Patience and answering volleys of compliments from Mrs. Snow.

"I don't see how you make sech beach–plum preserves, Miss Davis," exclaimed the lady from Nantucket. "I declare! I'm goin' to ask you for another sasserful. I b'lieve they're the best I ever ate."

"Well, now! Do you think so? I kind of suspected that the plums was a little mite too ripe. You know how 'tis with beach–plums, they've got to be put up when they're jest so, else they ain't good for much. I was at Luther for I don't know how long 'fore I could git him to go over to the P'int and pick 'em, and I was 'fraid he'd let it go too long. I only put up twenty–two jars of 'em on that account. How much sugar do you use?"

There was material here for the discussion that country housewives love, and the two ladies took advantage of it. When it was over the female portion of the company washed the dishes, while the men walked up and down the beach and smoked. Here they were joined after a while by the ladies, for even by the ocean it was as mild as early May, and the wind was merely bracing and had no sting in it.

The big blue waves shouldered themselves up from the bosom of the sea, marched toward the beach, and tumbled to pieces in a roaring tumult of white and green. The gulls skimmed along their tops or dropped like falling stones into the water after sand eels, emerging again, screaming, to repeat the performance.

The conversation naturally turned to wrecks, and Captain Davis, his reserve vanishing before the tactful inquiries of the captains and Ralph, talked shop and talked it well.

CHAPTER XI. HEROES AND A MYSTERY

Luther Davis had been commandant at the life−saving station for years and "Number One Man" before that, so his experience with wrecks and disabled craft of all kinds had been long and varied. He told them of disasters the details of which had been telegraphed all over the country, and of rescues of half−frozen crews from ice− crested schooners whose signals of distress had been seen from the observatory on the roof of the station. He told of long rows in midwinter through seas the spray of which turned to ice as they struck, and froze the men's mittens to the oar−handles. He told of picking up draggled corpses in the surf at midnight, when, as he said, "You couldn't tell whether 'twas a man or a roll of seaweed, and the only way to make sure was to reach down and feel."

Captain Eri left them after a while, as he had some acquaintances among the men at the station, and wished to talk with them. Miss Davis remembered that she had not fed the chickens, and hurried away to perform that humane duty, gallantly escorted by Captain Perez. The Captain, by the way, was apparently much taken with the plump spinster and, although usually rather bashful where ladies were concerned, had managed to keep up a sort of side conversation with Miss Patience while the storytelling was going on. But Ralph and Elsie and Mrs. Snow were hungry for more tales, and Captain Davis obligingly told them.

"One of the wust wrecks we ever had off here," he said, "was the Bluebell, British ship, she was: from Singapore, bound to Boston, and loaded with hemp. We see her about off that p'int there, jest at dusk, and she was makin' heavy weather then. It come on to snow soon as it got dark, and blow—don't talk! Seems to me 'twas one of the meanest nights I ever saw. 'Tween the snow flyin' and the dark you couldn't see two feet ahead of you. We was kind of worried about the vessel all evenin'—for one thing she was too close in shore when we see her last—but there wa'n't nothin' to be done except to keep a weather eye out for signs of trouble.

"Fust thing we knew of the wreck was when the man on patrol up the beach—Philander Vose 'twas—telephoned from the shanty that a ship's long-boat had come ashore at Knowles' Cove, two mile above the station. That was about one o'clock in the mornin'. 'Bout h'af-past two Sim Gould—he was drownded the next summer, fishin' on the Banks—telephoned from the shanty BELOW the station—the one a mile or so 'tother side of the cable house, Mr. Hazeltine—that wreckage was washin' up abreast of where he was; that was six miles from where the longboat come ashore. So there we was. There wa'n't any way of tellin' whereabouts she was layin'; she might have been anywheres along them six miles, and you couldn't hear nothin' nor see nothin'. But anyhow, the wreckage kept comin' in below the cable station, so I jedged she was somewheres in that neighborhood and we got the boat out—on the cart, of course—and hauled it down there.

"'Twas a tremendous job, too, that haulin' was. We had the horse and the whole of us helpin' him, but I swan! I begun to think we'd never git anywheres. 'Tween the wind and the sand and the snow I thought we'd flap to pieces, like a passel of shirts on a clothes line. But we got there after a spell, and then there was nothin' to do but wait for daylight.

"'Bout seven o'clock the snow let up a little bit, and then we see her. There was a bar jest about opposite the cable station—it's been washed away sence—and she'd struck on that, and the sea was makin' a clean breach over her. There was a ha'f a dozen of her crew lashed in the riggin', but I didn't see 'em move, so I presume likely they was froze stiff then, for 'twas perishin' cold. But we wrastled the boat down to the water and was jest goin' to launch her when the whole three masts went by the 'board, men and all. We put off to her, but she was in a reg'lar soapsuds of a sea and awash from stem to stern, so we knew there was nothin' livin' aboard.

"Yes, siree," continued the Captain meditatively, "that was a mean night. I had this ear frost-bit, and it's been tender ever sence. One of the fellers had a rib broke; he was a little light chap, and the wind jest slammed him up against the cart like as if he was a chip.

106

And jest to show you," he added, "how the tide runs around this place, the bodies of that crew was picked up from Wellmouth to Setuckit P'int—twenty-mile stretch that is. The skipper's body never come ashore. He had a son, nice young feller, that was goin' to meet him in Boston, and that boy spent a month down here, waitin' for his father's body to be washed up. He'd walk up and down this beach, and walk up and down. Pitiful sight as ever I see."

"And they were all lost?" asked Elsie with a shiver.

"Every man Jack. But 'twas cu'rus about that hemp. The Bluebell was loaded with it, as I told you, and when she went to pieces the tide took that hemp and strung it from here to glory. They picked it up all 'longshore, and for much as a month afterwards you'd go along the 'main road' over in the village, and see it hung over fences or spread out in the sun to dry. Looked like all the blonde girls in creation had had a hair-cut."

"Captain Davis," said Ralph, "you must have seen some plucky things in your life. What was the bravest thing you ever saw done?"

The life saver took the cigar that Hazeltine had given him from his mouth, and blew the smoke into the air over his head.

"Well," he said slowly, "I don't know exactly. I've seen some pretty gritty things done 'long-shore here, in the service. When there's somebody drownin', and you know there's a chance to save 'em, you'll take chances, and think nothin' of 'em, that you wouldn't take if you had time to set down and cal'late a little. I see somethin' done once that may not strike you as bein' anything out of the usual run, but that has always seemed to me clear grit and nothin' else. 'Twa'n't savin' life neither; 'twas jest a matter of bus'ness.

"It happened up off the coast of Maine 'long in the seventies. I was actin' as sort of second mate on a lumber schooner. 'Twas a pitch-black night, or mornin' rather, 'bout six o'clock, blowin' like all possessed and colder 'n Greenland. We struck a rock that wa'n't even down on an Eldredge chart and punched a hole in the schooner's side, jest above what ought to have been the water line, only she was heeled over so that 'twas consider'ble below it most of the time. We had a mean crew aboard, Portugees mainly, and poor ones at that. The skipper was below, asleep, and when he come on deck things was in a bad way. We'd got the canvas off her, but she was takin' in water every time she rolled, and there was a sea goin' that was tearin' things loose in great shape. We shipped one old grayback that ripped off a strip of the lee rail jest the same as you'd rip the edge off the cover of a pasteboard box—never made no more fuss about it, either.

"I didn't see nothin' to do but get out the boats, but the skipper he wa'n't that kind. He sized things up in a hurry, I tell you. He drove the crew—ha'f of 'em was prayin' to the Virgin and t'other ha'f swearin' a blue streak—to the pumps, and set me over 'em with a revolver to keep 'em workin'. Then him and the fust mate and one or two of the best hands rousted out a spare sail, weighted one edge of it to keep it down, and got it over the side, made fast, of course.

"Then him and the mate stripped to their underclothes, rigged a sort of bos'n's chair over where the hole in the side was, took hammers and a pocketful of nails apiece, and started in to nail that canvas over the hole.

"'Twas freezin' cold, and the old schooner was rollin' like a washtub. One minute I'd see the skipper and the mate h'isted up in the air, hammerin' for dear life, and then, swash! under they'd go, clear under, and stay there, seemed to me, forever. Every dip I thought would be the end, and I'd shet my eyes, expectin' to see 'em gone when she lifted; but no, up they'd come, fetch a breath, shake the salt water out of their eyes, and go to work again.

"Four hours and a quarter they was at it, four hours, mind you, and under water a good ha'f of the time; but they got that sail nailed fast fin'lly. We got 'em on deck when 'twas done, and we had to carry the fust mate to the cabin. But the skipper jest sent the cook for a pail of bilin' hot coffee, drunk the whole of it, put on dry clothes over his wet flannels, and stayed on deck and worked that schooner into Portland harbor, the men pumpin' clear green water out of the hold every minute of the way.

"Now, that always seemed to me to be the reel thing. 'Twa'n't a question of savin' life—we could have took to the boats and, nine chances out of ten, got ashore all right, for 'twa'n't very fur. But no, the skipper said he'd never lost a vessel for an owner yit and he wa'n't goin' to lose this one. And he didn't either, by Judas! No, sir!"

"That was splendid!" exclaimed Elsie. "I should like to have known that captain. Who was he, Captain Davis?"

Cap'n Eri

"Well, the fust mate was Obed Simmons—he's dead now—but he used to live over on the road towards East Harniss. The skipper—well, he was a feller you know."

"'Twas Cap'n Eri," said Mrs. Snow with conviction.

"That's right, ma'am. Perez told you, I s'pose."

"No, nobody told me. I jest guessed it. I've seen a good many folks in my time, and I cal'late I've got so I can tell what kind a man is after I've known him a little while. I jedged Cap'n Eri was that kind, and, when you said we knew that skipper, I was almost sartin 'twas him."

"Well!" exclaimed Ralph, "I don't believe I should have guessed it. I've always liked the Captain, but he has seemed so full of fun and so easy−going that I never thought of his doing anything quite so strenuous."

Captain Davis laughed. "I've seen fo'mast hands try to take advantage of that easy−goin' way 'fore now," he said, "but they never did it but once. Cap'n Eri is one of the finest fellers that ever stepped, but you can't stomp on his toes much, and he's clear grit inside. And say," he added, "don't you tell anybody I told that story, for he'd skin me alive if he knew it."

As they walked back toward the station Ralph and Elsie lingered a little behind the others, and then stopped to watch a big four− master that, under full sail, was spinning along a mile or two from the beach. They watched it for a moment or two without speaking. Elsie's cheeks were brown from the sun, stray wisps of her hair fluttered in the wind, and her trim, healthy figure stood out against the white sandhill behind them as if cut from cardboard. The electrician looked at her, and again the thought of that disgraceful "'Gusty" Black episode was forced into his mind. They had had many a good laugh over it since, and Elsie had apparently forgotten it, but he had not, by a good deal.

She was the first to speak, and then as much to herself as to him.

"I think they are the best people I ever knew," she said.

"Who?" he asked.

"Oh, all of them! The captains and Mrs. Snow, and Captain Davis and his sister. They are so simple and kind and generous. And the best of it is, they don't seem to know it, and wouldn't believe it if you told them."

Ralph nodded emphatically.

"I imagine it would take a good deal to convince Davis or any of these station men that there was anything heroic in their lives," he said. "As for Captain Eri, I have known him only a month or two, but I don't know of anyone to whom I would rather go if I were in trouble."

"He has been so kind to grandfather and me," said Elsie, "that I feel as though we were under an obligation we never could repay. When I came down here I knew no one in Orham, and he and Captain Jerry and Captain Perez have made me feel more at home than I have ever felt before. You know," she added, "grandfather is the only relative I have."

"I suppose you will go back to your studies when your grandfather recovers."

"I don't know. If grandfather is well enough I think I shall try to persuade him to come up to Boston and live with me. Then I might perhaps teach. This was to have been my last year at Radcliffe, so my giving it up will not make so much difference. Do you intend to stay here long? I suppose you do. Your profession, I know, means so much to you, and your work at the station must be very interesting."

"It would be more so if I had someone who was interested with me. Mr. Langley is kind, but he is so wrapped up in his own work that I see very little of him. I took the place because I thought it would give me a good deal of spare time that I might use in furthering some experiments of my own. Electricity is my hobby, and I have one or two ideas that I am foolish enough to hope may be worth developing. I have had time enough, goodness knows, but it's a lonesome sort of life. If it had not been for the captains—and you—I think I should have given it up before this."

"Oh, I hope you won't."

"Why?"

"Why—why, because it seems like running away, almost, doesn't it? If a thing is hard to do, but is worth doing, I think the satisfaction IN doing it is ever so much greater, don't you? I know it must be lonely for you; but, then, it is lonely for Mr. Langley and the other men, too."

"I doubt if Mr. Langley would be happy anywhere else, and the other men are married, most of them, and live over in the village."

Now, there isn't any real reason why this simple remark should have caused a halt in the conversation, but it did. Miss Preston said, "Oh, indeed!" rather hurriedly, and her next speech was concerning the height of a particularly big wave. Mr. Hazeltine answered this commonplace somewhat absent–mindedly. He acted like a man to whom a startling idea had suddenly occurred. Just then they heard Captain Eri calling them.

The Captain was standing on a sand dune near the station, shouting their names through a speaking trumpet formed by placing his hands about his mouth. As the pair came strolling toward him, he shifted his hands to his trousers pockets and stood watching the young couple with a sort of half smile.

"I s'pose if Jerry was here now," he mused, "he'd think his scheme was workin'. Well, maybe 'tis, maybe 'tis. You can't never tell. Well, I swan!"

The exclamation was called forth by the sight of Captain Perez and Miss Patience, who suddenly came into view around the corner of the station. The Captain was gallantly assisting his companion over the rough places in the path, and she was leaning upon his arm in a manner that implied implicit confidence. Captain Eri glanced from one couple to the other, and then grinned broadly. The grin had not entirely disappeared when Captain Perez came up, and the latter rather crisply asked what the joke was.

"Oh, nothin'!" was the reply. "I was jest thinkin' we must be playin' some kind of a game, and I was It."

"It?" queried Miss Patience, puzzled.

"Why, yes. I'm kinder like 'Rastus Bailey used to be at the dances when you and me was younger, Perez. Old man Alexander—he was the fiddler—used to sing out 'Choose partners for Hull's Vict'ry,' or somethin' like that, and it always took 'Ras so long to make up his mind what girl to choose that he gin'rally got left altogether. Then he'd set on the settee all through the dance and say he never cared much for Hull's Vict'ry, anyway. Seems to me, I'm the only one that ain't choosed partners. How 'bout it, Perez?"

"More fool you, that's all I've got to say," replied Captain Perez stoutly.

Miss Patience laughed so heartily at this rejoinder that Perez began to think he had said a very good thing indeed, and so repeated it for greater effect.

"You want to look out for him, Miss Davis," said Captain Eri. "He's the most fascinatin' youngster of his age I ever see. Me and Jerry's been thinkin' we'd have to build a fence 'round the house to keep the girls away when he's home. Why, M'lissy Busteed fairly—"

"Oh, give us a rest, Eri!" exclaimed Perez, with even more indignation than was necessary. "M'lissy Busteed!"

Just then Ralph and Elsie came up, and Captain Eri explained that he had hailed them because it was time to be going if they wanted to get across to the mainland without swimming. They walked around to the back door of the station and there found Mrs. Snow and Captain Davis by the hen–yard. The lady from Nantucket had discovered a sick chicken in the collection, and she was holding it in her lap and at the same time discoursing learnedly on the relative value of Plymouth Rocks and Rhode Island Reds, as layers.

"See there!" exclaimed Captain Eri delightedly, pointing to the suffering pullet, "what did I tell you? D'you wonder we picked her out for nuss for John, Luther? Even a sick hen knows enough to go to her."

They harnessed Daniel to the carryall, and stowed the living freight aboard somehow, although Captain Perez protested that he had eaten so much dinner he didn't know's he'd be able to hang on the way he did coming down. Then they said farewell to Captain Davis and his sister and started for home. The members of the crew, such of them as were about the station, waved good–by to them as they passed.

Cap'n Eri

"Things kind of average up in this world, don't they?" said Captain Eri reflectively, as he steered Daniel along the soft beach toward the ford. "We're all the time readin' 'bout fellers that work for the Gov'ment gittin' high sal'ries and doin' next to nothin'. Now there's a gang—the life–savin' crew, I mean—that does what you and me would call almighty hard work and git next to nothin' for it. Uncle Sam gits square there, it seems to me. A few dollars a month and find yourself ain't gilt–edged wages for bein' froze and drownded and blown to pieces ten months out of the year, is it?"

The tide was higher when they came to the crossing than it had been when they drove over before, but they made the passage all right, although there was some nervousness displayed by the feminine portion of the party. When they reached home they found Captain Jerry contentedly smoking his pipe, the sick man was asleep, and everything was serene. Josiah appeared from behind the barn, where he had been smoking a cigarette.

They pressed Mr. Hazeltine to stay to supper, but he declined, alleging that he had been away from business too long already. He had been remarkably silent during the homeward ride, and Elsie, too, had seemed busy with her thoughts. She was full of fun at the supper table, however, and the meal was a jolly one. Just as it was finished Captain Jerry struck the table a bang with his palm that made the knives and forks jump, and so startled Captain Perez as to cause him to spill half a cup of tea over his shirt bosom.

"Land of love!" ejaculated the victim, mopping his chin and his tie with his napkin. "It's bad enough to scare a feller to death, let alone drowndin' and scaldin' him at the same time. What did you do that for?"

"I jest thought of somethin'," exclaimed Captain Jerry, going through one pocket after the other.

"Well, I wish you'd have your thinkin' fits in the barn or somewheres else next time. I put this shirt on clean this mornin' and now look at it!"

His friend was too busy to pay any attention to this advice. The pocket search apparently being unsatisfactory, he rose from the table and hurriedly made a round of the room, looking on the mantelpiece and under chairs.

"I had it when I come in," he soliloquized. "I know I did, 'cause I was wearin' it when I went out to see to the hens. I don't see where—"

"If it's your hat you're looking for," observed Josiah, "I saw Mrs. Snow hang it up on the nail behind the door. There it is now."

The reply to this was merely a grunt, which may, or may not have expressed approval. At any rate, the hat was apparently the object of his search, for he took it from the nail, looked inside, and with a sigh of relief took out a crumpled envelope.

"I knew I put it somewheres," he said. "It's a letter for you, Elsie. Josiah, here, he brought it down from the post–office when he come from school this afternoon. I meant to give it to you afore."

Captain Eri, who sat next to the young lady, noticed that the envelope was addressed in an irregular, sprawling hand to "Miss Elizabeth Preston, Orham, Mass." Elsie looked it over in the absent way in which so many of us examine the outside of a letter which comes unexpectedly.

"I wonder who it is from," she said.

She did not open it at once, but, tucking it into her waist, announced that she must run upstairs, in order that Mrs. Snow might come down to supper. The housekeeper did come down a few minutes later, and, as she was interested to know more about Luther Davis and his sister, the talk became animated and general.

It was after eight o'clock when Mrs. Snow, having finished washing the dishes—she allowed no one to assist her in this operation since the time when she caught Captain Jerry absent–mindedly using the dust rag instead of the dishcloth—went upstairs to her patient. Shortly afterward Elsie came down, wearing her hat and jacket.

"I'm going out for a little while," she said. "No, I don't want anyone to go with me. I'll be back soon."

Her back was turned to the three captains as she spoke, but, as she opened the door, the lamplight shone for an instant on her face, and Captain Eri noticed, or fancied that he did, that she was paler than usual. He rose, and again offered to accompany her, but met with such a firm refusal that he could not insist further.

"Now, that's kind of funny, ain't it?" remarked Perez. "I don't b'lieve she's been out alone afore after dark sence she's been here."

"Where did you git that letter, Josiah?" asked Captain Eri.

It may as well be explained here that Captain Perez' grand–nephew was a thorn in the flesh to everyone, including his indulgent relative. He was a little afraid of Mrs. Snow, and obeyed her better than he did anyone else, but that is not saying a great deal. He was in mischief in school two–thirds of the time, and his reports, made out by the teacher, were anything but complimentary. He was a good–looking boy, the image of his mother, who had been her uncle's favorite, and he was popular with a certain class of youngsters. Also, and this was worse, his work at the livery stable had thrown him in contact with a crowd of men like "Squealer" Wixon, "Web" Saunders, and others of their class, and they appreciated his New York street training and made much of him. Captain Perez, mindful of his promise to the boy's mother, did not use the necessary measures to control him, and Captain Eri and Captain Jerry did not like to interfere.

Just now he was seated in the corner, and he looked up with a start, hurriedly folded up the tattered paper book he was reading, stuffed it into his pocket, and said, "What?"

"Who give you that letter that come for Elsie?"

"Miss Cahoon up at the office. It was in our box," said the boy.

"Humph! What are you readin' that's so interestin'?"

"Oh, nothin'. A book, that's all."

"Let me look at it."

Josiah hesitated, looked as if he would like to refuse, and then sullenly took the ragged volume from his pocket and handed it to the Captain, who deliberately unfolded it, and looked at the cover.

Cap'n Eri

"'Fightin' Fred Starlight, the Boy Rover of the Pacific,'" he read aloud. "Humph! Is it good?"

"Bet your life! It's a red–hot story."

"I want to know! Who was Mr. Moonshine—what's his name—Starlight?"

"He was a sailor," was the sulky answer. Josiah was no fool, and knew when he was being made fun of.

The Captain opened the book, and read a page or two to himself. Then he said, "I see he knocked the skipper down 'cause he insulted him. Nice, spunky chap; I'd like to have had him aboard a vessel of mine. And he called the old man a 'caitiff hound'? Awful thing to call a feller, that is. I'll bet that skipper felt ashamed. Looks like a good book. I'll borrow it to–night to read while you're doin' your lessons."

"I ain't got any lessons to do."

"Oh, ain't you? I thought that was a 'rithmetic over there."

"Well, I know 'em now. Besides, you ain't got any right to order me around. You ain't my uncle. Can't I read that book, Uncle Perez?"

Poor Perez! He hesitated, swallowed once or twice, and answered, "You can read it after you've studied a spell. You'll let him have it then, won't you, Eri? Now study, like a good boy."

Captain Eri looked as if he would like to say something further, but he evidently thought better of it, and tossed the paper novel across to Captain Perez, who put it on the table, saying, rather feebly:

"There now, it's right there, where you can have it soon's you've l'arned your examples. Now pitch in, so's the teacher can see how smart you are."

His nephew grumblingly got his paper and pencil, took the arithmetic and went to work. No one spoke for a while, Captain Perez twirling his thumbs and looking, as he felt,

116

uncomfortable. Soon Josiah, announcing that his studies were completed, grabbed the novel from the table, took a lamp from the kitchen and went off to bed. When he had gone Captain Jerry said, "Perez, you're sp'ilin' that boy."

"I s'pose I am, I s'pose I am, but I can't bear to be cross to him, somehow. Poor Lizzie, she made me promise I wouldn't be, and I jest can't; that's all. You understand how 'tis, don't you, Eri?"

The Captain nodded. "I understand," he said. "I'm sorry I said anything. I hadn't ought to be givin' orders 'bout what's none of my affairs. What time is it gittin' to be?"

Captain Jerry announced that it was bedtime, and that he was going to turn in. Perez, still looking worried and anxious, said that he also was going to bed. Captain Eri thought that he would sit up for a while.

Another hour and still another went by, and the Captain sat there in his rocker. His two friends were sound asleep. Mrs. Snow called twice from the head of the stairs to know if Elsie had come back, and where on earth she could be. Captain Eri's answers were cheery and to the effect that the young lady had an errand up town, and would be home pretty soon, he guessed. Nevertheless, it might have been noticed that he glanced at the clock every few minutes, and grew more and more fidgety.

It was after eleven when Elsie came in. She hurriedly and with some confusion apologized for being so late, and thanked the Captain for sitting up for her. She made no offer to explain her long absence and, as she went upstairs, Captain Eri noticed that her face was, if anything, paler than when she went out, and her eyes looked as if she had been crying. He wanted to ask her some questions, but didn't, because she evidently did not wish to talk. He pondered over the matter while undressing, and for a long time after that lay awake thinking. That the girl was in trouble of some sort was plain, but he could not understand why she said nothing about it, or what its cause might be. She had been her bright, happy self all day and a part of the evening. Then she had suddenly changed. The Captain wondered what was in that letter.

117

CHAPTER XII. A LITTLE POLITICS

Elsie, when she came down to breakfast next morning, was quieter than usual, and to the joking questions of Captain Jerry and Captain Perez, who were curious concerning her "errand" of the previous evening, and who pretended to believe that she had gone to a dance or "time" with some "feller" unknown, she gave evasive, but good–humored replies. Captain Eri was on his usual fishing trip, and after breakfast was over Perez departed to the Barry place, and Jerry to his beloved schoolhouse. The sacrifice, whose impending matrimonial doom had not been mentioned for some time by the trio interested, was gradually becoming his own garrulous self, and his principal topic of conversation recently had been the coming marriage of the "upstairs teacher"—that is, the lady who presided over the grammar grade of the school—and the question of her probable successor. In fact, this question of who the new teacher was to be was the prevailing subject of surmise and conjecture in the village just then.

When Captain Jerry came back to the house he went out to the barn to feed Lorenzo and the hens, and attend to Daniel's toilet. He was busy with the curry–comb when Elsie came in. She seated herself on a box, and watched the performance for a while without speaking. The Captain, who took this part of his duties very seriously, was too intent on crimping Daniel's rather scraggy forelock to talk much. At length Miss Preston broke the silence.

"Captain Jerry," she said, "you have never told me just where you found grandfather that night when he was taken sick. On the hill back of the post–office, wasn't it?"

"Yes, jest on the top. You see, he'd fell down when he was runnin' to the fire."

"Captain Eri found him, didn't he?"

"Yep. Whoa there, Dan'l; stand still, can't you? Yes, Eri found him."

"How was he dressed?"

"Who? John? Oh, he was bareheaded and in his shirtsleeves, jest as he run outdoors when he heard the bell. Queer, he didn't put on that old white hat of his. I never knew him to be without it afore; but a feller's li'ble to forgit 'most anything a night like that was. Did Eri tell you how Perez forgot his shoes? Funniest thing I ever see, that was."

He began the story of his friend's absent-mindedness, but his companion did not seem to pay much attention to it. In fact, it was evident that her thoughts were somewhere else, for when the Captain asked her a question that plainly called for a negative, she replied "Yes," very calmly, and didn't seem to know that she had said it. She went into the house soon after and Captain Jerry, after considering the matter, decided that she was probably thinking of Hazeltine. He derived much comfort from the idea.

When he, too, entered the dining room, Elsie said to him:

"Oh, Captain Jerry! Please don't tell the others that I asked about grandfather. They would think that I was worrying, and I'm not, a bit. You won't mention it, will you? Just promise, to please me."

So the Captain promised, although he did not understand why it was asked of him.

When Captain Eri came home that afternoon, and was cleaning his catch at the shanty, he was surprised to receive a call from Miss Preston.

"Hello!" he exclaimed. "Come to l'arn the trade?"

Elsie smiled, and disclaimed any intention of apprenticeship.

"Captain Eri," she said, "I want to have a talk with you, a business talk."

The Captain looked at her keenly. All he said, however, was, "You don't tell me!"

"Yes, I want to talk with you about getting me a position."

"A position?"

"Yes, I've been thinking a great deal lately, and, now that grandfather seems to be a little better, and I'm not needed to help take care of him, I want to do something to earn my living."

"Earn your livin'? Why, child alive, you don't need to do that. You ain't a mite of trouble at the house; fact is, I don't know how we'd get along without you, and, as for money, why I cal'late your grandpa ain't so poor but what, if I let you have a little change once in a while, he'd be able to pay me back, when he got better."

"But I don't want to use your money or his either. Captain Eri, you don't know what he has done for me ever since I was a little girl. He has clothed me and given me an education, and been so kind and good that, now that he is ill and helpless, I simply can't go on using his money. I can't, and I won't."

The tears stood in the girl's eyes, as she spoke, and the Captain, noticing her emotion, thought it better to treat the matter seriously, for the present at any rate.

"All right," he said. "'Independence shows a proper sperit and saves grocery bills,' as old man Scudder said when his wife run off with the tin–peddler. What kind of a place was you thinkin' of takin'?"

"I want to get the appointment to teach in the grammar school here. Miss Nixon is going to be married, and when she leaves I want her place—and I want you to help me get it."

Captain Eri whistled. "I want to know!" he exclaimed. Then he said, "Look here, Elsie, I don't want you to think I'm tryin' to be cur'ous 'bout your affairs, or anything like that, but are you sure there ain't some reason more 'n you've told me of for your wantin' this place? I ain't no real relation of yours, you understand, but I would like to have you feel that you could come to me with your troubles jest the same as you would to your grandpa. Now, honest and true, ain't there somethin' back of this?"

It was only for a moment that Elsie hesitated, but that moment's hesitation and the manner in which she answered went far toward confirming the Captain's suspicions.

"No, Captain Eri," she said. "It is just as I've told you. I don't want to be dependent on grandfather any longer."

"And there ain't a single other reason for— Of course, I ought to mind my business, but— Well, there! what was it you wanted me to do? Help you git the place?"

"Yes, if you will. I know Captain Perez has said that you were interested in the town–meetings and helped to nominate some of the selectmen and the school–committee, so I thought perhaps, if you used your influence, you might get the position for me."

"Well, I don't know. I did do a little electioneerin' for one or two fellers and maybe they'd ought to be willin' to do somethin' for me. Still, you can't never tell. A cat 'll jump over your hands if she knows there's a piece of fish comin' afterwards, but when she's swallowed that fish, it's a diff'rent job altogether. Same way with a politician. But, then, you let me think over it for a spell, and p'raps to–morrow we'll see. You think it over, too. Maybe you'll change your mind."

"No, I shan't change my mind. I'm ever and ever so much obliged to you, though."

She started toward the door, but turned impulsively and said, "Oh, Captain Eri, you don't think that I'm ungrateful, do you? You nor Captain Perez nor Captain Jerry won't think that I do not appreciate all your kindness? You won't think that I'm shirking my duty, or that I don't want to help take care of grandfather any longer? You won't? Promise me you won't."

She choked down a sob as she asked the question.

Captain Eri was as much moved as she was. He hastened to answer.

"No, no, no!" he exclaimed. "Course we won't do no such thing. Run right along, and don't think another word about it. Wait till to–morrer. I'll have a plan fixed up to land that school–committee, see if I don't."

But all that evening he worked at the model of the clipper, and the expression on his face as he whittled showed that he was puzzled, and not a little troubled.

He came back from his fishing next day a little earlier than usual, changed his working–clothes for his second best suit, harnessed Daniel into the buggy, and then came into the house, and announced that he was going over to the Neck on an errand, and if Elsie wanted to go with him, he should be glad of her company. As this was but part of a pre–arranged scheme, the young lady declared that a ride was just what she needed.

Cap'n Eri

Captain Eri said but little, as they drove up to the "main road"; he seemed to be thinking. Elsie, too, was very quiet. When they reached the fruit and candy shop, just around the corner, the Captain stopped the horse, got down, and went in. When he came out he had a handful of cigars.

"Why, Captain Eri," said Elsie, "I didn't know that you smoked cigars. I thought a pipe was your favorite."

"Well, gin'rally speakin', 'tis," was the answer, "but I'm electioneerin' now, and politics without cigars would be like a chowder without any clams. Rum goes with some kind of politics, but terbacker kind of chums in with all kinds. 'Tain't always safe to jedge a candidate by the kind of cigars he gives out neither; I've found that out.

"Reminds me of a funny thing that Obed Nickerson told me one time. Obed used to be in politics a good deal up and down the Cape, here, and he had consider'ble influence. 'Twas when Bradley up to Fall River was runnin' for Congress. They had a kind of pow-wow in his office—a whole gang of district leaders—and Obed he was one of 'em. Bradley went to git out the cigar-box, and 'twas empty, so he called in the boy that swept out and run errands for him, give the youngster a ten-dollar bill, and told him to go down to a terbacker store handy and buy another box. Well, the boy, he was a new one that Bradley'd jest hired, seemed kind of surprised to think of anybody's bein' so reckless as to buy a whole box of cigars at once, but he went and pretty soon come back with the box.

"The old man told him to open it and pass 'em round. Well, everybody was lookin' for'ard to a treat, 'cause Bradley had the name of smokin' better stuff than the average; but when they lit up and got a-goin', Obed said you could see that the gang was s'prised and some disgusted. The old man didn't take one at fust, but everybody else puffed away, and the smoke and smell got thicker 'n' thicker. Obed said it reminded him of a stable afire more 'n anything else. Pretty soon Bradley bit the end of one of the things and touched a match to it. He puffed twice—Obed swears 'twa'n't more'n that—and then he yelled for the boy.

"'For the Lord's sake!' he says, 'where'd you git them cigars?' Well, it come out that the boy hadn't told who the cigars was for, and he'd bought a box of the kind his brother that worked in the cotton mill smoked. Obed said you'd ought to have seen Bradley's face when the youngster handed him back seven dollars and seventy- five cents change."

Cap'n Eri

They reached that part of Orham which is called the Neck, and pulled up before a small building bearing the sign "Solomon Bangs, Attorney–at–Law, Real Estate and Insurance." Here the Captain turned to his companion and asked, "Sure you haven't changed your mind, Elsie? You want that school–teachin' job?"

"I haven't changed my mind, Captain Eri."

"Well, I wanted to be sure. I should hate to ask Sol Bangs for anything and then have to back out afterwards. Come on, now."

Mr. Soloman Bangs was the chairman of the Orham school–committee. He was a short, stout man with sandy side–whiskers and a bald head. He received them with becoming condescension, and asked if they wouldn't sit down.

"Why, I've got a little bus'ness I want to talk with you 'bout, Sol," said the Captain. "Elsie, you set down here, and make yourself comf'table, and Sol and me 'll go inside for a minute."

As he led the way into the little private office at the back of the building, and seemed to take it for granted that Mr. Bangs would follow, the latter gentleman couldn't well refuse. The private office was usually reserved for interviews with widows whose homestead mortgages were to be foreclosed, guileless individuals who had indorsed notes for friends, or others whose business was unpleasant and likely to be accompanied with weeping or profanity. Mr. Bangs didn't object to foreclosing a mortgage, but he disliked to have a prospective customer hear the dialogue that preceded the operation.

On this occasion the door of the sanctum was left ajar so that Elsie, although she did not try to listen, could not very well help hearing what was said.

She heard the Captain commenting on the late cranberry crop, the exceptionally pleasant weather of the past month, and other irrelevant subjects. Then the perfumes of the campaign cigars floated out through the doorway.

"Let's see," said Captain Eri, "when's town meetin' day?"

"First Tuesday in December," replied Mr. Bangs.

"Why, so 'tis, so 'tis. Gittin' pretty nigh, ain't it? What are you goin' to git off the school–committee for?"

"Me? Get off the committee? Who told you that?"

"Why, I don't know. You are, ain't you? Seems to me I heard Seth Wingate was goin' to run and he's from your district, so I thought, of course—"

"Is Seth going to try for the committee?"

"Seth's a good man," was the equivocal answer.

"A good man! He ain't any better man than I am. What's he know about schools, or how to run 'em?"

"Well, he's pretty popular. Folks like him. See here, Sol; what's this 'bout your turnin' Betsy Godfrey off her place?"

"Who said I turned her off? I've been carrying that mortgage for so long it's gray–headed. I can't be Santa Claus for the whole town. Business is business, and I've got to look out for myself."

"Ye–es, I s'pose that's so. Still, folks talk, and Seth's got lots of friends."

"Eri, I ain't denying that you could do a heap to hurt me if you wanted to, but I don't know why you should. I've always been square with you, far's I know. What have you got against me?"

"Oh, nuthin', nuthin'! Didn't I hear you was tryin' to get that Harniss teacher to come down here and take Carrie Nixon's place when she got married?"

"Well, I thought of her. She's all night, isn't she?"

"Yes, I s'pose she is. 'Twould be better if she lived in Orham, maybe, and folks couldn't say you went out of town for a teacher when you could have had one right from home. Then, she's some relation of your cousin, ain't she? 'Course, that's all right, but—well,

124

you can't pay attention to everything that's said."

"Could have got one right from home! Who'd we get? Dave Eldredge's girl, I suppose. I heard she was after it."

The conversation that followed was in a lower tone, and Elsie heard but little of it. She heard enough, however, to infer that Captain Eri was still the disinterested friend, and that Solomon was very anxious to retain that friendship. After a while the striking of matches indicated that fresh cigars were being lighted, and then the pair rose from their chairs, and entered the outer office. Mr. Bangs was very gracious, exceedingly so.

"Miss Preston," he said, "Cap'n Hedge tells me that it—er—might be possible for us—er—for the town to secure—er—to—in short, for us to have you for our teacher in the upstairs room. It ain't necessary for me to say that—er—a teacher from Radcliffe don't come our way very often, and that we—that is, the town of Orham, would—er—feel itself lucky if you'd be willing to come."

"Of course, I told him, Elsie," said Captain Eri, "that you wouldn't think of comin' for forty-five dollars a month or anything like that. Of course, 'tisn't as though you really needed the place."

"I understand, I understand," said the pompous committeeman. "I think that can be arranged. I really think—er—Miss Preston, that there ain't any reason why you can't consider it settled. Ahem!"

Elsie thanked him, trying her best not to smile, and they were bowed out by the great man, who, however, called the Captain to one side, and whispered eagerly to him for a moment or two. The word "Seth" was mentioned at least once.

"Why, Captain Eri!" exclaimed Elsie, as they drove away.

The Captain grinned. "Didn't know I was such a heeler, did you?" he said. "Well, I tell you. If you're fishin' for eels there ain't no use usin' a mack'rel jig. Sol, he's a little mite eely, and you've got to use the kind of bait that 'll fetch that sort of critter."

"But I shouldn't think he would care whether he was on the school– committee or not. It isn't such an exalted position."

Captain Eri's answer was in the form of a parable. "Old Laban Simpkins that lived 'round here one time," he said, "was a mighty hard ticket. Drank rum by the hogshead, pounded his wife till she left him, and was a tough nut gin'rally. Well, one evenin' Labe was comin' home pretty how–come–you–so, and he fell into Jonadab Wixon's well. Wonder he wa'n't killed, but he wa'n't, and they fished him out in a little while. He said that was the deepest well he ever saw; said he begun to think it reached clear through to the hereafter, and when he struck the water he was s'prised to find it wa'n't hot. He j'ined the church the next week, and somebody asked him if he thought religion would keep him from fallin' into any more wells. He said no; said he was lookin' out for somethin' further on.

"Well, that's the way 'tis with Sol. School–committee's all right, but this section of the Cape nominates a State representative next year.

"I mustn't forgit to see Seth," he added. "I promised I would, and besides," with a wink, "I think 'twould be better to do it 'cause, between you and me, I don't b'lieve Seth knows that he's been thinkin' of runnin' for the committee and has decided not to."

The second member of the school board, John Mullett, was, so the Captain said, a sort of "me too" to Mr. Bangs, and would vote as his friend directed. The third member was Mr. Langworthy, the Baptist minister and, although two to one was a clear majority, Captain Eri asserted that there was nothing like a unanimous vote, and so they decided to call upon the reverend gentleman.

They found him at home, and Elsie was surprised, after the previous interview, to see how differently her champion handled the case. There was no preliminary parley and no beating about the bush. Miss Preston's claim to the soon–to–be–vacant position was stated clearly and with vigor. Also the reasons why she should receive a higher salary than had previously been paid were set forth. It was something of a surprise to Elsie, as it had been to Ralph, to see how highly the towns–people, that is, the respectable portion of them, seemed to value the opinions of this good–natured but uneducated seaman. And yet when she considered that she, too, went to him for advice that she would not have asked of other and far more learned acquaintances, it did not seem so surprising after all.

Cap'n Eri

The clergyman had had several candidates in mind, but he was easily won over to Elsie's side, partly by the Captain's argument, and partly because he was favorably impressed by the young lady's appearance and manner. He expressed himself as being convinced that she would be exactly the sort of teacher that the school required and pledged his vote unconditionally.

And so, as Captain Eri said, the stump–speaking being over, there was nothing to do but to wait for the election, and Elsie and he agreed to keep the affair a secret until she received formal notice of the appointment. This was undoubtedly a good plan, but, unfortunately for its success, Solomon Bangs called upon his fellow in the committee, Mr. Mullett, to inform the latter that he, entirely unaided, had discovered the very teacher that Orham needed in the person of John Baxter's granddaughter. Mr. Mullett, living up to his "me too" reputation, indorsed the selection with enthusiasm, and not only did that, but also told everyone he met, so that Captain Perez heard of it at the post–office the very next afternoon.

The natural surprise of this gentleman and of Captain Jerry at their guest's sudden determination was met by plausible explanations from Captain Eri, to the effect that Elsie was a smart girl, and didn't like to be "hangin' 'round doin' nothin', now that her grandpa was some better." Elsie's own reason, as expressed to them, being just this, the pair accepted it without further questioning. Neither of them attached much importance to the letter which she had received, although Captain Perez did ask Mrs. Snow if she knew from whom it came.

The lady from Nantucket was not so easily satisfied. At her first opportunity she cornered Captain Eri, and they discussed the whole affair from beginning to end. There was nothing unusual in this proceeding, for discussions concerning household matters and questions of domestic policy were, between these two, getting to be more and more frequent. Mrs. Snow was now accepted by all as one of the family, and Captain Eri had come to hold a high opinion of her and her views. What he liked about her, he said, was her "good old–fashioned common–sense," and, whereas he had formerly trusted to his own share of this virtue almost altogether, now he was glad to have hers to help out.

The marriage idea, that which had brought the housekeeper to Orham, was now seldom mentioned. In fact, Captain Eri had almost entirely ceased to ruffle Jerry's feelings with reference to it. Mrs. Snow, of course, said nothing about it. But, for that matter, she said very little about herself or her affairs.

It was a curious fact that the lady from Nantucket had never referred, except in a casual way, to her past history. She had never told how she came to answer the advertisement in the Nuptial Chime, nor to explain how so matter–of–fact a person as she was had ever seen that famous sheet. As she said nothing concerning these things, no one felt at liberty to inquire, and, in the course of time, even Captain Perez' lively curiosity had lapsed into a trance.

Mrs. Snow was certain that Elsie's reason for wishing to obtain the position of school–teacher was something more specific than the one advanced. She was also certain that the girl was troubled about something. The root of the matter, she believed, was contained in the mysterious letter. As Captain Eri was of precisely the same opinion, speculation between the two as to what that letter might have contained was as lively as it was unfruitful.

One thing was certain, Elsie was not as she had formerly been. She did her best to appear the same, but she was much more quiet, and had fits of absentmindedness that the Captain and the housekeeper noticed. She had no more evening "errands," but she occasionally took long walks in the afternoons, and on these walks she evidently preferred to be alone.

Whether Mr. Hazeltine noticed this change in her was a question. The Captain thought he did, but at any rate, his calls were none the less frequent, and he showed no marked objection when Captain Jerry, who now considered himself bound in honor to bring about the union he had so actively championed, brought to bear his artful schemes for leaving the young folks alone. These devices were so apparent that Elsie had more than once betrayed some symptoms of annoyance, all of which were lost on the zealous match–maker. Ralph, like the others, was much surprised at Miss Preston's application for employment, but, as it was manifestly none of his business, he, of course, said nothing.

At the next committee meeting Elsie was unanimously chosen to fill Miss Nixon's shoes as trainer of the young idea at the grammar school, and, as Miss Nixon was very anxious to be rid of her responsibilities in order that she might become the carefree bride of a widower with two small children, the shoe–filling took place in a fortnight.

Cap'n Eri

From her first day's labors Elsie returned calm and unruffled. She had met the usual small rebellion against a new teacher, and had conquered it. She said she believed she had a good class and she should get on with them very nicely. It should be mentioned in passing, however, that Josiah Bartlett, usually the ring–leader in all sorts of trouble, was a trifle upset because the new schoolmistress lived in the same house with him, and so had not yet decided just how far it was safe to go in trespassing against law and order.

Thanksgiving day came, and the Captains entertained Miss Patience Davis and her brother and Ralph Hazeltine at dinner. That dinner was an event. Captain Eri and Mrs. Snow spent a full twenty minutes with the driver of the butcher's cart, giving him directions concerning the exact breed of turkey that was to be delivered, and apparently these orders were effectual, for Captain Luther, who was obliged to hurry back to the life–saving station as soon as dinner was over, said that he was so full of white meat and stuffing that he cal'lated he should "gobble" all the way to the beach. His sister stayed until the next day, and this was very pleasing to all hands, particularly Captain Perez.

They had games in the evening, and here the captains distinguished themselves. Seth Wingate and his wife, and Mr. and Mrs. Obed Nickerson came in, as did several other retired mariners and their better–halves. Obed brought his fiddle and sat in the corner and played the music for a Virginia reel, and Ralph laughed until he choked to see Captain Jerry—half of his shirt–collar torn loose from the button and flapping like a sail—convoy stout Mrs. Wingate from one end of the line to the other, throwing into the performance all the fancy "cuts" and "double–shuffles" he learned at the Thanksgiving balls of a good many years before. Captain Perez danced with Miss Patience, who assured him she had never had such a good time since she was born. The only scoffer was the bored Josiah, who, being a sophisticated New Yorker, sat in the best chair and gazed contemptuously upon the entire proceeding. He told "Web" Saunders the next day that he never saw such a gang of "crazy jays" in his life.

Even John Baxter was better that day. He seemed a trifle more rational, and apparently understood when they told him that it was Thanksgiving. There would have been no cloud anywhere had not Mrs. Snow, entering her room after Elsie had gone to bed, found that young lady awake and crying silently.

"And she wouldn't tell what the trouble was," said the housekeeper to Captain Eri, the next day. "Said it was nothin'; she was kind of worried 'bout her grandpa. Now, you and me know it wa'n't THAT. I wish to goodness we knew WHAT it was."

The Captain scratched his nose with a perplexed air. "There's one feller I'd like to have a talk with jest 'bout now," he said; "that's the one that invented that yarn 'bout a woman's not bein' able to keep a secret."

CHAPTER XIII. CAPTAIN JERRY MAKES A MESS OF IT

It was during the week that followed the holiday so gloriously celebrated that Captain Jerry made a mess of it, and all with the best intentions in the world. Elsie had had a hard day at the school, principally owing to the perversity of the irrepressible Josiah, whose love for deviltry was getting the better of his respect for the new teacher. The boy had discovered that Elsie never reported his bad conduct to Captain Perez, and, therefore, that the situation was not greatly different from what it had been during the reign of Miss Nixon.

On this particular day he had been a little worse than usual, and, as uneasiness and mischief in a schoolroom are as catching as the chickenpox, Elsie came home tired and nervous. Captain Eri and Mrs. Snow were certain that this increasing nervousness on the part of their guest was not due to school troubles alone, but, at any rate, nervous she was, and particularly nervous, and, it must be confessed, somewhat inclined to be irritable, during the supper and afterward, on this ill-starred night.

The beginning of the trouble was when Ralph Hazeltine called. Mrs. Snow was with her patient in the upper room, Captain Eri was out, and Captain Perez and Captain Jerry were with Elsie in the dining room. The electrician was made welcome by the trio—more especially by the captains, for Miss Preston was in no mood to be over-effusive—and a few minutes of general conversation followed. Then Captain Jerry, in accordance with his plan of campaign, laid down his newspaper, coughed emphatically to attract the attention of his partner, and said, "Well, I guess I'll go out and look at the weather for a spell. Come on, Perez."

"Why, Captain Jerry!" exclaimed Elsie, "you were out looking at the weather only ten minutes ago. I don't think it has changed much since then. Why don't you stay here and keep us company?"

"Oh, you can't never tell about the weather 'long this coast. It's likely to change most any time. Besides," with a wink that expressed comprehension unlimited, "I reckon you and Mr. Hazeltine don't care much 'bout the company of old fogies like me and Perez. Two's company and three's a crowd, you know. Ho, ho, ho!"

"Captain Jerry, come back this minute!"

But the Captain chuckled and shook out of the door, followed by the obedient Perez, who, having pledged fealty, stuck to his colors whatever might happen.

At another time, Elsie would probably have appreciated and enjoyed the joke as much as anyone, but this evening it did not appeal to her in the least. Ralph put in a very uncomfortable half−hour, and then cut his visit short and departed. It was rather sharp and chilly outside, but the breeze felt like a breath from the tropics compared with the atmosphere of that dining room.

It certainly was Captain Jerry's unlucky evening, for he left Perez chatting with a fisherman friend, who had left a favorite pipe in his shanty and had come down to get it, and entered the house alone. He had seen the electrician go, and was surprised at the brevity of his call, but he was as far from suspecting that he himself was the indirect cause of the said brevity as a mortal could be.

He came into the dining room, hung his cap on the back of a chair, and remarked cheerfully, "Well, Elsie, what did you send your company home so quick for? Land sake! twelve o'clock wa'n't none too late for me when I was young and goin' round to see the girls."

But Miss Preston did not smile. On the contrary, she frowned, and when she spoke the Captain had a vague feeling that someone had dropped an icicle inside his shirt collar.

"Captain Jerry," said the young lady, "I want to have a talk with you. Why do you think it necessary to get up and leave the room whenever Mr. Hazeltine calls? You do it every time, and to−night was no exception, except that by what you said you made me appear a little more ridiculous than usual. Now, why do you do it?"

Cap'n Eri

The Captain's jaw fell. He stared at his questioner to see if she was not joking, but, finding no encouragement of that kind, stammered, "Why do I do it? Why?"

"Yes, why?"

"Why, 'cause I thought you wanted me to."

"_I_ wanted you to! Why should you think that, please?"

"Well, I don't know. I thought you two would ruther be alone. I know, when I used to go to see my wife 'fore we was married, I—"

"Please, what has that got to do with Mr. Hazeltine's visits here?"

"Why, why, nothin', I s'pose, if you say so. I jest thought—"

"What right have you to suppose that Mr. Hazeltine is calling on me more than any other person or persons in this house?"

This was something of a poser, but the Captain did his best. He sat on the edge of a chair and rubbed his knee, and then blurted out, "Well, I s'pose I—that is, we thought he was, jest 'cause he nat'rally would; that's 'bout all. If I'd thought—why, see here, Elsie, don't YOU think he's comin' to see you?"

This was a return thrust that was hard to parry, but, although the young lady's color heightened just a bit, she answered without much hesitation:

"I don't know that I do. At any rate, I have given you no authority to act on any such assumption, and I DON'T want you to put me again in the ridiculous position you did this evening, and as you have done so often before. Why, his visits might be perfect torture to me, and still I should have to endure them out of common politeness. I couldn't go away and leave him alone."

Captain Jerry's face was a study of chagrin and troubled repentance.

"Elsie," he said, "I'm awful sorry; I am so. If I'd thought I was torturin' of you, 'stead of makin' it pleasant, I'd never have done it, sure. I won't go out again; I won't, honest. I hope you won't lay it up against me. I meant well."

Now, if Captain Perez had delayed his entrance to that dining room only two or three minutes longer, if he had not come in just in time to prevent Elsie's making the explanatory and soothing answer that was on her tongue, events would probably have been entirely different, and a good deal of trouble might have been saved. But in he came, as if some perverse imp had been waiting to give him the signal, and the interview between Captain Jerry and the young lady whom he had unwittingly offended broke off then and there.

Elsie went upstairs feeling a little conscience–stricken, and with an uneasy idea that she had said more than she should have. Captain Perez took up the newspaper and sat down to read. As for Captain Jerry, he sat down, too, but merely to get his thoughts assorted into an arrangement less like a spilled box of jackstraws. The Captain's wonderful scheme, that he had boasted of and worked so hard for, had fallen to earth like an exploded airship, and when it hit it hurt.

His first idea was to follow the usual procedure, and take the whole matter to Captain Eri for settlement, but the more he considered this plan the less he liked it. Captain Eri was an unmerciful tease, and he would be sure to "rub it in," in a way the mere thought of which made his friend squirm. There wasn't much use in confiding to Captain Perez, either. He must keep the secret and pretend that everything was working smoothly.

Then his thoughts turned to Hazeltine, and when he considered the wrong he had done that young man, he squirmed again. There wasn't a doubt in his mind that Ralph felt exactly as Elsie did about his interference. Captain Jerry decided that he owed the electrician an apology, and determined to offer it at the first opportunity.

And the opportunity came the very next morning, for Mrs. Snow wanted some clams for dinner, and asked him to dig some for her. The best clams in the vicinity were those in the flat across the bay near the cable station, and the Captain took his bucket and hoe and rowed over there. As he was digging, Ralph came strolling down to the shore.

Mr. Hazeltine's "Good—morning" was clear and hearty. Captain Jerry's was hesitating and formal. The talk that followed was rather one—sided. Finally, the Captain laid down his hoe, and came splashing over to where his friend was standing.

"Mr. Hazeltine," he said confusedly, "I kind of feel as if I ought to beg your pardon. I'm awful sorry I done what I did, but, as I said to Elsie, I meant well, and I'm sorry."

"Sorry? Sorry for what?"

"Why, for leavin' you and her alone so when you come to the house. You see, I never thought but what you'd both like it, and 'twa'n't till she raked me over the coals so for doin' it that I realized how things was."

"Raked you over the coals? I'm afraid I don't understand."

It is unnecessary to repeat the whole of the long and tangled conversation that ensued. The Captain tried to explain, tumbled down, metaphorically speaking, got up again, and started off on another tack. In his anxiety to make his position perfectly clear, he quoted from Elsie's remarks of the previous evening, and then, thinking perhaps he had gone too far, tried to smooth these over by more explanations. Repeating this process several times got him into such a snarl that he scarcely knew what he was saying. When the agony was over Ralph had received the impression that Miss Preston had said his visits were a perfect torture to her, that she objected to being left alone with him, that she held Captain Jerry responsible for these things, and that the latter was sorry for something or other, though what it was he, Ralph, didn't know or care particularly. To the Captain's continued apologies he muttered absently that it was "all right," and walked slowly away with his hands in his pockets. Captain Jerry was relieved by this expression of forgiveness. He felt that the situation wasn't what he would like to have it, but, at any rate, he had done his duty. This was a great consolation.

Ralph didn't call that evening or the next. When he did drop in it was merely to inquire concerning John Baxter's progress, and to chat for a moment with the captains. His next visit was a week later, and was just as brief and formal.

If Elsie noticed this sudden change she said nothing. There might have been some comment by the others, had not a new sensation so occupied their minds as to shut out everything else. This sensation was caused by Josiah Bartlett, who ran away one night, with his belongings tied up in a brown paper parcel, leaving a note saying that he had gone to enlist in the Navy and wasn't coming back any more.

There were lively times the next morning when the note was found. Captain Perez was for harnessing up immediately and starting off to find the lost one, hit or miss. Captain Eri soon showed him the folly of this proceeding and, instead, hurried to the railway station and sent a telegram describing the fugitive to the conductor of the Boston train. It caught the conductor at Sandwich, and the local constable at Buzzard's Bay caught the boy. Josiah was luxuriously puffing a five–cent cigar in the smoking car, and it was a crest–fallen and humiliated prodigal that, accompanied by the a fore–mentioned constable, returned to Orham that night.

But the stubbornness remained, and the next day Perez sought Captain Eri in a troubled frame of mind.

"Eri," he said dejectedly, "I don't know what I'm goin' to do with that boy. He's too many for ME, that boy is. Seems he's been plannin' this runnin' away bus'ness for more 'n a month; been doin' errands and odd jobs 'round town and savin' up his money on purpose. Says he won't go back to school again, no matter what we do to him, and that he's goin' to git into the Navy if it takes ten year. He says he'll run away again fust chance he gits, and he WILL, too. He's got the sperit of the Old Scratch in him, and I can't git it out. I'm clean discouraged and wore out, and I know that he'll do somethin' pretty soon that 'll disgrace us all."

"Humph!" exclaimed his friend. "Stuffy as all that, is he? You don't say! He ain't a bad boy, that is a REEL bad boy, either."

"No, that's jest it. He ain't reel bad—yit. But he will be if he ain't fetched up pretty sudden. 'Course, I know what he needs is to be made to mind fust, and then preached to afterwards. And I know that nat'rally I'm the one that ought to do it, but I jest can't—there! If I should start out to give him the dressin' down he needs, I'd be thinkin' of his mother every minute, and how I promised to treat him gentle and not be cross to him. But SOMETHIN'S got to be done, and if you can help me out any way I'll never forgit it, Eri."

Captain Eri scratched his chin. "Humph!" he grunted reflectively. "He couldn't git into the Navy, he's too young. More likely to be a stowaway on a merchantman and then roustabout on a cattle boat, or some such thing. Even if he lied 'bout his age and did git to be a sort of a ship's boy on a sailin' vessel, you and me know what that means nowadays. I presume likely 'twould end in his bein' killed in some rumshop scrimmage later on. Let—me—see. Bound to be a sailor, is he?"

"He's dead sot on it."

"More fool he. Comes from readin' them ridic'lous story books, I s'pose. He ain't been on the water much sence he's been down here, has he?"

"Not more 'n once or twice, except in a dory goin' to the beach, or somethin' like that."

"That's so, that's what I thought. Well, Perez, I'll tell you. The boy does need breakin' in, that's a fact, and I think maybe I could do it. I could use a young feller on my boat; to go coddin' with me, I mean. Let me have the boy under me—no meddlin' from anybody—for a couple of months. Let him sign reg'lar articles and ship 'long of me for that time. Maybe I could make a white man of him."

"I don't b'lieve he'd do it."

"I cal'late I could talk him into it. There's some butter on my tongue when it's necessary."

"You'd have to promise not to lay a hand on him in anger. That's what I promised his mother."

"All right, I promise it now. That's all right, Perez. You and me are old shipmates, and bound to help each other out. Just trust him to me, and don't ask too many questions. Is it a trade? Good! Shake."

They shook hands on it, and then Captain Eri went in to talk to the unreconciled runaway. That young gentleman, fresh from his triumph over his uncle, at first refused to have anything to do with the scheme. He wasn't going to be a "cheap guy fisherman," he was going into the Navy. The Captain did not attempt to urge him, neither did he preach or patronize. He simply leaned back in the rocker and began spinning sailor yarns. He told

136

of all sorts of adventures in all climates, and with all sorts of people. He had seen everything under the sun, apparently, and, according to him, there was no life so free and void of all restraint as that of an able seaman on a merchant ship, or, preferably, on a fisherman; but one point he made clear, and that was that, unless the applicant had had previous training, his lot was likely to be an unhappy one.

"Of course," he said, as he rose to go, "it was my idea to sort of train you up so's you could be ready when 'twas time to ship, but long's you don't want to, why it's all off."

"I'll go with you, Cap!" said Josiah, whose eyes were shining.

"Good! That's the talk! You might as well sign articles right away. Wait till I git 'em ready."

He brought pen, ink, and paper, and proceeded to indite a formidable document to the effect that "Josiah Bartlett, able seaman," was to ship aboard the catboat Mary Ellen for a term of two months. Wages, five dollars a month.

"You see," he said, "I've put you down as able seaman 'cause that's what you'll be when I git through with you. Now sign."

So Josiah signed, and then Captain Eri affixed his own signature with a flourish.

"There!" exclaimed the Captain, bringing his big palm down on the back of the "able seaman" with a thump that brought water into the eyes of that proud youth, "You're my man, shipmate. We sail to– morrer mornin' at four, rain or shine. I'll call you at quarter of. Be ready."

"You bet, old man!" said Josiah.

Captain Perez met his friend as they came out of the parlor.

"Now, Eri," he whispered, "be easy as you can with him, won't you?"

The Captain answered in the very words of his crew.

"You bet!" he said fervently, and went away whistling. Captain Perez slept better that night.

CHAPTER XIV. THE VOYAGE OF AN "ABLE SEAMAN"

Promptly at a quarter to four the next morning Captain Eri rapped on the parlor door. Josiah, who had been dressed since three, appeared almost instantly. They walked down to the shore together, and the Captain's eyes twinkled as he noted the elaborate roll in the boy's walk.

The Mary Ellen was anchored between the beaches, and they rowed off to her in a dory. It was pitch–dark, and cold and raw. Lanterns showed on two or three of the other boats near by, and, as Josiah and the Captain pulled up the eelgrass–covered anchor, a dim shape glided past in the blackness. It was the You and I, bound out. Ira Sparrow was at the helm, and he hailed the Mary Ellen, saying something about the weather.

"It 'll be kind of ca'm for a spell," replied Captain Eri, "but I wouldn't wonder if we had some wind 'fore night. Here you, fo'mast hand," he added, turning to Josiah, "stand by to git the canvas on her."

The mainsail was soon hoisted, and the catboat moved slowly out of the bay.

"Gee! it's dark," exclaimed Josiah. "what are you goin' way off here for? Why don't you go straight out?"

"I gin'rally take the short cut through the narrers," replied the Captain, "but I thought you mightn't like the breakers on the shoals, so I'm goin' 'round the p'int flat."

"Huh! I ain't a–scared of breakers. Can't be too rough for me. Wisht 'twould blow to beat the band."

"Maybe 'twill by and by. Pretty toler'ble slick now, though."

It was after sunrise when they reached the ledge where codfish most do congregate. The land was a mere yellow streak on the horizon. The stiff easterly blow of the day before had left a smooth, heavy swell that, tripping over the submerged ledge, alternately tossed the Mary Ellen high in air and dropped her toward the bottom. It was cold, and the newly risen December sun did not seem to have much warmth in it. Anchor over the side, the Captain proposed breakfast.

The "able seaman" did not feel very hungry, but he managed to swallow a hard−boiled egg and a sandwich, and then, just to show that he had reached the dignity of manhood, leaned back against the side of the cockpit, lit a cigarette, and observed cheerfully, "This is hot stuff, ain't it, Cap?"

Captain Eri wiped the crumbs from his mouth, leisurely produced his pipe, and proceeded to fill it with tobacco shaved from a chunky plug.

"What d'you smoke them things for?" he asked contemptuously, referring to the cigarette. "Nobody but dudes and sissies smoke that kind of truck. Here, take this pipe, and smoke like a man."

Josiah looked askance at the proffered pipe.

"Oh, no!" he said magnanimously, "you'll want it yourself. I'll get along with these things till I git ashore; then I'll buy a pipe of my own."

"Never you mind 'bout me. I've got two or three more below there, some'eres. Take it and light up."

The "able seaman" took the reeking, nicotine soaked affair, placed it gingerly between his teeth, held a match to the bowl and coughingly emitted a cloud of ill−smelling smoke. The pipe wheezed and gurgled, and the Mary Ellen rocked and rolled.

"Now, then," said Captain Eri, "we've sojered long enough. Go below, and bring up the bait bucket and the lines."

Josiah staggered into the little cabin, reappeared with the heavy cod lines and the bucket of mussels, and watched while the Captain "baited up."

"All ready!" said the skipper. "Two lines apiece, one over each side. Watch me."

Cap'n Eri

The cod bit almost immediately, and for ten minutes the work was exciting and lively. The Captain, watching from the corner of his eye, noticed that his assistant's pipe was wheezing less regularly, and that his lines were thrown over more and more listlessly. At length he said, "Haven't stopped smokin' so quick, have you? What's the matter—gone out? Here's a match."

"I guessed I've smoked enough for now. I can't fish so well when I'm smokin'."

"Bosh! If you want to be a reel sailor you must smoke all the time. Light up."

Reluctantly the boy obeyed, and puffed with feverish energy. Also he swallowed with vigor. The cod smelt fishy; so did the bait, and the catboat rolled and rolled. Suddenly Josiah pulled in his lines, and took the pipe from his lips.

"What's the matter?" inquired the watchful skipper.

"I—I guess I won't fish any more, Cap. Kind of slow sport, ain't it? Guess I'll go in there and take a snooze."

"I guess you won't! You shipped to fish, and you're goin' to fish. Pick up them lines."

The boy sullenly turned toward the cabin door. Was he, who had just declared himself independent of school restraint, he who had once been the thorn in the flesh of every policeman in the —th ward, to be ordered about by this Cape Cod countryman! "Aw, go chase yourself!" he said contemptuously. A minute after, when he picked himself up from the heap of slimy fish in the bottom of the boat, he saw the Captain standing solidly on one cowhide–shod foot, while the other was drawn easily back and rested on its toe. When Josiah recovered his breath, the burst of bad language with which he assailed his companion did credit to his street bringing up. It was as short as it was fierce, however, and ended amid the cod and the mussels from the overturned bait bucket. But, as the Captain said afterwards, he was "spunky" and rose again, incoherent with rage.

"You—you—I'll kill you!" he shrieked. "You promised not to touch me, you lyin' old—"

He tried to get out of the way, but didn't succeed, and this time merely sat up and sobbed as Captain Eri said in even tones:

"No, I'm not lyin'. I promised not to lay a hand on you in anger, that's all. Fust place, I don't kick with my hands, and, second place, I ain't angry. Now, then, pick up them lines."

The "able seaman" was frightened. This sort of treatment was new to him. He judged it best to obey now and "get square" later on. He sulkily picked up the codlines, and threw the hooks overboard. Captain Eri, calmly resuming his fishing, went on to say, "The fust thing a sailor has to l'arn is to obey orders. I see you've stopped smokin'. Light up."

"I don't want to."

"Well, I want you TO. Light up."

"I won't. Oh, yes, I will!"

He eyed the threatening boot fearfully and lit the awful pipe with shaking fingers. But he had taken but a few puffs when it went over the side, and it seemed to Josiah that the larger half of himself went with it. The Captain watched the paroxysm grimly.

"Sick, hey?" he grunted, "and not a capful of wind stirrin'. You're a healthy sailor! I thought I'd shipped a man, but I see 'twas only a sassy baby. My uncle Labe had a good cure for seasickness. You take a big hunk of fat salt pork, dip it in molasses, and—"

"Oh, d–o–n–'t!" Another spasm.

"Dip it in molasses," repeated Captain Eri.

"Don't, Cap! PLEASE don't!"

"Another thing a sailor learns is not to call his skipper 'Cap.' A fo'mast hand always says 'Aye, aye, sir,' when his off'cer speaks to him. Understand that?"

"Y–e–s. Oh, Lord!"

"WHAT?"

"Ye—I mean aye, aye."

"Aye, aye, WHAT?"

"Aye, aye, SIR! OH, dear me!"

"That's better. Now pick up them lines."

Well, 'twas a dreadful forenoon for Josiah; one not to be forgotten. The boat rolled unceasingly, his head ached, and pulling the heavy cod made his back and shoulders lame; also, he was wet and cold. The other boats scattered about the fishing grounds pulled up their anchors and started for home, but Captain Eri did not budge. At noon he opened his lunch basket again, and munched serenely. The sight of the greasy ham sandwiches was too much for the "able seaman." He suffered a relapse and, when it was over, tumbled on the seat which encircled the cockpit and, being completely worn out, went fast asleep. The Captain watched him for a minute or two, smiled in a not unkindly way, and, going into the cabin, brought out an old pea jacket and some other wraps with which he covered the sleeper. Then he went back to his fishing.

When Josiah awoke the Mary Ellen was heeled over on her side, her sail as tight as a drumhead. The wind was whistling through the cordage, and the boat was racing through seas that were steel–blue and angry, with whitecaps on their crests. The sun was hidden by tumbling, dust–colored clouds. The boy felt weak and strangely humble; the dreadful nausea was gone.

Captain Eri, standing at the tiller, regarded him sternly, but there was the suspicion of a twinkle in his eye.

"Feelin' better?" he asked.

"Ye—aye, aye, sir."

"Humph! Want to smoke again. Pipe right there on the thwart."

"No, thank you, sir."

Cap'n Eri

It was some time before anything more was said. Josiah was gazing at the yellow sand−cliffs that, on every tack, grew nearer. At length the Captain again addressed him.

"Perez ever tell you 'bout our fust v'yage? Never did, hey? Well, I will. Him and me run away to sea together, you know."

And then Captain Eri began a tale that caused the cold shivers to chase themselves from Josiah's big toe to the longest hair on his head. It was the story of two boys who ran away and shipped aboard an Australian sailing packet, and contained more first−class horrors than any one of his beloved dime novels. As a finishing touch the narrator turned back the grizzled hair on his forehead and showed a three−inch scar, souvenir of a first mate and a belaying pin. He rolled up his flannel shirtsleeve and displayed a slightly misshapen left arm, broken by a kick from a drunken captain and badly set by the same individual.

"Now," he said in conclusion, "I cal'late you think I was pretty hard on you this mornin', but what do you figger that you'd have got if you talked to a mate the way you done to me?"

"Don't know. S'pose I'd have been killed,—sir."

"Well, you would, mighty nigh, and that's a fact. Now, I'll tell you somethin' else. You wanted to enlist in the Navy, I understand. You couldn't git in the Navy, anyway, you're too young, but s'pose you could, what then? You'd never git any higher 'n a petty officer, 'cause you don't know enough. The only way to git into the Navy is to go through Annapolis, and git an education. I tell you, education counts. Me and Perez would have been somethin' more 'n cheap fishin' and coastin' skippers if we'd had an education; don't forgit that."

"I guess I don't want to be a sailor, anyway, sir. This one trip is enough for me, thank you."

"Can't help that. You shipped 'long with me for two months, and you'll sail with me for two months, every time I go out. You won't run away again neither, I'll look out for that. You'll sail with me and you'll help clean fish, and you'll mind me and you'll say 'sir.' You needn't smoke if you don't want to," with a smile. "I ain't p'tic'lar 'bout that.

143

"Then," went on the Captain, "when the two months is up you'll be your own master again. You can go back to 'Web' Saunders and 'Squealer' Wixon and 'Ily' Tucker and their tribe, if you want to, and be a town nuisance and a good–for–nuthin'. OR you can do this: You can go to school for a few years more and behave yourself and then, if I've got any influence with the Congressman from this district—and I sort of b'lieve I have, second–handed, at any rate— you can go to Annapolis and learn to be a Navy officer. That's my offer. You've got a couple of months to think it over in."

The catboat swung about on her final tack and stood in for the narrows, the route which the Captain had spoken of as the "short cut." From where Josiah sat the way seemed choked with lines of roaring, frothing breakers that nothing could approach and keep above water. But Captain Eri steered the Mary Ellen through them as easily as a New York cabdriver guides his vehicle through a jam on Broadway, picking out the smooth places and avoiding the rough ones until the last bar was crossed and the boat entered the sheltered waters of the bay.

"By gum!" exclaimed the enthusiastic "able seaman." "That was great—er—sir!"

"That's part of what I'll l'arn you in the next two months," said the Captain. "'Twon't do you any harm to know it when you're in the Navy neither. Stand by to let go anchor!"

CHAPTER XV. IN JOHN BAXTER'S ROOM

If Josiah expected any relaxation in Captain Eri's stern discipline he was disappointed, for he was held to the strict letter of the "shipping articles." The Captain even went to the length of transferring Perez to the parlor cot and of compelling the boy to share his own room. This was, of course, a precaution against further attempts at running away. Morning after morning the pair rose before daylight and started for the fishing grounds. There were two or three outbreaks on the part of the "able seaman," but they ended in but one way, complete submission. After a while Josiah, being by no means dull, came to realize that when he behaved like a man he was treated like one. He learned to steer the Mary Ellen, and to handle her in all weathers. Also, his respect for Captain Eri developed into a liking.

Captain Perez was gratified and delighted at the change in his grandnephew's behavior and manners, and was not a little curious to learn the methods by which the result had been brought about. His hints being fruitless, he finally asked his friend point–blank. Captain Eri's answer was something like this:

"Perez," he said, "do you remember old man Sanborn, that kept school here when you and me was boys? Well, when the old man run foul of a youngster that was sassy and uppish he knocked the sass out of him fust, and then talked to him like a Dutch uncle. He used to call that kind of treatment 'moral suasion.' That's what I'm doin' to Josiah; I'm 'moral suasionin' him."

Captain Perez was a little anxious concerning the first part of this course of training, but its results were so satisfactory that he asked no more questions. The fact is, Captain Perez' mind was too much occupied with another subject just at this time to allow him to be over–anxious. The other subject was Miss Patience Davis.

Miss Davis, her visit with her brother being over, was acting as companion to an old lady who lived in a little house up the shore, a mile or so above the station. This elderly female, whose name was Mayo, had a son who kept a grocery store in the village and was, therefore, obliged to be away all day and until late in the evening. Miss Patience found Mrs. Mayo's crotchets a bit trying, but the work was easy and to her liking, and she was, as she said, "right across the way, as you might say, from Luther." The "way" referred to was the stretch of water between the outer beach and the mainland.

And Captain Perez was much interested in Miss patience—very much so, indeed. His frequent visits to the Mayo homestead furnished no end of amusement to Captain Eri, and also to Captain Jerry, who found poking fun at his friend an agreeable change from the old programme of being the butt himself. He wasn't entirely free from this persecution, however, for Eri more than once asked him, in tones the sarcasm of which was elaborately veiled, if his match– making scheme had gotten tired and was sitting down to rest. To which the sacrifice would reply stoutly, "Oh, it's comin' out all right; you wait and see."

But in his heart Captain Jerry knew better. He had been wise enough to say nothing to his friends concerning his interviews with Elsie and Ralph, but apparently the breaking–off between the pair was final. Hazeltine called occasionally, it is true, but his stays were short and, at the slightest inclination shown by the older people to leave the room, he left the house. There was some comment by Eri and Mrs. Snow on this sudden change, but they were far from suspecting the real reason. Elsie continued to be as reticent as she had been of late; her school work was easier now that Josiah was no longer a pupil.

Christmas was rather a failure. There were presents, of course, but the planned festivities were omitted owing to a change in John Baxter's condition. From growing gradually better, he now grew slowly, but surely, worse. Dr. Palmer's calls were more frequent, and he did not conceal from Mrs. Snow or the captains his anxiety. They hid much of this from Elsie, but she, too, noticed the change, and was evidently worried by it. Strange to say, as his strength ebbed, the patient's mind grew clearer. His speech, that in his intervals of consciousness had heretofore dealt with events of the past, was now more concerned with recent happenings. But Captain Eri had never heard him mention the fire.

One afternoon in January Mrs. Snow and Captain Eri were together in the sick room. The rest of the household was absent on various errands; Captain Perez paying a visit to the life-saver's sister and Elsie staying after school to go over some examination papers. There was snow on the ground, and a "Jinooary thaw" was causing the eaves to drip, and the puddles in the road to grow larger. The door of the big stove was open, and the coals within showed red- hot. Captain Baxter was apparently asleep.

"Let me see," said Mrs. Snow musingly, in a low tone. "I've been here now, two, three, over four months. Seems longer, somehow."

"Seems almost as if you'd always been here," replied Captain Eri. "Queer how soon we git used to a change. I don't know how we got along afore, but we did some way or other, if you call it gittin' along," he added with a shrug. "I should hate to have to try it over again."

"It's always seemed funny to me," remarked the lady, "that you men, all sailors so—and used to doin' for yourselves, should have had such a time when you come to try keepin' house. I should have expected it if you was—well, doctors, or somethin' like that—used to havin' folks wait on you, but all sea captains, it seems queer."

"It does, don't it? I've thought of that myself. Anybody'd think we was the most shif'less lot that ever lived, but we wa'n't. Even Jerry—and he's the wust one of the three when it comes to leavin' things at loose ends—always had a mighty neat vessel, and had the name of makin' his crews toe the mark. I honestly b'lieve it come of us bein' on shore and runnin' the shebang on a share and share alike idee. If there'd been a skipper, a feller to boss things, we'd have done better, but when all hands was boss—nobody felt like doin' anything. Then, too, we begun too old. A feller gits sort of sot in his ways, and it's hard to give in to the other chap.

"Now, take that marryin' idee," he went on. "I laughed at that a good deal at fust and didn't really take any stock in it, but I guess 'twas real hoss sense, after all. Anyhow, it brought you down here, and what we'd done without you when John was took sick, _I_ don't know. I haven't said much about it, but I've felt enough, and I know the other fellers feel the same way. You've been so mighty good and put up with so many things that must have fretted you like the nation, and the way you've managed—my!"

The whole–souled admiration in the Captain's voice made the housekeeper blush like a girl.

"Don't say a word, Cap'n Eri," she protested. "It's been jest a pleasure to me, honest. I've had more comfort and—well, peace, you might say, sence I've been in this house than I've had afore for years."

"When I think," said the Captain, "of what we might have got for that advertisement, I swan it makes my hair curl. Advertisin' that way in that kind of a paper, why we might have had a—a play actress, or I don't know what, landed on us. Seems 's if there was a Providence in it: seems 's if you was kind of SENT—there!"

"I don't know what you must think of me answerin' an advertisement for a husband that way. It makes me 'shamed of myself when I think of it, I declare. And in that kind of a paper, too."

"I've wondered more times than a few how you ever got a hold of that paper. 'Tain't one you'd see every day nat'rally, you know."

Mrs. Snow paused before she answered. Then she said slowly, "Well, I'm s'prised you ain't asked that afore. I haven't said much about myself sence I've been here, for no p'tic'lar reason that I know of, except that there wasn't much to tell and it wasn't a very interestin' yarn to other folks. My husband's name was Jubal Snow—"

"You don't say!" exclaimed the Captain. "Why, Jerry used to know him."

"I shouldn't wonder. Jubal knew a lot of folks on the Cape here. He was a good husband—no better anywheres—and he and I had a good life together long as he was well. I've sailed a good many v'yages with him, and I feel pretty nigh as much at home on the water as I do on land. Our trouble was the same that a good many folks have; we didn't cal'late that fair weather wouldn't last all the time, that's all.

"It wasn't his fault any more than 'twas mine. We saved a little money, but not enough, as it turned out. Well, he was took down sick and had to give up goin' to sea, and we had a little place over in Nantucket, and settled down on it. Fust along, Jubal was able to do a little farmin' and so on, and we got along pretty well, but by and by he got so he wa'n't able to work, and then 'twas harder. What little we'd saved went for doctor's bills and this, that, and t'other. He didn't like to have me leave him, so I couldn't earn much of anything, and fin'lly we come to where somethin' had to be done right away, and we talked the thing over and decided to mortgage the house. The money we got on the mortgage lasted until he died.

"He had a little life insurance, not enough, of course, but a little. He was plannin' to take on more, but somehow it never seemed as if he could die, he so big and strong, and we put it off until he got so he couldn't pass the examination. When the insurance money come I took it to Jedge Briar, a mighty good friend of Jubal's and mine and the one that held the mortgage on the house, and I told him I wanted to pay off the mortgage with it, so's I'd have the house free and clear. But the Jedge advised me not to, said the mortgage was costin' me only six per cent., and why didn't I put the money where 'twas likely to be a good investment that would pay me eight or ten per cent.? Then I'd be makin' money, he said. I asked him to invest it for me, and he put it into the Bay Shore Land Company, where most of his own was."

"Sho! I want to know!" broke in the Captain. "He did, hey! Well, I had some there, too, and so did Perez. Precious few fam'lies on the Cape that didn't."

"Yes, he thought 'twas the safest and best place he knew of. The officers bein' sons of Cape people and their fathers such fine men, everybody said 'twas all right. I got my dividends reg'lar for a while, and I went out nussin' and did sewin' and got along reel well. I kept thinkin' some day I'd be able to pay off the mortgage and I put away what little I could towards it, but then _I_ was took sick and that money went, and then the Land Company went up the spout."

The Captain nodded. The failure of the company had brought poverty to hundreds of widows. Mrs. Snow's case was but another instance.

"Let me see," said the lady. "Where was I? Oh, yes! the Land Company's failin'. Well, it failed and the insurance money went with it. It was discouragin', of course, but I had my house, except for the mortgage, and I had my health again, and, if I do say it, I ain't afraid of work, so I jest made up my mind there was no use cryin' over spilt milk, and that I must git along and begin to save all over again. Then Jedge Briar died and his nephew up to Boston come into the property. I was behind in my payments a little, and they sent me word they should foreclose the mortgage, and they did."

"Well, I swan! The mean sculpins! Didn't you have NOBODY you could go to; no relations nor nothin'?"

"I've got a brother out in Chicago, but he married rich and his wife doesn't care much for her husband's relations. I never saw her but once, and then one of the first things she asked me was if it was true that there was more crazy people in Nantucket than in any other place of its size on earth, and afore I could answer she asked me what made 'em crazy. I told her I didn't know unless it was answerin' city folks' questions. She didn't like that very well, and I haven't heard from Job—that's my brother—for a long time. All my other near relations are dead.

"So they foreclosed the mortgage, and gave me notice to move out. I packed my things, and watered my flowers—I had quite a pretty flower garden—for the last time, and then come in and set down in the rocker to wait for the wagon that was goin' to move me. I got to thinkin' how proud Jubal and me was when we bought that house and how we planned about fixin' it up, and how our baby that died was born in it, and how Jubal himself had died there, and told me that he was glad he was leavin' me a home, at any rate; and I got so lonesome and discouraged that I jest cried, I couldn't help it. But I've never found that cryin' did much good, so I wiped my eyes and looked for somethin' to read to take up my mind. And that Chime paper was what I took up.

"You see, there'd been a big excursion from Boston down the day before, and some of the folks come down my way to have a sort of picnic. Two of 'em, factory girls from Brockton, they was, come to the house for a drink of water. They were gigglin', foolish enough critters, but I asked 'em in, and they eat their lunches on my table. They left two or three story papers and that Chime thing when they went away.

"Well, I looked it over, and almost the first thing I saw was that advertisement signed 'Skipper.' It didn't read like the other trashy things in there, and it sounded honest. And all of a sudden it come over me that I'd answer it. I was lonesome and tired and sort of didn't care, and I answered it right off without waitin' another minute. That's all there is to tell. When I come here to be housekeeper I wrote the folks that's takin' care of my furniture—they're reel kind people; I was goin' to board there if I had stayed in Nantucket—to keep it till I come back. There! I meant to tell you this long ago, and I don't know why I haven't."

The Captain knew why she hadn't. It was easy to read between the lines the tale of the years of disappointment and anxiety. Such stories are not easy to tell, and he respected the widow more than ever for the simple way in which she had told hers.

"That Land Company bus'ness," he said, "carried off a good lot of Cape Cod money. I never saw but one man that I thought was glad it busted, and that was old Caleb Weeks, over to Harniss. The old man was rich, but closer 'n the bark of a tree—he'd skin a flea for the hide and taller—and used to be a hard case into the bargain. One time they had a big revival over there and he got religion. The boys used to say what caught Caleb was the minister's sayin' salvation was free. Well, anyhow, he got converted and j'ined the church. That was all right, only while the fit was fresh he pledged himself to give five hundred dollars to help build the new chapel. When he cooled down a little he was sorry, and every time they'd hint at his comin' down with the cash, he'd back and fill, and put it off for a spell. When the Land Company went up he was the only happy one in town, 'cause he said he'd lost all his money. Course, under the circumstances, they couldn't ask him to pay, so he didn't. From what I hear he lost as much as fifty dollars."

They both laughed, and Mrs. Snow was about to answer when she was interrupted.

"Eri," said a weak voice. "Eri."

The Captain started, turned sharply, and saw the sick man watching him, his eyes fixed and unwavering.

"Eri," said John Baxter again, "come here."

Mrs. Snow hurried to her patient, but the latter impatiently bade her let him alone.

"Not you," he said, "I want Eri."

Captain Eri stooped down beside the bed.

"What is it, John?" he asked.

"Eri s'pose God called you to break man's law and keep his, what would you do?"

The Captain glanced anxiously at the house-keeper. Then he said soothingly:

"Oh, that's all right, John. Don't worry 'bout that. You and me settled that long ago. How are you feelin' now?"

"I know, I know," with the monotonous persistence of those whose minds are wandering,—and then cleanly once more, "Eri, I've been called."

"Ssh-h! That's all right, John; that's all right. Don't you want Mrs. Snow to fix your piller? P'raps you'd lay a little easier, then. Now, Mrs. Snow, if you'll jest turn it while I lift him. So; that's better now, ain't it, shipmate, hey?" But the sick man muttered an unintelligible something, and relapsed once more into the half-doze, half-stupor that was his usual state.

Captain Eri sighed in relief.

"That was queer, wa'n't it?" he observed.

"He's had two or three of those spells in the last day or two," was the answer.

Cap'n Eri

The Captain wondered what his friend might have said during those "spells," but he was afraid to inquire. Instead, he asked, "What did the doctor say when he was here this mornin'?"

"Nothin' very hopeful. I asked him plain what he thought of the case, and he answered jest as plain. He said Cap'n Baxter had failed dreadful in the last week, and that he wouldn't be s'prised if he dropped off most any time. Then again, he said he might live for months."

"I see, I see."

They were silent for a while, watching the sick man, whose sleep, or stupor, was not as tranquil as usual. Two or three times his eyes opened, and he muttered audibly.

"I never saw him so restless afore," commented Captain Eri anxiously.

"He was so last night."

"Did Elsie see him?"

"No, I was alone here, and she was asleep in the next room. I got up and shut the door."

The Captain glanced keenly at the housekeeper, but her face was placid and inscrutable. He shifted uneasily and then said, "Elsie's late to–night, ain't she? I wonder what's keepin' her."

"School work, I s'pose. She's workin' harder 'n she ought to, I think."

"FIRE!"

The word was shouted, and the room rang with it. John Baxter, whose weakness had hitherto been so great that he could not turn himself in bed, was leaning on his elbow and pointing with outstretched finger to the open stove door.

"Fire!" he shouted again. "It's blazin'! It's burnin'! It's wipin' the plague spot from the earth. I hear you, Lord! I'm old, but I hear you, and your servant's ready. Where will it be

152

to– morrer? Gone! burnt up! and the ways of the wicked shan't prevail."

They forced him back on the pillow, but he fought them fiercely for a moment or two. After they thought they had quieted him, he broke out again, talking rapidly and clearly.

"I hear the call, Lord," he said. "I thank thee for showin' it to me in your Book. 'And they burnt all their cities wherein they dwelt, and all their goodly castles, with fire.' With fire! With fire!"

"Ssh–h! There, there, John! Don't talk so," entreated the Captain.

"Where's the kerosene?" continued the old man. "And the matches? Now softly, softly. The shavin's. It's dark. Here, in the corner. Ah, ha! ah, ha! 'And all their goodly castles with fire!' Now, Web Saunders, you wicked man! Now! Burn! I've done it, Lord! I've done it!"

"Hush!" almost shouted the agonized Captain Eri. "Hush, John! Be still!"

"There, there, Cap'n Baxter," said Mrs. Snow soothingly, laying her hand on the sick man's forehead. Somehow, the touch seemed to quiet him; his eyes lost their fire, and he muttered absently that he was tired. Then the eyes closed and he lay still, breathing heavily.

"Land of love!" exclaimed the Captain. "That was awful! Hadn't I better go for the doctor?"

"I don't think so, unless he gits worse. He had jest such a turn, as I told you, last night."

"Did he talk like he did jest now?"

"Jest the same."

"'Bout the same things?"

"Yes."

Cap'n Eri

The Captain gasped. "Then you knew!" he said.

"That he set the billiard room afire? Yes. I've always rather suspicioned that he did, and last night, of course, made me sure of it."

"Well, well! You haven't said nothin' 'bout it to anybody?"

"Of course not."

"No, 'course you haven't. You must excuse me—I'm kind of upset, I guess. Dear! dear! Did you think _I_ knew it?"

"I sort of guessed that you did."

"Well, I did. I've known it ever sence that night he was found. He had his coat on when I found him, and 'twas all burnt, and there was an empty kerosene bottle in his pocket. I hid the coat, and threw the bottle away, and turned him so he was facin' towards the saloon 'stead of from it. And I lied when I told the doctor that he was jest as he fell. There! the murder's out! Now, what do you think of me?"

"Think? I think you did exactly right."

"You DO?"

"I sartinly do."

"Well, I snum! I've been over that thing time and time again, and I've felt like I was sort of a firebug myself sometimes. I've heard folks layin' it to fust one and then the other, and cal'latin' that Web did it himself to git the insurance, and all the time I've known who really did do it, and haven't said anything. I jest couldn't. You see, John and me's been brothers almost. But I didn't s'pose anybody else would see it the same way."

"Cap'n Eri, do you s'pose I blame you for tryin' to keep your best friend out of trouble that he got into by bein'—well—out of his head. Why, land of mercy! He ain't no more to be held responsible than a baby. You did what I'd have done if I'd been in your place, and I respect you for it."

154

The Captain's voice shook as he answered:

"Marthy Snow," he said, "you're the kind of woman that I'd like to have had for a sister."

It was perhaps a half–hour later when Captain Eri started for the schoolhouse to bring Elsie home. John Baxter had not wakened, and Mrs. Snow said she was not afraid to remain alone with him. The thaw had turned to a light rain and the Captain carried an umbrella. It was dark by this time, and when he came in sight of the schoolhouse he saw a light in the window.

One of the scholars—a by no means brilliant one—whose principal educational achievement was the frequency with which he succeeded in being "kept after school," was seated on the fence, doing his best to whittle it to pieces with a new jackknife.

"Hello, sonny!" said the Captain. "Miss Preston gone yit?"

"No, she ain't," replied the boy, continuing to whittle. "She's up there. Mr. Saunders is there, too."

"Saunders? WEB SAUNDERS?"

"Yup. I see him go in there a little while ago." Captain Eri started toward the schoolhouse at a rapid pace; then he suddenly stopped; and then, as suddenly, walked on again. All at once he dropped his umbrella and struck one hand into the palm of the other with a smack.

When he reached the door, he leaned the umbrella in the corner and walked up the stairs very softly, indeed.

CHAPTER XVI. A BUSINESS CALL

That enterprising business man, Mr. "Web" Saunders, opened the door of his renovated billiard room a little later than usual the next morning. It was common report about the village that Mr. Saunders occasionally sampled the contents of some of the "original packages" which, bearing the name and address of a Boston wholesale liquor dealer, came to him by express at irregular intervals. It was also reported, probably by unreliable total abstainers, that during these "sampling" seasons his temper was not of the best. Perhaps Mrs. Saunders might have said something concerning this report if she had been so disposed, but unless a discolored eye might be taken as evidence, she never offered any. The injury to her eye she explained by saying that something "flew up and hit her." This was no doubt true.

But, gossip aside, Mr. Saunders did not seem in good humor on this particular morning. A yellow cur, of nondescript breed, taken since the fire, in payment of a debt from "Squealer" Wixon, who had described it as a "fust–class watchdog," rose from its bed behind the cigar counter, yawned, stretched, and came slinking over to greet its master. "Web" forcibly hoisted it out of the door on the toe of his boot. Its yelp of pained surprise seemed to afford the business man considerable relief, for he moved more briskly afterward, and proceeded to sweep the floor with some degree of speed.

The forenoon trade at the billiard room was never very lively, and this forenoon was no exception. "Bluey" Batcheldor drifted in, stepped into the little room the door of which was lettered "Ice Cream Parlor," and busied himself with a glass and bottle for a few moments. Then he helped himself to a cigar from the showcase, and told his friend to "chalk it up." This Mr. Saunders didn't seem to care to do, and there was a lively argument. At length "Bluey's" promise to "square up in a day or so" was accepted, under protest, and the customer departed.

At half–past eleven the man of business was dozing in a chair by the stove, and the "watchdog," having found it chilly outside and venturing in, was dozing near him. The bell attached to the door rang vigorously, and both dog and man awoke with a start. The visitor was Captain Eri.

Now, the Captain was perhaps the last person whom the proprietor of the billiard room expected to see, but a stranger never would have guessed it. In fact, the stranger might reasonably have supposed that the visitor was Mr. Saunders' dearest friend, and that his call was a pleasure long looked forward to.

"Why, Cap'n!" exclaimed "Web," "how are you? Put her there! I'm glad to see you lookin' so well. I said to 'Squealer' the other day, s'I, 'Squealer, I never see a man hold his age like Cap'n Hedge. I'll be blessed if he looks a day over forty,' I says. Take off your coat,

156

won't you?"

Somehow or other, the Captain must have lost sight of "Web's" extended hand. Certainly, the hand was large enough to be seen, but he did not take it. He did, however, accept the invitation to remove his coat, and, slipping out of the faded brown pea jacket, threw it on a settee at the side of the room. His face was stern and his manner quiet, and in spite Of Mr. Saunders' flattering reference to his youthful appearance, this morning he looked at least more than a day past forty.

But, if Captain Eri was more than usually quiet and reserved, "Web" was unchanged, and, if he noticed that the handshake was declined, said nothing about it. His smile was sweetness itself, as he observed, "Well, Cap'n, mighty mod'rate weather we're having for this time of year, ain't it? What's new down your way? That's right, have a chair."

The Captain had no doubt anticipated this cordial invitation, for he seated himself before it was given, and, crossing his legs, extended his dripping rubber boots toward the fire. The rain was still falling, and it beat against the windows of the saloon in gusts.

"Web," said Captain Eri, "set down a minute. I want to talk to you."

"Why, sure!" exclaimed the genial man of business, pulling up another chair. "Have a cigar, won't you? You don't come to see me very often, and I feel's though we ought to celebrate. Ha! ha! ha!"

"No, I guess not, thank you," was the answer. "I'll smoke my pipe, if it's all the same to you."

Mr. Saunders didn't mind in the least, but thought he would have a cigar himself. So he lit one and smoked in silence as the Captain filled his pipe. "Web" knew that this was something more than an ordinary social visit. Captain Eri's calls at the billiard room were few and far between. The Captain, for his part, knew what his companion was thinking, and the pair watched each other through the smoke.

The pipe drew well, and the Captain sent a blue cloud whirling toward the ceiling. Then he asked suddenly, "Web, how much money has Elsie Preston paid you altogether?"

157

Mr. Saunders started the least bit, and his small eyes narrowed a trifle. But the innocent surprise in his reply was a treat to hear.

"Elsie? Paid ME?" he asked.

"Yes. How much has she paid you?"

"I don't know what you mean."

"Yes, you do. She's been payin' you money reg'lar for more 'n a month. I want to know how much it is."

"Now, Cap'n Hedge, I don't know what you're talkin' about. Nobody's paid me a cent except them that's owed me. Who did you say? Elsie Preston? That's the school–teacher, ain't it?"

"Web, you're a liar, and always was, but you needn't lie to me this mornin', 'cause it won't be healthy; I don't feel like hearin' it. You understand that, do you?"

Mr. Saunders thought it time to bluster a little. He rose to his feet threateningly.

"Cap'n Hedge," he said, "no man 'll call me a liar."

"There's a precious few that calls you anything else."

"You're an old man, or I'd—"

"Never you mind how old I am. A minute ago you said I didn't look more 'n forty; maybe I don't feel any older, either."

"If that Preston girl has told you any—"

"She hasn't told me anything. She doesn't know that I know anything. But I do know. I was in the entry upstairs at the schoolhouse for about ten minutes last night."

Mr. Saunders' start was perceptible this time. He stood for a moment without speaking. Then he jerked the chair around, threw himself into it, and said cautiously, "Well, what of it?"

"I come up from the house to git Elsie home 'cause 'twas rainin'. I was told you was with her, and I thought there was somethin' crooked goin' on; fact is, I had a suspicion what 'twas. So when I got up to the door I didn't go in right away; I jest stood outside."

"Listenin', hey! Spyin'!"

"Yup. I don't think much of folks that listens, gin'rally speakin', but there's times when I b'lieve in it. When I'm foolin' with a snake I'd jest as soon hit him from behind as in front. I didn't hear much, but I heard enough to let me know that you'd been takin' money from that girl right along. And I think I know why."

"You do, hey?"

"Yup."

Then Mr. Saunders asked the question that a bigger rascal than he had asked some years before. He leaned back in his chair, took a pull at his cigar, and said sneeringly, "Well, what are you goin' to do 'bout it?"

"I'm goin' to stop it, and I'm goin' to make you give the money back. How much has she paid you?"

"None of your d—n bus'ness."

The Captain rose to his feet. Mr. Saunders sprang up, also, and reached for the coal shovel, evidently expecting trouble. But if he feared a physical assault, his fear was groundless. Captain Eri merely took up his coat.

"Maybe it ain't none of my bus'ness," he said. "I ain't a s'lectman nor sheriff. But there's such things in town, and p'raps they'll be int'rested. Seems to me that I've heard that blackmailin' has got folks into State's prison afore now."

Cap'n Eri

"Is that so? Never heard that folks that set fire to other people's prop'ty got there, did you? Yes, and folks that helps 'em gits there, too, sometimes. Who was it hid a coat a spell ago?"

It was Captain Eri's turn to start. He hesitated a moment, tossed the pea jacket back on the settee and sat down once more. Mr. Saunders watched him, grinning triumphantly.

"Well?" he said with a sneer.

"A coat, you say?"

"Yes, a coat. Maybe you know who hid it; I can guess, myself. That coat was burned some. How do you s'pose it got burned? And say! who used to wear a big white hat round these diggin's? Ah, ha! Who did?"

There was no doubt about the Captain's start this time. He wheeled sharply in his chair, and looked at the speaker.

"Humph!" he exclaimed. "You found that hat, did you?"

"That's what I done! And where do you think I found it? Why, right at the back of my shed where the fire started. And there'd been a pile of shavin's there, too, and there'd been kerosene on 'em. Who smashed the bottle over in the field, hey?"

Captain Eri seemed to be thinking. "Web" evidently set his own interpretation on this silence, for he went on, raising his voice as he did so.

"Did you think I was fool enough not to know who set that fire? I knew the night she burned, and when I met Dr. Palmer jest comin' from your house, and he told me how old Baxter was took sick goin' to the fire—oh, yes, GOIN'—I went up on that hill right off, and I hunted and I found things, and what I found I kept. And what I found when I pulled that burned shed to pieces I kept, too. And I've got 'em yit!"

"You have, hey? Dear! dear!"

160

"You bet I have! And somebody's goin' to pay for 'em. Goin' to pay, pay, PAY! Is that plain?"

The Captain made no answer. He thrust his hands into his pockets and looked at the stove dolefully, so it seemed to the man of business.

"Fust off I thought I'd have the old cuss jailed," continued Mr. Saunders. "Then, thinks I, 'No, that won't pay me for my buildin' and my bus'ness hurt and all that.' So I waited for Baxter to git well, meanin' to make him pay or go to the jug. But he stayed sick a–purpose, I b'lieve, the mean, white–headed, psalm–singin'—"

Captain Eri moved uneasily and broke in, "You got your insurance money, didn't you?"

"Yes, I did, but whose fault is that? 'Twa'n't his, nor any other darned 'Come–Outer's.' It don't pay me for my trouble, nor it don't make me square with the gang. I gen'rally git even sometime or 'nother, and I'll git square now. When that girl come here, swellin' 'round and puttin' on airs, I see my chance, and told her to pay up or her granddad would be shoved into Ostable jail. That give her the jumps, I tell you!"

"You wrote her a letter, didn't you?"

"You bet I did! She come 'round to see me in a hurry. Said she didn't have no money. I told her her granddad did, an she could git that or go to work and earn some. I guess she thought she'd ruther work. Oh, I've got her and her prayin', house–burnin' granddad where I want 'em, and I've got you, too, Eri Hedge, stickin' your oar in. Talk to me 'bout blackmail! For two cents I'd jail the old man and you, too!"

This was the real Mr. Saunders. He usually kept this side of his nature for home use; his wife was well acquainted with it.

Captain Eri was evidently frightened. His manner had become almost apologetic.

"Well," he said, "I wouldn't do that if I was you, Web. I heard you tell Elsie last night she wa'n't payin' you enough, and I thought—"

"I know what you thought. You thought you could scare me. You didn't know I had the coat and hat, did you? Well, what I said I stand by. The girl AIN'T payin' me enough. Fourteen dollars a week she gits, and she's only been givin' up ten. I want more. I want—"

But here Captain Eri interrupted him.

"I guess that 'll do," he said calmly. "You've told me what I wanted to know. Ten dollars a week sence the middle of November. 'Bout seventy dollars, rough figgerin'. Now, then, hand it over."

"What?"

"Hand over that seventy dollars."

"Hand over hell! What are you talkin' 'bout?"

The Captain rose and, leaning over, shook his forefinger in Mr. Saunders' flabby red face.

"You low–lived, thievin' rascal," he said, "I'm givin' you a chance you don't deserve. Either you'll pay me that money you've stole from that girl or I'll walk out of that door, and when I come in again the sheriff 'll be with me. Now, which 'll it be? Think quick."

Web's triumphant expression was gone, and rage and malice had taken its place. He saw, now, that the Captain had tricked him into telling more than he ought. But he burst out again, tripping over words in his excitement.

"Think!" he yelled. "I don't need to think. Bring in your sheriff. I'll march down to your house and I'll show him the man that set fire to my buildin'. What 'll you and that snivelin' granddaughter of his do then? You make off to think a turrible lot of the old prayer–machine 'cause he's your chum. How'd you like to see him took up for a firebug, hey?"

"I ain't afraid of that."

"You ain't? You AIN'T! Why not?"

"'Cause he's gone where you can't git at him. He died jest afore I left the house."

Mr. Saunders' brandished fist fell heavily on the arm of his chair. His face turned white in patches, and then flamed red again.

"Died!" he gasped.

"Died."

"You—you're a liar!"

"No, I ain't. John Baxter's dead. He was a chum of mine—you're right there—and if I'd known a sneak like you was after him I'd have been here long afore this. Why, you—"

The Captain's voice shook, but he restrained himself and went on.

"Now, you see where you stand, don't you? Long's John lived you had the proof to convict him; I'll own up to that much. I hid the coat; I smashed the bottle. The hat I didn't know 'bout. I might have told you at fust that all that didn't amount to anything, but I thought I'd wait and let you tell me what more I wanted to know. John Baxter's gone, poor feller, and all your proof ain't worth a cent. Not one red cent. Understand?"

It was quite evident that Mr. Saunders did understand, for his countenance showed it. But the bluster was not out of him yet.

"All right," he said. "Anyhow, the girl's left, and if she don't pay I'll show her granddad up for what he was. And I'll show you up, too. Yes, I will!" he shouted, as this possibility began to dawn on him. "I'll let folks know how you hid that coat and—and all the rest of it."

"No, you won't."

"Why won't I?"

"'Cause you won't dare to. You've been hittin' at a sick man through a girl; neither of 'em could hit back. But now you're doin' bus'ness with me, and I ain't sick. If you open your

163

mouth to anybody,—if you let a soul know who set that fire,—I'll walk straight to Jedge Baker, and I'll tell him the whole story. I'll tell him what I did and why I did it. And THEN I'll tell him what you did—how you bullied money out of that girl that hadn't no more to do with the fire than a baby. If it comes to facin' a jury I'll take my chances, but how 'bout you? You, runnin' a town nuisance that the s'lectmen are talkin' of stoppin' already; sellin' rum by the drink when your license says it shan't be sold 'cept by the bottle. Where'll YOUR character land you on a charge of blackmail?

"And another thing. The folks in this town knew John Baxter afore he was like what he's been lately. A good many of 'em swore by him—yes, sir, by mighty, some of 'em loved him! This is a law- abidin' town, but s'pose—jest s'pose I should go to some of the fellers that used to sail with him, and tell 'em what you've been up to. Think you'd stay here long? _I_ think you'd move out—on a rail."

Captain Eri paused and sat on the arm of his chair, grimly watching his opponent, whose turn for thinking had come. The face of the billiard magnate was an interesting study in expression during the Captain's speech. From excited triumph it had fallen to fear and dejection; and now, out of the wreck, was appearing once more the oily smile, the sugared sweetness of the every-day Mr. Saunders.

"Now, Cap'n Hedge," purred the reconstructed one, "you and me has always been good friends. We hadn't ought to fight like this. I don't think either of us wants to go to court. Let's see if we can't fix the thing up some way."

"We'll fix it up when you pay me the seventy dollars."

"Now, Cap'n Hedge, 'tain't likely I've got seventy dollars in my pocket. Seems to me you're pretty hard on a poor feller that's jest been burnt out. I think we'd ought to—"

"How much HAVE you got?"

After a good deal of talk and protestation Mr. Saunders acknowledged being the possessor of twenty-six dollars, divided between the cash drawer and his pocket. This he reluctantly handed to the Captain.

Then the Captain demanded pen, ink, and paper; and when they were brought he laboriously wrote out a screed to the effect that Webster Saunders had received of Elsie Preston forty-four dollars, which sum he promised to pay on demand.

"There," he said, pushing the writing materials across the table. "Sign that."

At first Mr. Saunders positively refused to sign. Then he intimated that he had rather wait and think it over a little while. Finally he affixed his signature and spitefully threw the pen across the room.

Captain Eri folded up the paper and put it in his pocket. Then he rose and put on his pea jacket.

"Now, there's jest one thing more," he said. "Trot out that coat and hat."

"What do you mean?"

"Trot out that coat and hat of John's. I want 'em."

"I shan't do it."

"All right, then. It's all off. I'll step over and see the Jedge. You'll hear from him and me later."

"Hold on a minute, Cap'n. You're in such a everlastin' hurry. I don't care anything 'bout the old duds, but I don't know's I know where they are. Seems to me they're up to the house somewheres. I'll give 'em to you to-morrer."

"You'll give 'em to me right now. I'll tend shop while you go after 'em."

For a moment it looked as though the man of business would rebel outright. But the Captain was so calm, and evidently so determined to do exactly what he promised, that "Web" gave up in despair. Muttering that maybe they were "'round the place, after all," he went into the back room and reappeared with the burned coat and the scorched white felt hat. Slamming them down on the counter, he said sulkily, "There they be. Any more of my prop'ty you'd like to have?"

Captain Eri didn't answer. Coolly tearing off several sheets of wrapping paper from the roll at the back of the counter, he made a bundle of the hat and coat, and tucked it under his arm. Then he put on his own hat and started for the door.

"Good—mornin'," he said.

The temper of the exasperated Mr. Saunders flared up in a final outburst.

"You think you're almighty smart, don't you?" he growled between his teeth. "I'll square up with you by and by."

The Captain turned sharply, his hand on the latch.

"I wish you'd try," he said. "I jest wish to God you'd try. I've held in more 'n I thought I could when I come up here, but if you want to start a reel fust—class rumpus, one that 'll land you where you b'long and rid this town of you for keeps, jest try some of your tricks on me. And if I hear of one word that you've said 'bout this whole bus'ness, I'll know it's time to start in. Now, you can keep still or fight, jest as you please. I tell you honest, I 'most wish you'd fight."

The door slammed. Mr. Saunders opened it again and gazed vindictively after the bulky figure splashing through the slush. The dog came sneaking up and rubbed his nose against his master's hand; it was an impolitic move on his part.

"Git out! " roared "Web," delighted at the opportunity. "You good— for—nothin' pup! How's that set?"

"That" was a kick that doubled the cur up against the settee. As it scrambled to its feet, Mr. Saunders kicked it again. And then the "watchdog" exhibited the first evidence of spirit that it had ever been known to show. With a snarl, as the man turned away, it settled its teeth into the calf of his leg, and then shot out of the door and, with its tail between its legs, went down the road like a yellow cannon ball.

CHAPTER XVII. THROUGH FIRE AND WATER

It was true—John Baxter was dead. His violent outbreak of the previous afternoon had hastened the end that the doctor had prophesied. There was no harrowing death scene. The weather- beaten old face grew calmer, and, the sleep sounder, until the tide went out—that was all. It was like a peaceful coming into port after a rough voyage. No one of the watchers about the bed could wish him back, not even Elsie, who was calm and brave through it all. When it was over, she went to her room and Mrs. Snow went with her. Captain Eri went out to make his call upon Mr. Saunders.

The funeral was one of the largest ever held in Orham. The little house was crowded. Old friends, who had drifted away from the fanatic in his latter days, came back to pay tribute to the strong man whom they had known and loved. There was some discussion among the captains as to who should preach the funeral sermon. Elsie had left this question to Captain Eri for settlement, and the trio and Mrs. Snow went into executive session immediately.

"If John had had the settlin' of it himself," observed Eri, "he'd have picked Perley, there ain't no doubt 'bout that."

"I know it," said Captain Perez, "but you must remember that John wa'n't himself for years, and what he'd have done now ain't what he'd have done 'fore he broke down. I hate to think of Perley's doin' it, somehow."

"Isn't Mr. Perley a good man?" asked the housekeeper.

"He's good enough, fur's I know," replied Captain Jerry, "but I know what Perez means. A funeral, seems to me, ought to be a quiet, soothin' sort of a thing, and there ain't nothin' soothin' 'bout Come−Outer' preachin'. He'll beller and rave 'round, I'm 'fraid, and stir up poor Elsie so she won't never git over it."

"I know it," agreed Captain Eri. "That's what I've been afraid of. And yit," he added, "I should feel we was doin' somethin' jest opposite from what John would like, if we had anybody else."

167

Cap'n Eri

"Couldn't you see Mr. Perley beforehand," suggested Mrs. Snow, "and tell him jest the kind of sermon he must preach. Tell him it must be quiet and comfortin' and—"

"And short." Captain Eri finished the sentence for her. "I guess that's the way we'll have to settle it. I'll make him understand one thing, though—he mustn't drag in rum sellin' and all the rest of it by the heels. If he does I'll—I don't know what I'll do to him."

The interview with the Reverend Perley that followed this conversation must have been effective, for the sermon was surprisingly brief and as surprisingly calm. In fact, so rational was it that a few of the more extreme among the preacher's following were a bit disappointed and inquired anxiously as to their leader's health, after the ceremony was over.

The procession of carryalls and buggies followed the hearse to the cemetery among the pines, and, as the mourners stood about the grave, the winter wind sang through the evergreen branches a song so like the roar of the surf that it seemed like a dirge of the sea for the mariner who would sail no more. As they were clearing away the supper dishes that night Captain Eri said to Mrs. Snow, "Well, John's gone. I wonder if he's happier now than he has been for the last ten years or so."

"I think he is," was the answer.

"Well, so do I, but if he hadn't been a 'Come Outer' I don't s'pose Brother Perley and his crowd would have figgered that he had much show. Seems sometimes as if folks like that—reel good–hearted folks, too, that wouldn't hurt a fly—git solid comfort out of the feelin' that everybody that don't agree with 'em is bound to everlastin' torment. I don't know but it's wicked to say it, but honest, it seems as if them kind would 'bout as soon give up the hopes of Heaven for themselves as they would the satisfaction of knowin' 'twas t'other place for the other feller."

To which remark the somewhat shocked housekeeper made no reply.

The following day Elsie went back to her school. Captain Eri walked up with her, and, on the way, told her of his discovery of her secret, and of his interview with "Web" Saunders. It was exactly as the Captain had surmised. The note she had received on the evening of the return from the life–saving station was from the proprietor of the billiard

168

saloon, and in it he hinted at some dire calamity that overshadowed her grandfather, and demanded an immediate interview. She had seen him that night and, under threat of instant exposure, had promised to pay the sum required for silence. She had not wished to use her grandfather's money for this purpose, and so had taken the position as teacher.

"Well," said the Captain, "I wish you'd have come to me right away, and told me the whole bus'ness. 'Twould have saved a pile of trouble."

The young lady stopped short and faced him.

"Captain Eri," she said, "how could I? I was sure grandfather had set the fire. I knew how ill he was, and I knew that any shock might kill him. Besides, how could I drag you into it, when you had done so much already? It would have been dreadful. No, I thought it all out, and decided I must face it alone."

"Well, I tell you this, Elsie; pretty gin'rally a mean dog 'll bite if he sees you're afraid of him. The only way to handle that kind is to run straight at him and kick the meanness out of him. The more he barks the harder you ought to kick. If you run away once it 'll be mighty uncomf'table every time you go past that house. But never mind; I cal'late this p'tic'lar pup won't bite; I've pulled his teeth, I guess. What's your plans, now? Goin' to keep on with the school, or go back to Boston?"

Miss Preston didn't know; she said she had not yet decided, and, as the schoolhouse was reached by this time, the Captain said no more.

There was, however, another question that troubled him, and that seemed to call for almost immediate settlement. It was: What should be done with Mrs. Snow? The housekeeper had been hired to act as such while John Baxter was in the house. Now he was gone, and there remained the original marriage agreement between Captain Jerry and the widow, and honor called for a decision one way or the other. Mrs. Snow, of course, said nothing about it, neither did Captain Jerry, and Captain Eri felt that he must take the initiative as usual. But, somehow, he was not as prompt as was his wont, and sat evening after evening, whittling at the clipper and smoking thoughtfully. And another week went by.

Cap'n Eri

Captain Perez might, and probably would, have suggested action upon this important matter, had not his mind been taken up with what, to him, was the most important of all. He had made up his mind to ask Patience Davis to marry him.

Love is like the measles; it goes hard with a man past fifty, and Captain Perez was severely smitten. The decision just mentioned was not exactly a brand–new one, his mind had been made up for some time, but he lacked the courage to ask the momentous question. Something the lady had said during the first stages of their acquaintance made a great impression on the Captain. She gave it as her opinion that a man who loved a woman should be willing to go through fire and water to win her. Captain Perez went home that night pondering deeply.

"Fire and water!" he mused. "That's a turrible test. But she's a wonderful woman, and would expect it of a feller. I wonder if I could do it; seems 's if I would now, but flesh is weak, and I might flunk, and that would settle it. Fire and water! My! my! that's awful!"

So the Captain delayed and Miss Patience, who had cherished hopes, found need of a good share of the virtue for which she was named.

But one afternoon at the end of the week following that of the funeral, Perez set out for a call upon his intended which he meant should be a decisive one. He had screwed his courage up to the top notch, and as he told Captain Eri afterwards, he meant to "hail her and git his bearin's, if he foundered the next minute."

He found the lady alone, for old Mrs. Mayo had gone with her son, whose name was Abner, to visit a cousin in Harniss, and would not be back until late in the evening. Miss Patience was very glad to have company, and it required no great amount of urging to persuade the infatuated swain to stay to tea. When the meal was over—they washed the dishes together, and the Captain was so nervous that it is a wonder there was a whole plate left—the pair were seated in the parlor. Then said Captain Perez, turning red and hesitating, "Pashy, do you know what a feller told me 'bout you?"

Now, this remark was purely a pleasant fiction, for the Captain was about to undertake a compliment, and was rather afraid to shoulder the entire responsibility.

"No; I'm sure I don't, Perez," replied Miss Davis, smiling sweetly.

170

"Well, a feller told me you was the best housekeeper in Orham. He said that the man that got you would be lucky."

This was encouraging. Miss Patience colored and simpered a little.

"Land sake!" she exclaimed. "Whoever told you such rubbish as that? Besides," with downcast eyes, "I guess no man would ever want me."

"Oh, I don't know." The Captain moved uneasily in his chair, as if he contemplated hitching it nearer to that occupied by his companion. "I guess there's plenty would be mighty glad to git you. Anyhow, there's—there's one that—that—I cal'late the fog's thick as ever, don't you?"

But Miss Patience didn't mean to give up in this way.

"What was it you was goin' to say?" she asked, by way of giving the bashful one another chance.

"I was goin' to say, Pashy, that—that—I asked if you thought the fog was as thick as ever."

"Oh, dear me! Yes, I s'pose likely 'tis," was the discouraged answer.

"Seems to me I never see such weather for this time of year. The ice is all out of the bay, and there ain't a bit of wind, and it's warm as summer, pretty nigh. Kind of a storm–breeder, I'm afraid."

"Well, I'm glad you're here to keep me comp'ny. I've never been sole alone in this house afore, and I should be dreadful lonesome if you hadn't come." This was offered as a fresh bait.

"Pashy, I've got somethin' I wanted to ask you. Do you think you could—er—er—"

"What, Perez?"

Cap'n Eri

"I wanted to ask you"—the Captain swallowed several times—"to ask you—What in the nation is that?"

"Oh, that's nothin' only the hens squawkin'. Go on!"

"Yes, but hens don't squawk this time of night 'thout they have some reason to. It's that fox come back; that's what 'tis."

Miss Patience, earlier in the evening, had related a harrowing tale of the loss of two of Mrs. Mayo's best Leghorns that had gone to furnish a Sunday meal for a marauding fox. As the said Leghorns were the pride of the old lady's heart, even the impending proposal was driven from Miss Davis' mind.

"Oh, Perez! you don't s'pose 'tis the fox, do you?"

"Yes, MA'AM, I do! Where's the gun?"

"There 'tis, behind the door, but there ain't a mite of shot in the house. Abner's been goin' to fetch some from the store for I don't know how long, but he's always forgot it."

"Never mind. I'll pound the critter with the butt. Come quick, and bring a lamp."

The noise in the henyard continued, and when they opened the door it was louder than ever.

"He's in the henhouse," whispered Miss Patience. "He must have gone in that hole at the side that had the loose board over it."

"All right," murmured the Captain. "You go 'round with the lamp and open the door. That 'll scare him, and I'll stand at the hole and thump him when he comes out."

So, shielding the lamp with her apron, the guardian of Mrs. Mayo's outraged Leghorns tiptoed around to the henhouse door, while Captain Perez, brandishing the gun like a club, took up his stand by the hole at the side.

172

Without the lamp the darkness was pitchy. The Captain, stooping down to watch, saw something coming out of the hole—something that was alive and moved. He swung the gun above his head, and, bringing it down with all his might, knocked into eternal oblivion the little life remaining in the finest Leghorn rooster.

"Consarn it!" yelled the executioner, stooping and laying his hand on the victim, "I've killed a hen!"

Just then there came a scream from the other side of the henhouse, followed by a crash and the sound of a fall. Running around the corner the alarmed Perez saw his lady–love stretched upon the ground, groaning dismally.

"Great land of Goshen!" he cried. "Pashy, are you hurt?"

"Oh, Perez!" gasped the fallen one. "Oh, Perez!"

This pitiful appeal had such an effect upon the Captain that he dropped upon his knees and, raising Miss Davis' head in his hands, begged her to say she wasn't killed. After some little time she obligingly complied, and then, having regained her breath, explained the situation.

What had happened was this: The fox, having selected his victim the rooster, had rendered it helpless, and was pushing it out of the hole ahead of him. The Captain had struck the rooster just as Miss Patience opened the door, and the fox, seizing this chance of escape, had dodged by the lady, upsetting her as he went.

"Well," she said, laughing, "there's no great harm done. I'm sorry for the rooster, but I guess the fox had fixed him anyway. Oh, my soul and body! look there!"

Perez turned, looked as directed, and saw the henhouse in flames.

The lighted lamp, which Miss Patience had dropped as she fell, lay broken on the floor, and the blazing oil had run in every direction. The flames were making such headway that they both saw there was practically no chance of saving the building. The frightened hens were huddled in the furthest corner, gazing stupidly at the fire.

Cap'n Eri

"Oh, those poor Leghorns!" wailed Miss Patience. "Those hens Mrs. Mayo thought the world of, and left me to look out for. Last thing she asked me was to be sure they was fed. And now they'll be all burned up! What SHALL I do?"

Here the lady began to cry.

"Pashy!" roared the Captain, whom the sight of his charmer's tears had driven almost wild, "don't say another word. I'll save them hens or git cooked along with 'em!"

And turning up his coat collar, as though he was going into a refrigerator instead of a burning building, Captain Perez sprang through the door.

Miss Davis screamed wildly to him to come back, and danced about, wringing her hands. The interior of the henhouse was now a mass of black smoke, from which the voices of the Captain and the Leghorns floated in a discordant medley, something like this:

"Hold still, you lunatics! ("Squawk! squawk!") Druther be roasted than have me catch you, hadn't you? ("Squawk! squawk!") A— kershew! Land! I'm smothered! NOW I've got you! Thunderation! Hold STILL! HOLD STILL, I tell you!"

Just as the agonized Miss Patience was on the point of fainting, the little window at the back of the shanty was thrown open and two hens, like feathered comets, shot through it. Then the red face of the Captain appeared for an instant as he caught his breath with a "Woosh!" and dived back again. This performance was repeated six times, the Captain's language and the compliments he paid the hens becoming more picturesque every moment.

At length he announced, "That's all, thank goodness!" and began to climb through the window. This was a difficult task; for the window was narrow and, in spite of what Captain Eri had called his "ingy–rubber" make up, Captain Perez stuck fast.

"Catch hold of my hands and haul, will you, Pashy?" he pleaded. "That's it; pull hard! It's gittin' sort of muggy in behind here. I'll never complain at havin' cold feet ag'in if I git out of this. Now, then! Ugh! Here we be!"

Cap'n Eri

He came out with a jerk, like a cork out of a bottle, and rolled on the ground at his lady's feet.

"Oh, Perez!" she exclaimed, "are you hurt?"

"Nothin' but my feelin's," growled the rescuer, scrambling upright. "I read a book once by a feller named Joshua Billin's, or somethin' like it. He was a ignorant chap—couldn't spell two words right— but he had consider'ble sense. He said a hen was a darn fool, and he was right; she's all that."

The Captain's face was blackened, and his clothes were scorched, but his spirit was undaunted.

"Pashy," he said, "do you realize that if we don't git help, this whole shebang, house and all, will burn down?"

"Perez, you don't mean it!"

"I wouldn't swear that I didn't. Look how that thing's blazin'! There's the barn t'other side of it, and the house t'other side of that."

"But can't you and me put it out?"

"I don't dare resk it. No, sir! We've got to git help, and git it in a hurry, too!"

"Won't somebody from the station see the light and come over?"

"Not in this fog. You can't see a hundred foot. No, I've got to go right off. Good land! I never thought! Is the horse gone?"

"No; the horse is here. Abner took one of the store horses to go to Harniss with. But he did take the buggy, and there's no other carriage but the old carryall, and that's almost tumblin' to pieces."

"I was cal'latin' to go horseback."

175

"What! and leave me here alone with the house afire? No, indeed! If you go, I'm goin', too."

"Well, then, the carryll's got to do, whether or no. Git on a shawl or somethin', while I harness up."

It was a frantic harnessing, but it was done in a hurry, and the ramshackle old carryall, dusty and cobwebbed, was dragged out of the barn, and Horace Greeley, the horse, was backed into the shafts. As they drove out of the yard the flames were roaring through the roof of the henhouse, and the lath fence surrounding it was beginning to blaze.

"Everything's so wet from the fog and the melted snow," observed the Captain, "that it 'll take some time for the fire to git to the barn. If we can git a gang here we can save the house easy, and maybe more. By mighty!" he ejaculated, "I tell you what we'll do. I'll drive across the ford and git Luther and some of the station men to come right across. Then I'll go on to the village to fetch more. It was seven when I looked at the clock as we come in from washin' dishes, so the tide must be still goin' out, and the ford jest right. Git dap!"

"Hurry all you can, for goodness' sake! Is this as fast as we can go?"

"Fast as we can go with this everlastin' Noah's Ark. Heavens! how them wheels squeal!"

"The axles ain't been greased for I don't know when. Abner was going to have the old carriage chopped up for kindlin' wood."

"Lucky for him and us 'tain't chopped up now. Git dap, slow−poke! Better chop the horse up, too, while he's 'bout it."

The last remark the Captain made under his breath.

"My gracious, how dark it is! Think you can find the crossin'?"

"GOT to find it; that's all. 'Tis dark, that's a fact."

It was. They had gone but a few hundred yards; yet the fire was already merely a shapeless, red smudge on the foggy blackness behind them. Horace Greeley pounded along at a jog, and when the Captain slapped him with the end of the reins, broke into a jerky gallop that was slower than the trot.

"Stop your hoppin' up and down!" commanded Perez, whose temper was becoming somewhat frayed. "You make me think of the walkin' beam on a steamboat. If you'd stop tryin' to fly and go straight ahead we'd do better."

They progressed in this fashion for some distance. Then Miss Davis, from the curtained depths of the back seat, spoke again.

"Oh, dear me!" she exclaimed. "Are you sure you're on the right track? Seems 's if we MUST be abreast the station, and this road's awful rough."

Captain Perez had remarked the roughness of the road. The carryall was pitching from one hummock to another, and Horace Greeley stumbled once or twice.

"Whoa!" commanded the Captain. Then he got down, lit a match, and, shielding it with his hands, scrutinized the ground. "I'm kind of 'fraid," he said presently, "that we've got off the road somehow. But we must be 'bout opposite the crossin'. I'm goin' to drive down and see if I can find it."

He turned the horse's head at right angles from the way they were going, and they pitched onward for another hundred yards. Then they came out upon the hard, smooth sand, and heard the water lapping on the shore. Captain Perez got out once more and walked along the strand, bending forward as he walked. Soon Miss Patience heard him calling.

"I've found it, I guess," he said, coming back to the vehicle. "Anyhow, it looks like it. We'll be over in a few minutes now. Git dap, you!"

Horace Greeley shivered as the cold water splashed his legs, but waded bravely in. They moved further from the shore and the water seemed to grow no deeper.

"Guess this is the crossin' all right," said the Captain, who had cherished some secret doubts. "Here's the deep part comin'. We'll be across in a jiffy."

Cap'n Eri

The water mounted to the hubs, then to the bottom of the carryall. Miss Davis' feet grew damp and she drew them up.

"Oh, Perez!" she faltered, "are you sure this is the ford?"

"Don't git scared, Pashy! I guess maybe we've got a little to one side of the track. I'll turn 'round and try again."

But Horace Greeley was of a different mind. From long experience he knew that the way to cross a ford was to go straight ahead. The bottom of the carryall was awash.

"Port your hellum, you lubber!" shouted the driver, pulling with all his might on one rein. "Heave to! Come 'bout! Gybe! consarn you! gybe!"

Then Horace Greeley tried to obey orders, but it was too late. He endeavored to touch bottom with his forelegs, but could not; tried to swim with his hind ones, but found that impossible; then wallowed wildly to one side and snapped a shaft and the rotten whiffletree short off. The carryall tipped alarmingly and Miss Patience screamed.

"Whoa!" yelled the agitated Perez. "'Vast heavin'! belay!"

The animal, as much frightened by his driver's shouts as by the water, shot ahead and tried to tear himself loose. The other sun– warped and rotten shaft broke. The carryall was now floating, with the water covering the floor.

"No use; I'll have to cut away the wreck, or we'll be on our beam ends!" shouted the Captain.

He took out his jackknife, and reaching over, severed the traces. Horace Greeley gave another wallow, and finding himself free, disappeared in the darkness amid a lather of foam. The carriage, now well out in the channel, drifted with the current.

"Don't cry, Pashy!" said the Captain, endeavoring to cheer his sobbing companion, "we ain't shark bait yit. As the song used to say:

"'We're afloat, we're afloat, And the rover is free.'

"I've shipped aboard of 'most every kind of craft," he added, "but blessed if I ever expected to be skipper of a carryall!"

But Miss Patience, shut up in the back part of the carriage like a water nymph in her cave, still wept hysterically. So Captain Perez continued his dismal attempt at facetiousness.

"The main thing," he said, "is to keep her on an even keel. If she teeters to one side, you teeter to t'other. Drat that fox!" he ejaculated. "I thought when Web's place burned we'd had fire enough to last for one spell, but it never rains but it pours."

"Oh, dear!" sobbed the lady. "Now everything 'll burn up, and they'll blame me for it. Well, I'll be drownded anyway, so I shan't be there to hear 'em. Oh, dear! dear!"

"Oh, don't talk that way. We're driftin' somewheres, but we're spinnin' 'round so I can't tell which way. Judas!" he exclaimed, more soberly, "I remember, now; it ain't but a little past seven o'clock, and the tide's goin' out."

"Of course it is," resignedly, "and we'll drift into the breakers in the bay, and that 'll be the end."

"No, no, I guess not. We ain't dead yit. If I had an oar or somethin' to steer this clipper with, maybe we could git into shoal water. As 'tis, we'll have to manage her the way Ote Wixon used to manage his wife, by lettin' her have her own way."

They floated in silence for a few moments. Then Miss Patience, who had bravely tried to stifle her sobs, said with chattering teeth, "Perez, I'm pretty nigh froze to death."

It will be remembered that the Captain had spoken of the weather as being almost as warm as summer. This was a slight exaggeration. It happened, fortunately for the castaways, that this particular night, coming as it did just at the end of the long thaw, was the mildest of the winter and there was no wind, but the air was chill, and the damp fog raw and biting.

"Well, now you mention it," said Captain Perez, "it IS cold, ain't it? I've a good mind to jump overboard, and try to swim ashore and tow the carryall."

179

Cap'n Eri

"Don't you DO it! My land! if YOU should drown what would become of ME?"

It was the tone of this speech, as much as the words, that hit the Captain hard. He himself almost sobbed as he said:

"Pashy, I want you to try to git over on this front seat with me. Then I can put my coat 'round you, and you won't be so cold. Take hold of my hand."

Miss Patience at first protested that she never could do it in the world, the carriage would upset, and that would be the end. But her companion urged her to try, and at last she did so. It was a risky proceeding, but she reached the front seat somehow, and the carryall still remained right–side–up. Luckily, in the channel between the beaches there was not the slightest semblance of a wave.

Captain Perez pulled off his coat, and wrapped it about his protesting companion. He was obliged to hold it in place, and he found the task rather pleasing.

"Oh, you're SO good!" murmured Miss Patience. "What should I have done without you?"

"Hush! Guess you'd have been better off. You'd never gone after that fox if it hadn't been for me, and there wouldn't have been none of this fuss."

"Oh, don't say that! You've been so brave. Anyhow, we'll die together, that's a comfort."

"Pashy," said Captain Perez solemnly, "it's mighty good to hear you say that."

It is, perhaps, needless to explain that the "dying" portion of the lady's speech was not that referred to by the Captain; the word "together" was what appealed to him. Miss Patience apparently understood.

"Is it?" she said softly.

"Yes—yes, 'tis." The arm holding the coat about the lady's shoulder tightened just a little. The Captain had often dreamed of something like this, but never with quite these surroundings. However, he was rapidly becoming oblivious to such trivial details as

180

surroundings.

"Pashy," he said huskily, "I've been thinkin' of you consider'ble lately. Fact is, I—I—well, I come down to–day a–purpose to ask you somethin'. I know it's a queer place to ask it, and—and I s'pose it's kind of sudden, but—will—will you— Breakers! by mighty!"

The carryall had suddenly begun to rock, and there were streaks of foam about it. Now, it gave a most alarming heave, grounded, swung clear, and tipped yet more.

"We're capsizin'," yelled Perez. "Hang on to me, Pashy!"

But Miss Patience didn't intend to let this, perhaps the final opportunity, slip. As she told her brother afterward, she would have made him say it then if they had been "two fathom under water."

"Will I what, Perez?" she demanded.

The carryall rose on two wheels and begun to turn over, but the Captain did not notice it. The arms of his heart's desire were about his neck, and he was looking into her eyes.

"Will you marry me?" he gasped.

"Yes," answered Miss Patience, and they went under together.

The Captain staggered to his feet, and dragged his chosen bride to hers. The ice–cold water reached their shoulders. And, like a flash, as they stood there, came a torrent of rain and a wind that drove the fog before it like smoke. Captain Perez saw the shore, with its silhouetted bushes, only a few yards away. Beyond that, in the blackness, was a light, a flickering blaze, that rose and fell and rose and fell again.

The Captain dragged Miss Patience to the beach.

"Run!" he chattered, "run, or we'll turn into icicles. Come on!"

With his arm about her waist Perez guided his dripping companion, as fast as they could run, toward the light. And as they came nearer to it they saw that it flickered about the blackened ruins of a hen–house and a lath fence.

It was Mrs. Mayo's henhouse, and Mrs. Mayo's fence. Their adventurous journey had ended where it began.

"You see, Eri," said Captain Perez, as he told his friend the story that night, "that clock in the dining room that I looked at hadn't been goin' for a week; the mainspring was broke. 'Twa'n't seven o'clock, 'twas nearer nine when the fire started, and the tide wa'n't goin' out, 'twas comin' in. I drove into the water too soon, missed the crossin', and we jest drifted back home ag'in. The horse had more sense than I did. We found him in the barn waiting for us."

Abner Mayo had piled against the back of his barn a great heap of damp seaweed that he intended using in the spring as a fertilizer. The fire had burned until it reached this seaweed and then had gone no further. The rain extinguished the last spark.

"Well, by mighty!" exclaimed Captain Perez for at least the tenth time, as he sat in the kitchen, wrapped in an old ulster of Mr. Mayo's, and toasting his feet in the oven, "if I don't feel like a fool. All that scare and wet for nothin'."

"Oh, not for nothin', Perez," said Miss Patience, looking tenderly down into his face.

"Well, no, not for nothin' by a good deal! I've got you by it, and that's everything. But say, Pashy!" and the Captain looked awed by the coincidence, "I went through fire and water to git you!"

CHAPTER XVIII. THE SINS OF CAPTAIN JERRY

Captain Perez made a clean breast of it to Captain Eri when he reached home that night. It was after twelve o'clock, but he routed his friend out of bed to tell him the news and the story. Captain Eri was not as surprised to hear of the engagement as he pretended to be, for he had long ago made up his mind that Perez meant business this time. But the tale of the fire and the voyage in the carryall tickled him immensely, and he rolled back and forth in the rocker and laughed until his side ached.

"I s'pose it does sound kind of ridic'lous," said the accepted suitor in a rather aggrieved tone, "but it wa'n't ha'f so funny when 'twas goin' on. Fust I thought I'd roast to death, then I thought I'd freeze, and then I thought I'd drown."

"Perez," said the panting Eri, "you're a wonder. I'm goin' to tell Sol Bangs 'bout you next time I see him. He'll want you to enter in the races next Fourth of July. We've had tub races and the like of that, but a carryall sailin' match 'll be somethin' new. I'll back you against the town, though. You can count on me."

"Now, look here, Eri Hedge, if you tell a livin' soul 'bout it, I'll—"

"All right, shipmate, all right; but it's too good to keep. You ought to write a book, one of them kind like Josiah used to read. Call it 'The Carryall Pirate, or The Terror of the Channel,' hey? Gee! you'd be famous! But, say, old man," he added more seriously, "I'll shake hands with you. I b'lieve you've got a good woman, one that 'll make it smooth sailin' for you the rest of your life. I wish you both luck."

Captain Perez shook hands very gravely. He was still a little suspicious of his chum's propensity to tease. It did not tend to make him less uneasy when, a little later, Captain Eri opened the parlor door and whispered, "Say, Perez, I've jest thought of some– thin'. What are you goin' to say to M'lissy Busteed? Her heart 'll be broke."

"Aw, git out!" was the disgusted answer.

"Well, I only mentioned it. Folks have had to pay heavy for breach of promise 'fore now. Good–night."

Perez manfully told of his engagement at the breakfast table next morning, although he said nothing concerning the rest of his adventures. He was rather taken aback to find that no one seemed greatly surprised. Everyone congratulated him, of course, and it was gratifying to discern the high opinion of the future Mrs. Ryder held by Mrs. Snow and the rest. Captain Jerry solemnly shook hands with him after the meal was over and said, "Perez, you done the right thing. There's nothin' like married life, after all."

"Then why don't you try it yourself?" was the unexpected question. "Seems to me we'll have to settle that matter of yours pretty soon. I meant to speak to Eri 'bout it 'fore this, but I've had so much on my mind. I will to–night when he comes back from fishin'."

Captain Jerry made no further remarks, but walked thoughtfully away.

So that evening, when they were together in Captain Jerry's room after supper, Perez, true to his promise, said:

"Eri, it seems to me we've got to do somethin' 'bout Mrs. Snow. She was hired to be housekeeper while John was sick. Now he's dead, and she'll think it's queer if we don't settle that marryin' bus'ness. Ain't that so?"

"Humph!" grunted Captain Jerry. "Perez is in a mighty sweat to git other folks married jest 'cause he's goin' to be. I don't see why she can't keep on bein' housekeeper jest the same as she's always been."

"Well, I do, and so do you, and you know it. We agreed to the housekeepin' bus'ness jest as a sort of put off. Now we can't put off no longer. Mrs. Snow come down here 'cause we advertised for a wife, and she's been so everlastin' good that I feel 'most ashamed every time I think of it. No use, you've got to ask her to marry you. He has, hasn't he, Eri?"

"Yes," answered Captain Eri laconically.

The sacrifice squirmed. "I hate to ask," he said. "Why don't we wait a spell, and let her say somethin' fust?"

"That WOULD be nice, wouldn't it? She's that kind of a woman, ain't she?" sputtered Perez. "No, you bet she ain't! What she'd say would be to give her opinion of us and our manners, and walk out of the house bag and baggage, and I wouldn't blame her for doin' it."

"P'raps she wouldn't have me. She never said she would."

"Never said she would! Have you ever asked her? She's had all this time to l'arn to know you in, and I cal'late if she was willin' to think 'bout it 'fore she ever see you, she'd be more willin' now. Ain't that so, Eri?

And again Captain Eri said shortly, "Yes."

"I wish you'd mind your own consarns, and give me time," protested Captain Jerry.

"Time! How much time do you want? Land of Goshen! I should think you'd had time enough. Why—"

"Oh, let up!" snorted the persecuted. "Why don't you git married yourself, and bring Pashy over to keep house? What we started to git in the fust place was jest a wife for one of us that would keep things shipshape, and now—"

The withering look of scorn that Perez bent upon him caused him to hesitate and stop. Captain Perez haughtily marched to the door.

"Eri," he said, "I ain't goin' to waste my time talkin' to a—a dogfish like him. He ain't wuth it."

"Hold on, now, Perez!" pleaded the discomfited sacrifice, alarmed at his comrade's threatened desertion. "I was only foolin'. Can't you take a joke? I haven't said I wouldn't do it. I think a heap of Mrs. Snow; it's only that I ain't got the spunk to ask her, that's all."

"Humph! it don't take much spunk," replied the successful wooer, forgetful of his own past trepidation.

"Well," Captain Jerry wriggled and twisted, but saw no loophole. "Well, give me a month to git up my courage in and—"

"A month! A month's ridic'lous; ain't it, Eri"

"Yes."

"Well, three weeks, then."

This offer, too, was rejected. Then Captain Jerry held out for a fortnight—for ten days. Finally, it was settled that within one week from that very night he was to offer his heart and hand to the lady from Nantucket. He pledged his solemn word to do it.

"There!" exclaimed the gratified Captain Perez. "That's a good job done. He won't never be sorry for it, will he, Eri?"

And Captain Eri made his fourth contribution to the conversation.

"No," he said.

Josiah went up to the post–office late in the afternoon of the next day. The "able seaman" was behaving himself remarkably well. He had become a real help to Captain Eri, and the latter said that sailing alone would be doubly hard when his foremast hand went back to school again, which he was to do very shortly, for Josiah meant to accept the Captain's offer, and to try for the Annapolis appointment when the time came.

The boy came back with the mail and an item of news. The mail, a paper only, he handed to Mrs. Snow, and the news he announced at the supper table as follows:

"Mr. Hazeltine's goin' to leave the cable station," he said.

"Goin' to leave!" repeated the housekeeper, "what for?"

"I don't know, ma'am. All I know is what I heard Mr. Wingate say. He said Mr. Hazeltine was goin' to get through over at the station pretty soon. He said one of the operators told him so."

"Well, for the land's sake! Did you know anything 'bout it, Eri?"

"Why, yes, a little. I met Hazeltine yesterday, and he told me that some folks out West had made him a pretty good offer, and he didn't know whether to take it or not. Said the salary was good, and the whole thing looked sort of temptin'. He hadn't decided what to do yit. That's all there is to it."

Cap'n Eri

There was little else talked about during the meal. Captain Perez, Captain Jerry, and Mrs. Snow argued, surmised, and questioned Captain Eri, who said little. Elsie said almost nothing, and went to her room shortly after the dishes were washed.

"Humph!" exclaimed Captain Perez, when they were alone, "I guess your match−makin' scheme's up spout, Jerry."

And, for a wonder, Captain Jerry did not contradict him.

The weather changed that night, and it grew cold rapidly. In the morning the pump was frozen, and Captain Jerry and Mrs. Snow spent some time and much energy in thawing it out. It was later than usual when the former set out for the schoolhouse. As he was putting on his cap, Elsie suggested that he wait for her, as she had some lessons to prepare, and wanted an hour or so to herself at her desk. So they walked on together under a cloudy sky. The mud in the road was frozen into all sorts of fantastic shapes, and the little puddles had turned to ice.

"That thaw was a weather−breeder, sure enough," observed Captain Jerry. "We'll git a storm out of this, 'fore we're done."

"It seems to me," said Elsie, "that the winter has been a very mild one. From what I had heard I supposed you must have some dreadful gales here, but there has been none so far."

"We'll git 'em yit. February's jist the time. Git a good no'theaster goin', and you'll think the whole house is comin' down. Nothin' to what they used to have, though, 'cordin' to tell. Cap'n Jonadab Wixon used to swear that his grandfather told him 'bout a gale that blew the hair all off a dog, and then the wind changed of a sudden, and blew it all on again."

Elsie laughed. "That must have been a blow," she said.

"Yes. Cap'n Jonadab's somethin' of a blow himself, so he ought to be a good jedge. The outer beach is the place that catches it when there's a gale on. Oh, say! that reminds me. I s'pose you was glad to hear the news last night?"

187

Cap'n Eri

"What news?"

"Why, that 'bout Mr. Hazeltine's goin' away. You're glad he's goin', of course."

Miss Preston did not answer immediately. Instead, she turned and looked wonderingly at her companion.

"Why should I be glad, pray?" she asked.

"Why, I don't know. I jest took it for granted you would be. You didn't want him to come and see you, and if he was gone he couldn't come, so—"

"Just a minute, please. What makes you think I didn't want Mr. Hazeltine to call?"

And now it was the Captain's turn to stare and hesitate.

"What makes me think—" he gasped. "Why—you told me so, yourself."

"_I_ told you so? I'm certain that I never told you anything of the kind."

Captain Jerry stood stock−still, and if ever a face expressed complete amazement, it was his.

"Elsie Preston!" he ejaculated, "are you losin' your mem'ry or what? Didn't you pitch into me hot−foot for lettin' him be alone with you? Didn't you give me 'hark from the tomb' for gittin' up and goin' away? Didn't you say his calls was perfect torture to you, and that you had to be decent to him jest out of common politeness? Now, didn't you?"

"Oh, that was it! No, of course I didn't say any such thing."

"You DIDN'T! Why, I heard you! Land of love! my ears smarted for a week afterward. I ain't had sech a goin' over sence mother used to git at me for goin' in swimmin' on Sunday. And now you say you didn't say it."

"I didn't. You misunderstood me. I did object to your leaving the room every time he called, and making me appear so ridiculous; and I did say that his visits might be a torture

188

for all that you knew to the contrary, but I certainly didn't say that they WERE."

"SUFFERIN'! And you ain't glad he stopped comin'?"

The air of complete indifference assumed by the young lady was a triumph.

"Why, of course," she said, "Mr. Hazeltine is a free agent, and I don't know of any reason why he should be compelled to go where he doesn't wish to go. I enjoyed his society, and I'm sure Captain Eri and Mrs. Snow enjoyed it, too; but it is quite evident that he did not enjoy ours, so I don't see that there need be any more said on the subject."

Captain Jerry was completely crushed. If the gale described by the redoubtable grandsire of Jonadab Wixon had struck him, he could not have been more upset.

"My! my! my!" he murmured. "And after my beggin' his pardon and all!"

"Begging his pardon? For what?"

"Why, for leavin' you two alone. Of course, after you pitched into me so I see how foolish I'd been actin', and I—honest, I didn't sleep scursely a bit that night thinkin' 'bout it. Thinks I, 'If Elsie feels that way, why, there ain't no doubt that Mr. Hazeltine feels the same.' There wa'n't but one thing to be done. When a man makes a mistake, if he is any kind of a man, he owns up, and does his best to straighten things out. 'Twa'n't easy to do, but duty's duty, and the next time I see Mr. Hazeltine I told him the whole thing, and—"

"You DID!"

"Sartin I did."

"What did you tell him?"

They had stopped on the sidewalk nearly opposite the post-office. Each was too much engrossed in the conversation to pay any heed to anything else. If the few passersby thought it strange that the schoolmistress should care to loiter out of doors on that cold and disagreeable morning, they said nothing about it. One young man in particular, who, standing just inside the post-office door, was buttoning his overcoat and putting on his

189

gloves, looked earnestly at the pair, but he, too, said nothing.

"Why, I told him," said Captain Jerry, in reply to the question, "how you didn't like to have me go out of the room when he was there. Course, I told him I didn't mean to do nothin' out of the way. Then he asked me some more questions, and I answered 'em best I could, and—well, I guess that's 'bout all."

"Did you tell him that I said his visits were a torture?"

"Why—" the Captain shuffled his feet uneasily—"seems to me I said somethin' 'bout it—not jest that, you know, but somethin'. Fact is, I was so muddle-headed and upset that I don't know exactly what I did say. Anyhow, he said 'twas all right, so there ain't nothin' to worry 'bout."

"Captain Jeremiah Burgess!" exclaimed Elsie. Then she added, "What MUST he think of me?"

"Oh, I'll fix that!" exclaimed the Captain. "I'll see him some time to-day, and I'll tell him you didn't mean it. Why, I declare! Yes, 'tis! There he is, now! Hi! Mr. Hazeltine! Come here a minute."

A mischievous imp was certainly directing Captain Jerry's movements. Ralph had, almost for the first time since he came to Orham, paid an early morning visit to the office in order to send an important letter in the first mail. The slamming of the door had attracted the Captain's attention and, in response to the hail, Mr. Hazeltine crossed the road.

And then Captain Jerry felt his arm clutched with a grip that meant business, as Miss Preston whispered, "Don't you dare say one word to him about it. Don't you DARE!"

If Ralph had been surprised by the request to join the couple, he was more surprised by the reception he received. Elsie's face was crimson, and as for the Captain, he looked like a man who had suddenly been left standing alone in the middle of a pond covered with very thin ice.

The electrician bowed and shook hands gravely. As no remark seemed to be forthcoming from those who had summoned him, he observed that it was an unpleasant morning. This commonplace reminded him of one somewhat similar that he had made to a supposed Miss "Gusty" Black, and he, too, colored.

"Did you want to speak with me, Captain?" he asked, to cover his confusion.

"Why—why, I did," stammered poor Captain Jerry, "but—but I don't know's I do now." Then he realized that this was not exactly complimentary, and added, "That is, I don't know—I don't know's I— Elsie, what was it I was goin' to say to Mr. Hazeltine?"

At another time it is likely that the young lady's quick wit would have helped her out of the difficulty, but now she was too much disturbed.

"I'm sure I don't know," she said coldly.

"You don't know! Why, yes you do? 'Twas—'twas—" The Captain was frantically grasping at straws. "Why, we was wonderin' why you didn't come to see us nowadays."

If the Captain had seen the look that Elsie shot at him, as he delivered this brilliant observation, he might have been more, instead of less, uncomfortable. As it was, he felt rather proud of having discovered a way out of the difficulty. But Ralph's embarrassment increased. He hurriedly said something about having been very busy.

"Well," went on the Captain, intent on making the explanation as plausible as possible, "we've missed you consider'ble. We was sayin' we hoped you wouldn't give us up altogether. Ain't that so, Elsie?"

Miss Preston's foot tapped the sidewalk several times, but she answered, though not effusively:

"Mr. Hazeltine is always welcome, of course." Then, she added, turning away, "Really, Captain Jerry, I must hurry to school. I have a great deal of work to do before nine o'clock. Good–morning, Mr. Hazeltine."

The Captain paused long enough to say, "We'll expect you now, so come," and then hurried after her. He was feeling very well satisfied with himself.

"By mighty! Elsie," he chuckled, "I got out of that nice, didn't I?"

He received no answer, even when he repeated the remark, and, although he endeavored, as he swept out the schoolroom, to engage the teacher in conversation, her replies were as cold as they were short. The Captain went home in the last stages of dismalness.

That afternoon, when Captain Eri returned from the fishing grounds, he found Captain Jerry waiting for him at the shanty. The humiliated matchmaker sent Josiah up to the grocery store on an errand, and then dragged his friend inside and shut the door.

Captain Eri looked at the woe–begone face with some concern.

"What ails you, Jerry?" he demanded. "Have you—have you spoken to Mrs. Snow 'bout that—that marriage?"

"No, I ain't, Eri, but I'm in a turrible mess, and I don't know why, neither. Seems to me the more I try to do for other folks the wuss off I am; and, instead of gittin' thanks, all I git is blame."

"Why, what's the matter?"

"Well, now I know you'll think I'm a fool, and 'll jest pester the life out of me. See here, Eri Hedge! If I tell you what I want to, will you promise not to pitch into me, and not to nag and poke fun? If you don't promise I won't tell one single word, no matter what happens."

So Captain Eri promised, and then Captain Jerry, stammering and hesitating, unburdened his mind of the whole affair, telling of his first reproof by Elsie, his "explanation" to Ralph, and the subsequent developments. Long before he finished, Captain Eri rose and, walking over to the door, stood looking out through the dim pane at the top, while his shoulders shook as if there was a smothered earthquake inside.

"There!" exclaimed the injured matrimonial agent, in conclusion. "There's the whole fool thing, and I 'most wish I'd never seen either of 'em. I thought I did fust–rate this mornin' when I was tryin' to think up somethin' to show why I hailed Hazeltine, but no, Elsie won't hardly speak to me. I wish to goodness you'd tell me what to do."

192

Cap'n Eri

Captain Eri turned away from the door. His eyes were watery, and his face was red, but he managed to say:

"Oh, Jerry, Jerry! Your heart's big as a bucket, but fishin' 's more in your line than gittin' folks married to order is, I'm 'fraid. You stay here, and unload them fish in the dory. There ain't many of 'em, and Josiah 'll help when he gits back. I'm goin' out for a few minutes."

He went down to the beach, climbed into a dory belonging to a neighbor, and Captain Jerry saw him row away in the direction of the cable station.

That evening, after the dishes were washed and the table cleared, there came a knock at the door. Mrs. Snow opened it.

"Why, for goodness sake! Mr. Hazeltine!" she exclaimed. "Come right in. What a stranger you are!"

Ralph entered, shook the snow, which had just begun to fall, from his hat and coat, took off these articles, in response to the hearty invitation of Captain Eri, and shook hands with all present. Elsie's face was an interesting study. Captain Jerry looked scared.

After a few minutes' talk, Captain Eri rose.

"Mrs. Snow," he said, "come upstairs a little while. I want to talk to you 'bout somethin'. You come, too, Jerry."

Captain Jerry looked from Elsie to the speaker, and then to Elsie again. But Captain Eri's hand was on his arm, and he rose and went.

Elsie watched this wholesale desertion with amazement. Then the door opened again, and Captain Eri put in his head.

"Elsie," he said, "I jest want to tell you that this is my doin's, not Jerry's. That's all." And the door shut.

Elsie faced the caller with astonishment written on her face.

Cap'n Eri

"Mr. Hazeltine," she said icily, "you may know what this means, but I don't."

Ralph looked at her and answered solemnly, but with a twinkle in his eye:

"I'm afraid I can guess, Miss Preston. You see Captain Jerry paid Captain Eri a call this afternoon and, as a result, Captain Eri called upon me. Then, as a result of THAT, I—well, I came here."

The young lady blushed furiously. "What did Captain Eri tell you?" she demanded.

"Just what Captain Jerry told him."

"And that was?"

"What you told Captain Jerry this morning concerning something that you told him before, I believe."

There was no answer to this. Miss Preston looked as if she had a mind to run out of the room, then as if she might cry, and finally as if she wanted to laugh.

"I humbly apologize," said the electrician contritely.

"YOU apologize? For what?"

"For my stupidity in believing that Captain Jerry was to be accepted seriously."

"You were excusable, certainly. And now I must apologize; also for taking the Captain too seriously."

"Suppose we pair the apologies as they do the votes in the Senate. Then one will offset the other."

"I'm afraid that isn't fair, for the blunder was all on my part."

"Well, if we can't pair apologies, suppose we pair blunders. I don't accept your statement of guilt, mind, but since you are determined to shoulder it, we might put it on one side

194

and on the other we'll put—"

"What?"

"'Gusty' Black."

And then they both laughed.

A little later Captain Eri knocked at the door.

"Is it safe for a feller to come in?" he asked.

"Well," said Elsie severely, "I don't know whether talebearers should be admitted or not, but if they do come they must beg pardon for interfering in other people's affairs."

"Ma'am," and the Captain made a profound bow, "I hope you'll be so 'kind and condescendin', and stoop so low, and be so bendin'' as to forgive me. And, while I'm 'bout it, I'll apologize for Jerry, too."

"No, sir," said the young lady decidedly. "Captain Jerry must apologize for himself. Captain Jeremiah Burgess," she called up the stairway, "come into court, and answer for your sins."

And Captain Jerry tremblingly came.

CHAPTER XIX. A "NO'THEASTER" BLOWS

It had begun to snow early in the evening, a light fall at first, but growing heavier every minute, and, as the flakes fell thicker and faster, the wind began to blow, and its force increased steadily. Ralph, hearing the gusts as they swooped about the corners of the house, and the "swish" of the snow as it was thrown against the window panes, several times rose to go, but Captain Eri in each instance urged him to stay a little longer. Finally, the electrician rebelled.

"I should like to stay, Captain," he said, "but how do you think I am going to get over to the station if this storm grows worse, as it seems to be doing?"

"I don't think," was the calm reply. "You're goin' to stay here."

"Well, I guess not."

"I guess yes. S'pose we're goin' to let you try to row over to the beach a night like this? It's darker 'n a nigger's pocket, and blowin' and snowin' great guns besides. Jest you look out here."

He rose, beckoned to Ralph, and then opened the outer door. He had to use considerable strength to do this, and a gust of wind and a small avalanche of snow roared in, and sent the lighter articles flying from the table. Elsie gave a little scream, and Mrs. Snow exclaimed, "For the land's sake, shut that door this minute! Everything 'll be soppin' wet."

The Captain pulled the door shut again, and dropped the hook into the staple.

"Nice night for a pull, ain't it?" he observed, smiling. "No, sir, I've heard it comin' on, and I made up my mind you'd have to stay on dry land for a spell, no matter if all creation wanted you on t'other side."

Ralph looked troubled. "I ought to be at the station," he said.

"Maybe so, but you ain't, and you'll have to put up at this boardin' house till mornin'. When it's daylight one of us 'll set you across. Mr. Langley ain't foolish. He won't expect you to– night."

"Now, Mr. Hazeltine," said the housekeeper, "you might jest as well give it up fust as last. You KNOW you can't go over to that station jest as well as I do."

So Ralph did give it up, although rather against his will. There was nothing of importance to be done, but he felt a little like a deserter, nevertheless.

"Perez won't git home neither," observed Captain Eri. "He's snowed in, too."

Cap'n Eri

Captain Perez had that afternoon gone down to the Mayo homestead to take tea with Miss Davis.

"Git home! I should think not!" said Mrs. Snow decidedly. "Pashy's got too much sense to let him try it."

"Well, Elsie," commented Captain Jerry, "I told you we'd have a no'theaster 'fore the winter was over. I guess there'll be gale enough to satisfy you, now. No school to–morrer."

"Well, that's settled! Let's be comf'table. Ain't there some of that cider down cellar? Where's the pitcher?" And Captain Eri hurried off to find it.

When bedtime came there was some argument as to where the guest should sleep. Ralph insisted that the haircloth sofa in the parlor was just the thing, but Captain Eri wouldn't hear of it.

"Haircloth's all right to look at," he said, "but it's the slipperiest stuff that ever was, I cal'late. Every time I set on a haircloth chair I feel's if I was draggin' anchor."

The cot was declared ineligible, also, and the question was finally settled by Josiah and Captain Eri going upstairs to the room once occupied by John Baxter, while Ralph took that which they vacated.

It was some time before he fell asleep. The gale seemed to be tearing loose the eternal foundations. The house shook and the bed trembled as if a great hand was moving them, and the snow slapped against the windows till it seemed that they must break.

In the morning there was little change in the weather. The snow had turned to a sleet, half rain, that stuck to everything and coated it with ice. The wind was blowing as hard as ever. Captain Eri and Ralph, standing just outside the kitchen door, and in the lee of the barn, paused to watch the storm for a minute before they went down to the beach. At intervals they caught glimpses of the snow–covered roofs of the fish shanties, and the water of the inner bay, black and threatening and scarred with whitecaps; then another gust would come, and they could scarcely see the posts at the yard gate.

Cap'n Eri

"Think you want to go over, do you?" asked the Captain.

"I certainly do, if I can get there."

"Oh, we can git there all right. I've rowed a dory a good many times when 'twas as bad as this. This ain't no picnic day, though, that's a fact," he added, as they crossed the yard, and caught the full force of the wind. "Lucky you put on them ileskins."

Ralph was arrayed in Captain Jerry's "dirty−weather rig," and although, as Captain Eri said, the garments fitted him "like a shirt on a handspike," they were very acceptable.

They found the dory covered with snow and half−full of slush, and it took some few minutes to get her into condition. When this was accomplished they hauled her down to the shore, and Captain Eri, standing knee−deep in water, steadied her while Ralph climbed in. Then the Captain tumbled in himself, picked up the oars, and settled down for the pull to the outer beach.

A dory, as everyone acquainted alongshore knows, is the safest of all small craft for use in heavy weather. It is unsinkable for one thing, and, being flat−bottomed, slips over the waves instead of plowing through them. But the high freeboard is a mark for the wind, and to keep a straight course on such a morning as this requires skill, and no small amount of muscle. Ralph, seated in the stern, found himself wondering how on earth his companion managed to row as he did, and steer at the same time. The strokes were short, but there was power in them, and the dory, although moving rather slowly, went doggedly on.

"Let me take her," shouted Ralph after a while, "you must be tired."

"Who, me?" Captain Eri laughed. "I could keep this up for a week. There ain't any sea in here. If we was outside now, 'twould be diff'rent, maybe."

They hit the beach almost exactly at the right spot, a feat which the passenger considered a miracle, but which the Captain seemed to take as a matter of course. They beached and anchored the dory, and, bending almost double as they faced the wind, plowed through the sand to the back door of the station. There was comparatively little snow here on the outer beach—the gale had swept it nearly all away.

Cap'n Eri

Mr. Langley met them as they tramped into the hall. The old gentleman was glad to see his assistant, for he had begun to fear that the latter might have tried to row over during the evening, and met with disaster. As they sat round the stove in his room he said, "We don't need any wrecks inside the beach. We shall have enough outside, I'm afraid. I hear there is one schooner in trouble now."

"That so?" asked Captain Eri. "Where is she?"

"On the Hog's Back shoal, they think. One of the life–saving crew told McLaughlin that they saw her last night, when the gale first began, trying to make an offing, and that wreckage was coming ashore this morning. Captain Davis was going to try to reach her with the boat, I believe."

"I should like to be at the life–saving station when they land," said Ralph. "It would be a new experience for me. I've seen the crew drill often enough, but I have never seen them actually at work."

"What d'you say if we go down to the station?" asked the Captain. "That is, if Mr. Langley here can spare you."

"Oh, I can spare him," said the superintendent. "There is nothing of importance to be done here just now. But it will be a terrible walk down the beach this morning."

"Wind 'll be at our backs, and we're rigged for it, too. What d'you say, Mr. Hazeltine?"

Ralph was only too glad of the opportunity to see, at least, the finish of a rescuing expedition, and he said so. So they got into the oilskins again, pulled their "sou'westers" down over their ears, and started on the tramp to the life–saving station.

The electrician is not likely to forget that walk. The wind was, as the Captain said, at their backs, but it whistled in from the sea with terrific strength, and carried the sleet with it. It deluged them with water, and plastered them with flying seaweed and ice. The wet sand came in showers like hail, and beat against their shoulders until they felt the sting, even through their clothes. Toward the bay was nothing but gray mist, streaked with rain and sleet; toward the sea was the same mist, flying with the wind over such a huddle of tossing green and white as Ralph had never seen. The surf poured in in rollers that leaped

199

over each other's humped backs in their savage energy to get at the shore, which trembled as they beat upon it. The ripples from one wave had not time to flow back before those of the next came threshing in. Great blobs of foam shot down the strand like wild birds, and the gurgle and splash and roar were terrific.

They walked as near the water line as they dared, because the sand was harder there. Captain Eri went ahead, hands in his pockets and head down. Ralph followed, sometimes watching his companion, but oftener gazing at the sea. At intervals there would be a lull, as if the storm giant had paused for breath, and they could see for half a mile over the crazy water; then the next gust would pull the curtain down again, and a whirl of rain and sleet would shut them in. Conversation meant only a series of shrieks and they gave it up.

At length the Captain turned, grinned pleasantly, while the rain drops splashed on his nose, and waved one arm. Ralph looked and saw ahead of them the clustered buildings of the life–saving station. And he was glad to see them.

"Whew!" puffed Captain Eri as they opened the door. "Nice mornin' for ducks. Hey, Luther!" he shouted, "wake up here; you've got callers."

They heard footsteps in the next room, the door opened, and in came—not Luther Davis, but Captain Perez.

"Why, Eri!" he exclaimed amazedly.

"For the land's sake, Perez! What are you doin' here?"

"What are YOU doin' here, I should say. How d'you do, Mr. Hazeltine?"

Captain Eri pushed back his "sou'wester," and strolled over to the stove. Ralph followed suit.

"Well, Perez," said the former, extending his hands over the fire, "it's easy enough to tell you why we're here. We heard there was a wreck."

"There is. She's a schooner, and she's off there on the Hog's Back. Luther and the crew put off to her more 'n two hours ago, and I'm gittin' worried."

Then Perez went on to explain that, because of the storm, he had been persuaded to stay at Mrs. Mayo's all night; that Captain Davis had been over for a moment that evening on an errand, and had said that the schooner had been sighted and that, as the northeaster was coming on, she was almost certain to get into trouble; that he, Perez, had rowed over the first thing in the morning to get the news, and had been just in time to see the launching of the lifeboat, as the crew put off to the schooner.

"There ain't nothin' to worry 'bout," observed Captain Eri. "It's no slouch of a pull off to the Hog's Back this weather, and besides, I'd trust Lute Davis anywhere on salt water."

"Yes, I know," replied the unconvinced Captain Perez, "but he ought to have been back afore this. There was a kind of let-up in the storm jest afore I got here, and they see her fast on the shoal with the crew in the riggin'. Luther took the small boat 'cause he thought he could handle her better, and that's what's worryin' me; I'm 'fraid she's overloaded. I was jest thinkin' of goin' out on the p'int to see if I could see anything of 'em when you folks come."

"Well, go ahead. We'll go with you, if Mr. Hazeltine's got any of the chill out of him."

Ralph was feeling warm by this time and, after Perez had put on his coat and hat, they went out once more into the gale. The point of which Perez had spoken was a wedge-shaped sand ridge that, thrown up by the waves and tide, thrust itself out from the beach some few hundred yards below the station. They reached its tip, and stood there in the very midst of the storm, waiting for the lulls, now more frequent, and scanning the tumbling water for the returning lifeboat.

"Schooner's layin' right over there," shouted Captain Perez in Ralph's ear, pointing off into the mist. "'Bout a mile off shore, I cal'late. Wicked place, the Hog's Back is, too."

"Wind's lettin' up a little mite," bellowed Captain Eri. "We've had the wust of it, I guess. There ain't so much—"

He did not finish the sentence. The curtain of sleet parted, leaving a quarter-mile-long lane, through which they could see the frothing ridges racing one after the other, endlessly. And across this lane, silent and swift, like a moving picture on a screen, drifted a white turtleback with black dots clinging to it. It was in sight not more than a half minute, then the lane closed again, as the rain lashed their faces.

Captain Perez gasped, and clutched the electrician by the arm.

"Godfrey mighty!" he exclaimed.

"What was it?" shouted Ralph. "What was it, Captain Eri?"

But Captain Eri did not answer. He had turned, and was running at full speed back to the beach. When they came up they found him straining at the side of the dory that Luther Davis used in tending his lobster pots. The boat, turned bottom up, lay high above tide mark in the little cove behind the point.

"Quick, now!" shouted the Captain, in a tone Ralph had never heard him use before. "Over with her! Lively!"

They obeyed him without question. As the dory settled right side up two heavy oars, that had been secured by being thrust under the seats, fell back with a clatter.

"What was it, Captain?" shouted Ralph.

"The lifeboat upset. How many did you make out hangin' onto her, Perez? Five, seemed to me."

"Four, I thought. Eri, you ain't goin' to try to reach her with this dory? You couldn't do it. You'll only be drownded yourself. My Lord!" he moaned, wringing his hands, "what 'll Pashy do?"

"Catch a–holt now," commanded Captain Eri. "Down to the shore with her! Now!"

They dragged the dory to the water's edge with one rush. Then Eri hurriedly thrust in the tholepins. Perez protested again.

"Eri," he said, "it ain't no use. She won't live to git through the breakers."

His friend answered without looking up. "Do you s'pose," he said, "that I'm goin' to let Lute Davis and them other fellers drown without makin' a try for 'em? Push off when I tell you to."

"Then you let me go instead of you."

"Don't talk foolish. You've got Pashy to look after. Ready now!"

But Ralph Hazeltine intervened.

"I'm going myself," he said firmly, putting one foot over the gunwale. "I'm a younger man than either of you, and I'm used to a boat. I mean it. I'm, going."

Captain Eri looked at the electrician's face; he saw nothing but determination there.

"We'll all go," he said suddenly. "Mr. Hazeltine, run as fast as the Lord 'll let you back to the station and git another set of oars. Hurry!"

Without answering, the young man sprang up the beach and ran toward the buildings. The moment that he was inside Captain Eri leaped into the dory.

"Push off, Perez!" he commanded. "That young feller's got a life to live."

"You don't go without me," asserted Perez stoutly.

"All right! Push off, and then jump in."

Captain Perez attempted to obey. He waded into the water and gave the dory a push, but, just as he was about to scramble in, he received a shove that sent him backwards.

"Your job's takin' care of Pashy!" roared Captain Eri.

Perez scrambled to his feet, but the dory was already half-way across the little patch of comparatively smooth water in the cove. As he looked he saw it enter the first line of breakers, rise amid a shower of foam, poise on the crest, and slip over. The second line of roaring waves came surging on, higher and more threatening than the first. Captain Eri glanced over his shoulder, turned the dory's bow toward them and waited. They broke, and, as they did so, the boat shot forward into the whirlpool of froth. Then the sleet came pouring down and shut everything from sight.

When Ralph came hurrying to the beach, bearing the oars, he found Captain Perez alone.

CHAPTER XX. ERI GOES BACK ON A FRIEND

Captain Eri knew that the hardest and most dangerous portion of his perilous trip was just at its beginning. If the dory got through the surf without capsizing, it was an even bet that she would stay right–side–up for a while longer, at any rate. So he pulled out of the little cove, and pointed the boat's bow toward the thundering smother of white, his shoulders squared, his hands tightened on the oar handles, and his under–jaw pushed out beyond the upper. Old foremast hands, those who had sailed with the Captain on his coasting voyages, would, had they seen these signs, have prophesied trouble for someone. They were Captain Eri's battle–flags, and just now his opponent was the gray Atlantic. If the latter won, it would only be after a fight.

The first wave tripped over the bar and whirled beneath him, sending the dory high into the air and splashing its occupant with spray. The Captain held the boat stationary, waiting for the second to break, and then, half rising, put all his weight and strength on the oars. The struggle had begun.

They used to say on board the Hannah M. that the skipper never got rattled. The same cool head and steady nerve that Josiah had admired when the catboat threaded the breakers at the entrance of the bay, now served the same purpose in this more tangled and infinitely more wicked maze. The dory climbed and ducked, rolled and slid, but gained, inch by inch, foot by foot. The advancing waves struck savage blows at the bow, the wind did its best to swing her broadside on, but there was one hundred and eighty pounds of clear grit and muscle tugging at the oars, and, though the muscles were not as young as they had been, there were years of experience to make every pound count. At last the preliminary round was over. The boat sprang clear of the breakers and crept out farther and farther, with six inches of water slopping in her bottom, but afloat and seaworthy.

It was not until she was far into deep water that the Captain turned her bow down the shore. When this was done, it was on the instant, and, although a little more water came inboard, there was not enough to be dangerous. Then, with the gale astern and the tide to help, Captain Eri made the dory go as she, or any other on that coast, had never gone before.

The Captain knew that the wind and the tide that were now aiding him were also sweeping the overturned lifeboat along at a rapid rate. He must come up with it before it reached the next shoal. He must reach it before the waves, and, worse than all, the cold had caused the poor fellows clinging to it for life to loose their grip.

The dory jumped from crest to crest like a hurdler. The sleet now beat directly into the Captain's face and froze on his eyebrows and lashes, but he dared not draw in an oar to free a hand. The wind caught up the spindrift and poured it over him in icy baths, but he was too warm from the furious exercise to mind.

In the lulls he turned his head and gazed over the sea, looking for the boat. Once he saw it, before the storm shut down again, and he groaned aloud to count but two black dots on its white surface. He pulled harder than ever, and grunted with every stroke, while the perspiration poured down his forehead and froze when it reached the ice dams over his eyes.

At last it was in plain sight, and the two dots, now clearly human beings, were still there. He pointed the bow straight at it and rowed on. When he looked again there was but one, a figure sprawled along the keel, clinging to the centerboard.

The flying dory bore down upon the lifeboat, and the Captain risked what little breath he had in a hail. The clinging figure raised its head, and Captain Eri felt an almost selfish sense of relief to see that it was Luther Davis. If it had to be but one, he would rather it was that one.

The bottom of the lifeboat rose like a dome from the sea that beat and roared over and around it. The centerboard had floated up and projected at the top, and it was about this that Captain Davis' arms were clasped. Captain Eri shot the dory alongside, pulled in one oar, and the two boats fitted closely together. Then Eri reached out, and, seizing his friend by the belt round his waist, pulled him from his hold. Davis fell into the bottom of the dory, only half conscious and entirely helpless.

Cap'n Eri

Captain Eri lifted him so that his head and shoulders rested on a thwart, and then, setting his oar against the lifeboat's side, pushed the dory clear. Then he began rowing again.

So far he had been more successful than he had reason to expect, but the task that he must now accomplish was not less difficult. He must reach the shore safely, and with another life beside his own to guard.

It was out of the question to attempt to get back to the cove; the landing must be made on the open beach, and, although Captain Eri had more than once brought a dory safely through a high surf, he had never attempted it when his boat had nearly a foot of water in her and carried a helpless passenger.

Little by little, still running before the wind, the Captain edged in toward the shore. Luther Davis moved once or twice, but said nothing. His oilskins were frozen stiff and his beard was a lump of ice. Captain Eri began to fear that he might die from cold and exhaustion before the attempt at landing was made. The Captain resolved to wait no longer, but to take the risk of running directly for the beach.

He was near enough now to see the leaping spray of the breakers, and their bellow sounded louder than the howl of the wind or the noises of the sea about him. He bent forward and shouted in the ear of the prostrate life–saver.

"Luther!" he yelled, "Lute!"

Captain Davis' head rolled back, his eyes opened, and, in a dazed way, he looked at the figure swinging back and forth with the oars.

"Lute!" shouted Captain Eri, "listen to me! I'm goin' to try to land. D'you hear me?"

Davis' thoughts seemed to be gathering slowly. He was, ordinarily, a man of strong physique, courageous, and a fighter every inch of him, but his strength had been beaten out by the waves and chilled by the cold, and the sight of the men with whom he had lived and worked for years drowning one by one, had broken his nerve. He looked at his friend, and then at the waves.

"What's the use?" he said feebly. "They're all gone. I might as well go, too."

206

Cap'n Eri

Captain Eri's eyes snapped. "Lute Davis," he exclaimed, "I never thought I'd see you playin' crybaby. Brace up! What are you, anyway?"

The half−frozen man made a plucky effort.

"All right, Eri," he said. "I'm with you, but I ain't much good."

"Can you stand up?"

"I don't know. I'll try."

Little by little he raised himself to his knees.

"'Bout as fur's I can go, Eri," he said, between his teeth. "You look out for yourself. I'll do my durndest."

The dory was caught by the first of the great waves, and, on its crest, went flying toward the beach. Captain Eri steered it with the oars as well as he could. The wave broke, and the half−filled boat paused, was caught up by the succeeding breaker, and thrown forward again. The Captain, still trying to steer with one oar, let go of the other, and seizing his companion by the belt, pulled him to his feet.

"Now then," he shouted, "stand by!"

The boat poised on the curling wave, went down like a hammer, struck the sand, and was buried in water. Just as it struck, Captain Eri jumped as far shoreward as he could. Davis sprang with him, but it was really the Captain's strength that carried them clear of the rail.

They kept their feet for an instant, but, in that instant, Captain Eri dragged his friend a yard or so up the shelving beach. Then they were knocked flat by the next wave. The Captain dug his toes into the sand and braced himself as the undertow sucked back. Once more he rose and they staggered on again, only to go down when the next rush of water came. Three times this performance was repeated, and, as they rose for the fourth time, the Captain roared, "Now!"

Another plunge, a splashing run, and they were on the hard sand of the beach. Then they both tumbled on their faces and breathed in great gasps.

But the Captain realized that this would not do, for, in their soaked condition, freezing to death was a matter of but a short time. He seized Davis by the shoulder and shook him again and again.

"Come on, Lute! Come on!" he insisted. "Git up! You've GOT to git up!"

And, after a while, the life–saver did get up, although he could scarcely stand. Then, with the Captain's arm around his waist, they started slowly up the beach toward the station.

They had gone but a little way when they were met by Ralph Hazeltine and Captain Perez.

Mrs. Snow had been, for her, rather nervous all that forenoon. She performed her household duties as thoroughly as usual, but Elsie, to whom the storm had brought a holiday, noticed that she looked out of the window and at the clock frequently. Once she even went so far as to tell the young lady that she felt "kind of queer; jest as if somethin' was goin' to happen." As the housekeeper was not the kind to be troubled with presentiments, Elsie was surprised.

Dinner was on the table at twelve o'clock, but Captain Eri was not there to help eat it, and they sat down without him. And here again Mrs. Snow departed from her regular habit, for she ate little and was very quiet. She was the first to hear an unusual sound outside, and, jumping up, ran to the window.

"Somebody's drivin' into the yard," she said. "Who on airth would be comin' here such a day as this?"

Captain Jerry joined her at the window.

"It's Abner Mayo's horse," he said. "Maybe it's Perez comin' home."

It was not Captain Perez, but Mr. Mayo himself, as they saw when the rubber blanket fastened across the front of the buggy was dropped and the driver sprang out. Mrs. Snow

Cap'n Eri

opened the door for him.

"Hello, Abner!" exclaimed Captain Jerry, as the newcomer stopped to knock the snow from his boots before coming in, "what have you done to Perez? Goin' to keep him for a steady boarder?"

But Mr. Mayo had important news to communicate, and he did not intend to lose the effect of his sensation by springing it without due preparation. He took off his hat and mittens and solemnly declined a proffered chair.

"Cap'n Burgess," he said, "I've got somethin' to tell you— somethin' awful. The whole life–savin' crew but one is drownded, and Cap'n Eri Hedge—"

An exclamation from Mrs. Snow interrupted him. The housekeeper clasped her hands together tightly and sank into a chair. She was very white. Elsie ran to her.

"What is it, Mrs. Snow?" she asked.

"Nothin', nothin'! Go on, Mr. Mayo. Go on!"

The bearer of ill–tidings, gratified at the result of his first attempt, proceeded deliberately:

"And Cap'n Hedge and Luther Davis are over at the station pretty nigh dead. If it wa'n't for the Cap'n, Luther'd have gone, too. Eri took a dory and went off and picked him up. Perez come over to my house and told us about it, and Pashy's gone back with him to see to her brother. I didn't go down to the store this mornin', 'twas stormin' so, but as soon as I heard I harnessed up to come and tell you."

Then, in answer to the hurried questions of Captain Jerry and Elsie, Mr. Mayo told the whole story as far as he knew it. Mrs. Snow said nothing, but sat with her hands still clasped in her lap.

"Luther is ha'f drownded and froze," concluded Abner, "and the Cap'n got a bang with an oar when they jumped out of the dory that, Perez is afraid, broke his arm. I'm goin' right back to git Dr. Palmer. They tried to telephone him, but the wire's down."

209

"Dear! dear! dear!" exclaimed Captain Jerry, completely demoralized by the news. "That's dreadful! I must go right down there, mustn't I? The poor fellers!"

Mrs. Snow rose to her feet quietly, but with a determined air.

"Are you goin' right back soon's you've got the Doctor, Mr. Mayo?" she asked.

"Why, no, I wa'n't. I ain't been to my store this mornin', and I'm 'fraid I ought to be there."

To be frank, Abner was too great a sensation lover to forfeit the opportunity of springing his startling news on the community.

"Then, Josiah, you'll have to harness Dan'l and take me down. I mustn't wait another minute."

"Why, Mrs. Snow!" expostulated Captain Jerry, "you mustn't go down there. The Doctor's goin', and I'll go, and Pashy's there already."

But the housekeeper merely waved him aside.

"I want you to stay here with Elsie," she said. "There's no tellin' how long I may be gone. Josiah 'll drive me down, won't you, Josiah?"

There was no lack of enthusiasm in the "able seaman's" answer. The boy was only too glad of the chance.

"But it ain't fit weather for you to be out in. You'll git soakin' wet."

"I guess if Pashy Davis can stand it, I can. Elsie, will you come and help me git ready, while Josiah's harnessin'?"

As they entered the chamber above, Elsie was thunderstruck to see her companion seat herself in the rocker and cover her face with her hands. If it had been anyone else it would not have been so astonishing, but the cool, self-possessed housekeeper—she could scarcely believe it.

Cap'n Eri

"Why, Mrs. Snow!" she exclaimed, "what IS it?"

The lady from Nantucket hastily rose and wiped her eyes with her apron.

"Oh, nothin'," she answered, with an attempt at a smile. "I'm kind of fidgety this mornin', and the way that man started off to tell his yarn upset me; that's all. I mustn't be such a fool."

She set about getting ready with a vim and attention to detail that proved that her "fidgets" had not affected her common–sense. She was pale and her hands trembled a little, but she took a covered basket and packed in it cloth for bandages, a hot–water bottle, mustard, a bottle of liniment, and numerous other things likely to be of use. Last of all, she added a bottle of whisky that had been prescribed as a stimulant for John Baxter.

"I s'pose some folks would think 'twas terrible carryin' this with me," she observed. "A woman pitched into me once for givin' it to her husband when he was sick. I told her I didn't favor RHUBARB as a steady drink, but I hoped I knew enough to give it when 'twas necessary."

Ralph and Captain Perez were surprised men when the housekeeper, dripping, but cheerful, appeared on the scene. She and Josiah had had a stormy passage on the way down, for the easy–going Daniel had objected to being asked to trot through drifts, and Mrs. Snow had insisted that he should be made to do it. The ford was out of the question, so they stalled the old horse in the Mayo barn and borrowed Abner's dory to make the crossing.

Mrs. Snow took charge at once of the tired men, and the overtaxed Miss Patience was glad enough to have her do it. Luther Davis was in bed, and Captain Eri, after an hour's sojourn in the same snug harbor, had utterly refused to stay there longer, and now, dressed in a suit belonging to the commandant, was stretched upon a sofa in the front room.

The Captain was the most surprised of all when Mrs. Snow appeared. He fairly gasped when she first entered the room, and seemed to be struck speechless, for he said scarcely a word while she dosed him with hot drinks, rubbed his shoulder—the bone was not broken, but there was a bruise there as big as a saucer—with the liniment, and made him

211

generally comfortable. He watched her every movement with a sort of worshipful wonder, and seemed to be thinking hard.

Captain Davis, although feeling a little better, was still very weak, and his sister and Captain Perez were with him. Josiah soon returned to the Mayo homestead to act as ferryman for Dr. Palmer when the latter should arrive, and Ralph, finding that there was nothing more that he could do, went back to the cable station. The storm had abated somewhat and the wind had gone down. Captain Eri and Mrs. Snow were alone in the front room, and, for the first time since she entered the house, the lady from Nantucket sat down to rest. Then the Captain spoke.

"Mrs. Snow," he said gravely, "I don't believe you've changed your clothes sence you got here. You must have been soaked through, too. I wish you wouldn't take such risks. You hadn't ought to have come over here a day like this, anyway. Not but what the Lord knows it's good to have you here," he added hastily.

The housekeeper seemed surprised.

"Cap'n Eri," she said, "I b'lieve if you was dyin' you'd worry for fear somebody else wouldn't be comf'table while you was doing it. 'Twould be pretty hard for me to change my clothes," she added, with a laugh, "seein' that there probably ain't anything but men's clothes in the place." Then, with a sigh, "Poor fellers, they won't need 'em any more."

"That's so. And they were all alive and hearty this mornin'. It's an awful thing for Luther. Has he told anything yit 'bout how it come to happen?"

"Yes, a little. The schooner was from Maine, bound to New York. Besides her own crew she had some Italians aboard, coal–handlers, they was, goin' over on a job for the owner. Cap'n Davis says he saw right away that the lifeboat would be overloaded, but he had to take 'em all, there wa'n't time for a second trip. He made the schooner's crew and the others lay down in the boat where they wouldn't hinder the men at the oars, but when they got jest at the tail of the shoal, where the sea was heaviest, them Italians lost their heads and commenced to stand up and yell, and fust thing you know, she swung broadside on and capsized. Pashy says Luther don't say much more, but she jedges, from what he does say, that some of the men hung on with him for a while, but was washed off and drownded."

"That's right; there was four or five there when we saw her fust. 'Twas Lute's grip on the centerboard that saved him. It's an awful thing—awful!"

"Yes, and he would have gone, too, if it hadn't been for you. And you talk about MY takin' risks!"

"Well, Jerry hadn't ought to have let you come."

"LET me come! I should like to have seen him try to stop me. The idea! Where would I be if 'twa'n't helpin' you, after all you've done for me?"

"I'VE done? I haven't done anything!"

"You've made me happier 'n I've been for years. You've been so kind that—that—"

She stopped and looked out of the window.

"It's you that's been kind," said the Captain. "You've made a home for me; somethin' I ain't had afore sence I was a boy."

Mrs. Snow went on as if he had not spoken.

"And to think that you might have been drownded the same as the rest," she said. "I knew somethin' was happenin'. I jest felt it, somehow. I told Elsie I was sure of it. I couldn't think of anything but you all the forenoon."

The Captain sat up on the couch.

"Marthy," he said in an awed tone, "do you know what I was thinkin' of when I was pullin' through the wust of it this mornin'? I was thinkin' of you. I thought of Luther and the rest of them poor souls, of course, but I thought of you most of the time. It kept comin' back to me that if I went under I shouldn't see you ag'in. And you was thinkin' of me!"

"Yes, when that Mayo man said he had awful news, I felt sure 'twas you he was goin' to tell about. I never fainted away in my life that I know of, but I think I 'most fainted then."

Cap'n Eri

"And you cared as much as that?"

"Yes."

Somehow both were speaking quietly, but as if it was useless longer to keep back anything. To speak the exact truth without reserve seemed the most natural thing in the world.

"Well, well, well!" said the Captain reverently, and still in the same low tone. "I said once afore that I b'lieved you was sent here, and now I'm sure of it. It seems almost as if you was sent to ME, don't it?"

The housekeeper still looked out of the window, but she answered simply, "I don't know."

"It does, it does so. Marthy, we've been happy together while you've been here. Do you b'lieve you could be happy with me always—if you married me, I mean?"

Mrs. Snow turned and looked at him. There were tears in her eyes, but she did not wipe them away.

"Yes," she said.

"Think now, Marthy. I ain't very young, and I ain't very rich."

"What am I?" with a little smile.

"And you really think you could be happy if you was the wife of an old codger like me?"

"Yes." The answer was short, but it was convincing.

Captain Eri rose to his feet.

"Gosh!" he said in a sort of unbelieving whisper. "Marthy, are you willin' to try?"

And again Mrs. Snow said "Yes."

When Dr. Palmer came he found Luther Davis still in bed, but Captain Eri was up and dressed, and there was such a quiet air of happiness about him that the man of medicine was amazed.

"Good Lord, man!" he exclaimed, "I expected to find you flat on your back, and you look better than I've seen you for years. Taking a salt–water bath in mid–winter must agree with you."

"It ain't so much that," replied the Captain serenely. "It's the pay I got for takin' it."

When the Doctor saw Perez alone, he asked the latter to keep a close watch on Captain Eri's behavior. He said he was afraid that the exertion and exposure might have affected the Captain's brain.

Perez, alarmed by this caution, did watch his friend very closely, but he saw nothing to frighten him until, as they were about to start for home, Captain Eri suddenly struck his thigh a resounding slap

"Jerry!" he groaned distressfully. "I clean forgot. I've gone back on Jerry!"

CHAPTER XXI. "DIME–SHOW BUS'NESS"

Elsie and Captain Jerry were kept busy that afternoon. Abner Mayo's news spread quickly, and people gathered at the post–office, the stores, and the billiard room to discuss it. Some of the men, notably "Cy" Warner and "Rufe" Smith, local representatives of the big Boston dailies, hurried off to the life–saving station to get the facts at first hand. Others came down to talk with Captain Jerry and Elsie. Melissa Busteed's shawl was on her shoulders and her "cloud" was tied about her head in less than two minutes after her next–door neighbor shouted the story across the back yards. She had just left the house, and Captain Jerry was delivering a sarcastic speech concerning "talkin' machines," when Daniel plodded through the gate, drawing the buggy containing Josiah, Mrs. Snow, and Captain Eri.

For a man who had been described as "half–dead," Captain Eri looked very well, indeed. Jerry ran to help him from the carriage, but he jumped out himself and then assisted the housekeeper to alight with an air of proud proprietorship. He was welcomed to the house like a returned prodigal, and Captain Jerry shook his well hand until the arm belonging to it seemed likely to become as stiff and sore as the other. While this handshaking was going on Captain Eri was embarrassed. He did not look his friend in the face, and most of his conversation was addressed to Elsie.

As soon as he had warmed his hands and told the story of the wreck and rescue, he said, "Jerry, come up to my room a minute, won't you? I've got somethin' I want to say."

Vaguely wondering what the private conversation might be, Jerry followed his friend upstairs. When they were in the room, Captain Eri closed the door and faced his companion. He was confused, and stammered a little, as he said, "Jerry, I've—I've got somethin' to say to you 'bout Mrs. Snow."

Then it was Captain Jerry's turn to be confused.

"Now, Eri," he protested, "'tain't fair to keep pesterin' me like this. I know I ain't said nothin' to her yit, but I'm goin' to. I had a week, anyhow, and it ain't ha'f over. Land sake!" he burst forth, "d'you s'pose I ain't been thinkin' 'bout it? I ain't thought of nothin' else, hardly. I bet you I've been over the whole thing every night sence we had that talk. I go over it and GO over it. I've thought of more 'n a million ways to ask her, but there ain't one of 'em that suits me. If I was goin' to be hung 'twouldn't be no worse, and now you've got to keep a–naggin'. Let me alone till my time is up, can't you?"

"I wa'n't naggin'. I was jest goin' to tell you that you won't have to ask. I've been talkin' to her myself, and—"

The sacrifice sprang out of his chair.

"Eri Hedge!" he exclaimed indignantly. "I thought you was a friend of mine! I give you my word I'd do it in a week, and the least you could have done, seems to me, would have been to wait and give me the chance. But no! all you think 'bout's yourself. So 'fraid she'd say no and you'd lose your old housekeeper, wa'n't you? The idea! She must think I'm a good one—can't do my own courtin', and have to git somebody to do it for me! What did she say?" he asked suddenly.

"She said yes to what I asked her," was the reply with a half smile.

Upon Captain Jerry's face settled the look of one who accepts the melancholy inevitable. He sat down again.

"I s'posed she would," he said with a sigh. "She's known me for quite a spell now, and she's had a chance to see what kind of a man I be. Well, what else did you do? Ain't settled the weddin' day, have you?" This with marked sarcasm.

"Not yit. Jerry, you've made a mistake. I didn't ask her for you."

"Didn't ask her—didn't— What are you talkin' 'bout, then?"

"I asked her for myself. She's goin' to marry me."

Captain Jerry was too much astonished even to get up. Instead, he simply sat still with open mouth while his friend continued.

"I've come to think a lot of Mrs. Snow since she's been here," Captain Eri said slowly, "and I've found out that she's felt the same way 'bout me. I've kept still and said nothin' 'cause I thought you ought to have the fust chance and, besides, I didn't know how she felt. But to–day, while we was talkin', it all come out of itself, seems so, and—well, we're goin' to be married."

The sacrifice—a sacrifice no longer—still sat silent, but curious changes of expression were passing over his face. Surprise, amazement, relief, and now a sort of grieved resignation.

"I feel small enough 'bout the way I've treated you, Jerry," continued Captain Eri. "I didn't mean to—but there! it's done, and all I can do is say I'm sorry and that I meant to give you your chance. I shan't blame you if you git mad, not a bit; but I hope you won't."

Captain Jerry sighed. When he spoke it was in a tone of sublime forgiveness.

"Eri," he said, "I ain't mad. I won't say my feelin's ain't hurt, 'cause—'cause—well, never mind. If a wife and a home ain't for me, why I ought to be glad that you're goin' to have

217

'em. I wish you both luck and a good v'yage. Now, don't talk to me for a few minutes. Let me git sort of used to it."

So they shook hands and Captain Eri, with a troubled look at his friend, went out. After he had gone, Captain Jerry got up and danced three steps of an improvised jig, his face one broad grin. Then, with an effort, he sobered down, assumed an air of due solemnity, and tramped downstairs.

If the announcement of Captain Perez' engagement caused no surprise, that of Captain Eri's certainly did—surprise and congratulation on the part of those let into the secret, for it was decided to say nothing to outsiders as yet. Ralph came over that evening and they told him about it, and he was as pleased as the rest. As for the Captain, he was only too willing to shake hands with any and everybody, although he insisted that the housekeeper had nothing to be congratulated upon, and that she was "takin' big chances." The lady herself merely smiled at this, and quietly said that she was willing to take them.

The storm had wrecked every wire and stalled every train, and Orham was isolated for two days. Then communication was established once more, and the Boston dailies received the news of the loss of the life–savers and the crew of the schooner. And they made the most of it; sensational items were scarce just then, and the editors welcomed this one. The big black headlines spread halfway across the front pages. There were pictures of the wreck, "drawn by our artist from description," and there were "descriptions" of all kinds. Special reporters arrived in the village and interviewed everyone they could lay hands on. Abner Mayo felt that for once he was receiving the attention he deserved.

The life–saving station and the house by the shore were besieged by photographers and newspaper men. Captain Eri indignantly refused to pose for his photograph, so he was "snapped" as he went out to the barn, and had the pleasure of seeing a likeness of himself, somewhat out of focus, and with one leg stiffly elevated, in the Sunday Blanket. The reporters waylaid him at the post–office, or at his fish shanty, and begged for interviews. They got them, brief and pointedly personal, and, though these were not printed, columns describing him as "a bluff, big–hearted hero," were.

If ever a man was mad and disgusted, that man was the Captain. In the first place, as he said, what he had done was nothing more than any other man 'longshore would have done, and, secondly, it was nobody's business. Then again, he said, and with truth:

"This whole fuss makes me sick. Here's them fellers in the crew been goin' out, season after season, takin' folks off wrecks, and the fool papers never say nothin' 'bout it; but they go out this time, and don't save nobody and git drownded themselves, and they're heroes of a sudden. I hear they're raisin' money up to Boston to give to the widders and orphans. Well, that's all right, but they'd better keep on and git the Gov'ment to raise the sal'ries of them that's left in the service."

The climax came when a flashily dressed stranger called, and insisted upon seeing the Captain alone. The interview lasted just about three minutes. When Mrs. Snow, alarmed by the commotion, rushed into the room, she found Captain Eri in the act of throwing after the fleeing stranger the shiny silk hat that the latter had left behind.

"Do you know what that—that swab wanted?" hotly demanded the indignant Captain. "He wanted me to rig up in ileskins and a sou'wester and show myself in dime museums. Said he'd buy that dory of Luther's that I went out in, and show that 'long with me. I told him that dory was spread up and down the beach from here to Setuckit, but he said that didn't make no diff'rence, he'd have a dory there and say 'twas the reel one. Offered me a hundred dollars a week, the skate! I'd give ten dollars right now to tell him the rest of what I had to say."

After this the Captain went fishing every day, and when at home refused to see anybody not known personally. But the agitation went on, for the papers fed the flames, and in Boston they were raising a purse to buy gold watches and medals for him and for Captain Davis.

Shortly after four o'clock one afternoon of the week following that of the wreck, Captain Eri ventured to walk up to the village, keeping a weather eye out for reporters and smoking his pipe. He made several stops, one of them being at the schoolhouse where Josiah, now back at his desk, was studying overtime to catch up with his class.

As the Captain was strolling along, someone touched him from behind, and he turned to face Ralph Hazeltine. The electrician had been a pretty regular caller at the house of late, but Captain Eri had seen but little of him, for reasons unnecessary to state.

"Hello, Captain!" said Ralph. "Taking a constitutional? You want to look out for Warner; I hear he's after you for another rescue 'special.'"

"He'll need somebody to rescue him if he comes pesterin' 'round me," was the reply. "You ain't seen my dime show friend nowheres, have you? I'd sort of like to meet HIM again; our other talk broke off kind of sudden."

Ralph laughed, and said he was afraid that the museum manager wouldn't come to Orham again very soon.

"I s'pose likely not," chuckled Captain Eri. "I ought to have kept his hat; then, maybe, he'd have come back after it. Oh, say!" he added, "I've been meanin' to ask you somethin'. Made up your mind 'bout that western job yit?"

Ralph shook his head. "Not yet," he said slowly. "I shall very soon, though, I think."

"Kind of puzzlin' you, is it? Not that it's really any of my affairs, you understand. There's only a few of us good folks left, as the feller said, and I'd hate to see you leave, that's all."

"I am not anxious to go, myself. My present position gives me a good deal of leisure time for experimental work—and—well, I'll tell you in confidence—there's a possibility of my becoming superintendent one of these days, if I wish to."

"Sho! you don't say! Mr. Langley goin' to quit?"

"He is thinking of it. The old gentleman has saved some money, and he has a sister in the West who is anxious to have him come out there and spend the remainder of his days with her. If he does, I can have his position, I guess. In fact, he has been good enough to say so."

"Well, that's pretty fine, ain't it? Langley ain't the man to chuck his good opinions round like clam shells. You ought to feel proud."

"I suppose I ought."

They walked on silently for a few steps, the Captain waiting for his companion to speak, and the latter seeming disinclined to do so. At length the older man asked another question.

"Is t'other job so much better?"

"No."

Silence again. Then Ralph said, "The other position, Captain, is very much like this one in some respects. It will place me in a country town, even smaller than Orham, where there are few young people, no amusements, and no society, in the fashionable sense of the word."

"Humph! I thought you didn't care much for them things."

"I don't."

To this enigmatical answer the Captain made no immediate reply. After a moment, however, he said, slowly and with apparent irrelevance, "Mr. Hazeltine, I can remember my father tellin' 'bout a feller that lived down on the South Harniss shore when he was a boy. Queer old chap he was, named Elihu Bassett; everybody called him Uncle Elihu. In them days all hands drunk more or less rum, and Uncle Elihu drunk more. He had a way of stayin' sober for a spell, and then startin' off on a regular jamboree all by himself. He had an old flat−bottomed boat that he used to sail 'round in, but she broke her moorin's one time and got smashed up, so he wanted to buy another. Shadrach Wingate, Seth's granddad 'twas, tried to fix up a dicker with him for a boat he had. They agreed on the price, and everything was all right 'cept that Uncle Elihu stuck out that he must try her 'fore he bought her.

"So Shad fin'lly give in, and Uncle Elihu sailed over to Wellmouth in the boat. He put in his time 'round the tavern there, and when he come down to the boat ag'in, he had a jugful of Medford in his hand, and pretty nigh as much of the same stuff under his hatches. He got afloat somehow, h'isted the sail, lashed the tiller after a fashion, took a nip out of the jug and tumbled over and went fast asleep. 'Twas a still night or 'twould have been the finish. As 'twas he run aground on a flat and stuck there till mornin'.

"Next day back he comes with the boat all scraped up, and says he, 'She won't do, Shad; she don't keep her course.'

"'Don't keep her course, you old fool!' bellers Shad. 'And you tight as a drumhead and sound asleep! Think she can find her way home herself?' he says.

"'Well,' says Uncle Elihu, 'if she can't she ain't the boat for me.'"

Ralph laughed. "I see," he said. "Perhaps Uncle Elihu was wise. Still, if he wanted the boat very much, he must have hated to put her to the test."

"That's so," assented the Captain, "but 'twas better to know it then than to be sorry for it afterwards."

Both seemed to be thinking, and neither spoke again until they came to the grocery store, where Hazeltine stopped, saying that he must do an errand for Mr. Langley. They said good−night, and the Captain turned away, but came quickly back and said:

"Mr. Hazeltine, if it ain't too much trouble, would you mind steppin' up to the schoolhouse when you've done your errand? I've left somethin' there with Josiah, and I'd like to have you git it. Will you?"

"Certainly," was the reply, and it was not until the Captain had gone that Ralph remembered he did not know what he was to get.

When he reached the school he climbed the stairs and opened the door, expecting to find Josiah alone. Instead, there was no one there but Elsie, who was sitting at the desk. She sprang up as he entered. Both were somewhat confused.

"Pardon me, Miss Preston," he said. "Captain Eri sent me here. He said he left something with Josiah, and wished me to call for it."

"Why, I'm sure I don't know what it can be," replied Elsie. "Josiah has been gone for some time, and he said nothing to me about it."

"Perhaps it is in his desk," suggested Ralph. "Suppose we look."

So they looked, but found nothing more than the usual assortment contained in the desk of a healthy schoolboy. The raised lid shut off the light from the window, and the desk's interior was rather dark. They had to grope in the corners, and occasionally their hands touched. Every time this happened Ralph thought of the decision that he must make so soon.

He thought of it still more when, after the search was abandoned, Elsie suggested that he help her with some problems that she was preparing for the next day's labors of the first class in arithmetic. In fact, as he sat beside her, pretending to figure, but really watching her dainty profile as it moved back and forth before his eyes, his own particular problem received far more attention than did those of the class. Suddenly he spoke:

"Teacher," he said, "please, may I ask a question?"

"You should hold up your hand if you wish permission to speak," was the stern reply.

"Please consider it held up."

"Is the question as important as 'How many bushels did C. sell?' which happens to be my particular trouble just now."

"It is to me, certainly." Ralph was serious enough now. "It is a question that I have been wrestling with for some time. It is, shall I take the position that has been offered me in the West, or shall I stay here and become superintendent of the station? The superintendent's place may be mine, I think, if I want it."

Elsie laid down her pencil and hesitated for a moment before she spoke. When she did reply her face was turned away from her companion.

"I should think that question might best be decided by comparing the salaries and prospects of the two positions," she said quietly.

"The two positions are much alike in one way. You know what the life at the station means the greater portion of the year—no companions of your own age and condition, no society, no amusements. The Western offer means all this and worse, for the situation is the same all the year. I say these things because I hope you may be willing to consider them, not from my point of view solely, but from yours."

"From mine?"

"Yes. You see I am recklessly daring to hope that, whichever lot is chosen, you may be willing to share it with me—as my wife. Elsie, do you think you could consider the question from that viewpoint?"

And—well—Elsie thought she could.

The consideration—we suppose it was the consideration—took so long that it was nearly dark when Elsie announced that she simply MUST go. It was Ralph's duty as a gentleman to help her in putting on her coat, and this took an astonishingly long time. Finally it was done, however, and they came downstairs.

"Dearest," said Ralph, after the door was locked, "I forgot to have another hunt for whatever it was that Captain Eri wanted me to get."

Elsie smiled rather oddly.

"Are you sure you haven't got it?" she asked demurely.

"Got it! Why—why, by George, what a numbskull I am! The old rascal! I thought there was a twinkle in his eye."

"He said he should come back after me."

"Well, well! Bless his heart, it's sound and sweet all the way through. Yes, I HAVE got it, and, what's more, I shall tell him that I mean to keep it."

The gold watches from the people to the heroes of the Orham wreck having been duly bought and inscribed and the medals struck, there came up the question of presentation, and it was decided to perform the ceremony in the Orham town hall, and to make the occasion notable. The Congressman from the district agreed to make the necessary speech. The Harniss Cornet Band was to furnish music. All preparations were made, and it remained only to secure the consent of the parties most interested, namely, Captain Eri and Luther Davis.

And this was the hardest task of all. Both men at first flatly refused to be present. The Captain said he might as well go to the dime museum and be done with it; he was much obliged to the Boston folks, but his own watch was keeping good time, and he didn't need a new one badly enough to make a show of himself to get it. Captain Davis said very much the same.

But Miss Patience was proud of her brother's rise to fame, and didn't intend to let him forfeit the crowning glory. She enlisted Captain Perez as a supporter, and together they finally got Luther's unwilling consent to sit on the platform and be stared at for one evening. Meanwhile, Captain Jerry, Elsie, Ralph, and Mrs. Snow were doing their best to win Captain Eri over. When Luther surrendered, the forces joined, and the Captain threw up his hands.

"All right," he said. "Only I ought to beg that dime museum feller's pardon. 'Tain't right to be partial this way."

The hall was jammed to the doors. Captain Eri, seated on the platform at one end of the half−circle of selectmen, local politicians, and minor celebrities, looked from the Congressman in the middle to Luther on the other end, and then out over the crowded settees. He saw Mrs. Snow's pleasant, wholesome face beaming proudly beside Captain Jerry's red one. He saw Captain Perez and Miss Patience sitting together close to the front, and Ralph and Elsie a little further back. The Reverend Mr. Perley was there; so were the Smalls and Miss Abigail Mullett. Melissa Busteed was on the very front bench with the boys, of whom Josiah was one. The "train committee" was there—not a member missing— and at the rear of the hall, smiling and unctuous as ever, was "Web" Saunders. In spite of his stage fright the Captain grinned when he saw "Web."

Mr. Solomon Bangs, his shirt−bosom crackling with importance, introduced the Congressman. The latter's address was, so the Item said, "a triumph of oratorical effort." It really was a good speech, and when it touched upon the simple sacrifice of the men who had given up their lives in the course of what, to them, was everyday work, there were stifled sobs all through the hall. Luther Davis, during this portion of the address, sat with his big hand shading his eyes. Later on, when the speaker was sounding the praises of the man who "alone, forgetful of himself, braved the sea and the storm to save his friends," those who looked at Captain Eri saw his chair hitched back, inch by inch, until, as the final outburst came, little more than his Sunday shoes was in sight. He had retired, chair and all, to the wings.

But they called him to the platform again and, amid—we quote from the Item once more—"a hurricane of applause," the two heroes were adorned with the watches and the medals.

There was a sort of impromptu reception after the ceremony, when Captain Eri, with Mrs. Snow on his arm, struggled through the crowd toward the door.

"'Twas great, shipmate, and you deserved it!" declared magnanimous Captain Jerry, wringing his hand.

"'Tain't ha'f what you ought to have, Eri," said Captain Perez.

"I haven't said much to thank you for savin' Luther," whispered Miss Patience, "but I hope you know that we both appreciate what you done and never 'll forget it."

Ralph and Elsie also shook hands with him, and said some pleasant things. So did many others, Dr. Palmer among the number. Altogether, the journey through the hall was a sort of triumphal progress.

"Whew!" gasped the Captain, as they came out into the clear air and the moonlight, "let's hope that's the last of the dime–show bus'ness."

"Eri," whispered Mrs. Snow, "I'm so proud of you, I don't know what to do."

And that remark was sweeter to the Captain's ears than all those that had preceded it.

They turned into the shore road and were alone. It was a clear winter night, fresh, white snow on the ground, not a breath of wind, and the full moon painting land and sea dark blue and silver white. The surf sounded faint and far off. Somewhere in the distance a dog was barking, and through the stillness came an occasional laugh or shout from the people going home from the hall.

"Lots of things can happen in a few months, can't they?" said Mrs. Snow, glancing at the black shadow of the shuttered Baxter homestead.

"They can so," replied the Captain. "Think what's happened sence last September. I didn't know you then, and now it seems 's if I'd always known you. John was alive then, and Elsie nor Ralph hadn't come. Perez hadn't met Pashy neither. My! my! Everybody's choosed partners but Jerry," he chuckled, "and Jerry looked the most likely candidate 'long at the beginnin'. I'm glad," he added, "that Ralph's made up his mind to stay here. We shan't lose him nor Elsie for a few years, anyhow."

They paused at the knoll by the gate.

"Fair day to–morrer," observed the Captain, looking up at the sky.

"I hope it 'll be fair weather for us the rest of our days," said Mrs. Snow.

"You've HAD it rough enough, that's sure. Well, I hope you'll have a smooth v'yage, now."

The lady from Nantucket looked up into his face with a happy laugh.

"I guess I shall," she said. "I know I've got a good pilot."